WAR ROOM

✦ ✦ ✦

Other Novels
by Chris Fabry

Dogwood

June Bug

Almost Heaven

Not in the Heart

Borders of the Heart

Every Waking Moment

A Marriage Carol
(with Dr. Gary Chapman)

The Song
(based on the screenplay by Richard L. Ramsay)

WAR ROOM

PRAYER IS A POWERFUL WEAPON

TYNDALE HOUSE PUBLISHERS, INC.
CAROL STREAM, ILLINOIS

A NOVELIZATION BY
CHRIS FABRY

BASED ON THE MOTION PICTURE BY
ALEX KENDRICK & STEPHEN KENDRICK

Visit Tyndale online at www.tyndale.com.

Visit Chris Fabry's website at www.chrisfabry.com.

For more information on *War Room*, visit www.warroomthemovie.com and www.kendrickbrothers.com.

TYNDALE and Tyndale's quill logo are registered trademarks of Tyndale House Publishers, Inc.

War Room

Edited by Sarah Mason

Published in association with the literary agency Working Title Agency, WTA Services, LLC, Franklin, TN.

Unless otherwise indicated, all Scripture quotations are taken from the Holman Christian Standard Bible,® copyright © 1999, 2000, 2002, 2003, 2009 by Holman Bible Publishers. Used by permission. Holman Christian Standard Bible,® Holman CSB,® and HCSB® are federally registered trademarks of Holman Bible Publishers.

James 5:16 is taken from the *Holy Bible*, King James Version.

War Room is a work of fiction. Where real people, events, establishments, organizations, or locales appear, they are used fictitiously. All other elements of the novel are drawn from the authors' imaginations.

Library of Congress Cataloging-in-Publication Data

Fabry, Chris, date.
  War room : prayer is a powerful weapon / by Chris Fabry.
    pages ; cm
  "Based on the screenplay by Alex Kendrick and Stephen Kendrick."
  ISBN 978-1-4964-0729-0 (hc : alk. paper) — ISBN 978-1-4964-0728-3 (sc : alk. paper)
  1. Dysfunctional families—Fiction. 2. Marriage—Fiction. 3. Domestic fiction.
I. Kendrick, Alex, date. II. Kendrick, Stephen, date. III. War room (Motion picture)
IV. Title.
  PS3556.A26W37 2015
  813'.54—dc23
                                      2015011970

Printed in the United States of America

21 20 19 18 17 16 15
7   6   5   4

To get nations back on their feet,
we must first get down
on our knees.

BILLY GRAHAM

Miss Clara

✦ ✦ ✦

She was an old woman with gray hair and dark skin, and she gave a sigh of relief as she pulled into the cemetery parking lot, as if just being able to apply the brake was an answer to prayer. She shuffled among the tombstones resolutely, nodding in recognition as she passed familiar names. It was becoming difficult to dredge up faces along with the names. Her gait was steady, and each footstep took her closer to her destination, a tombstone that read *Williams*. When she reached it, she stood and let the fresh, earthy smell wash over her. It felt like rain.

"You always loved the rain, didn't you, Leo?" she said aloud. "Yes, you did. You loved the rain."

In these sacred moments of Clara Williams's life, she knew she was not talking to her husband. She knew where his soul was, and it was not under the green earth below her. Still, the exercise cleared her mind and connected her with the past in a way nothing else could. She could look at pictures of Leo in his military uniform and a few tattered photographs he had carried with him after he'd come home from Vietnam, and those brought her closer, but there was nothing like the feeling of running her hand across the cut stone and feeling the carved-out name and adjusting the little flag on top of his grave. There always had to be a flag there.

Clara had no concept of military warfare, except for those pictures her husband kept. She couldn't bring herself to watch war movies, especially the documentaries with grainy footage of men in combat. Falling napalm and the recoil of M16s against naked shoulders. She flipped as fast as she could past the PBS station that aired those. It hit too close to the bone.

But Clara did know another conflict. It was waged every day on six billion battlefields of the human heart. She knew enough about warfare to realize that tucked away in some place protected from the onslaught of bullets and bombs, someone had developed a strategy.

She pictured her husband staring at maps and coordinates. Sweaty and tired and scared, he and his men would analyze what the enemy was doing and mobilize resources to push back against their advance. In the years since his death, she had heard stories of his bravery, his sacrifice for his men.

"We need men with a steel backbone today, Leo," she said. "Like you. Steel backbone and a heart of gold."

But Leo's heart had given out early and left her alone with a ten-year-old son. His death had been sudden. She hadn't prepared for it. In her thirties she thought she had plenty of time and that life would stretch out forever. But life had not worked that way. Life had its own strategy and time had cut like a river into her heart.

Clara gingerly knelt by the tombstone and pulled at weeds, thinking of a day forty years earlier when she stood at this same spot with her only son.

"I wish you could see Clyde," she said. "He looks so much like you, Leo. Talks like you. Has some of the same mannerisms. The way he laughs kind of low and easylike. I wish you could see the man he's become."

Forty years earlier she had stood here with Clyde, looking at the stones covering the landscape and loved ones. "Why do people have to die, Mama?" he had said.

She had answered him too quickly. She told him death comes to everyone and quoted the verse about it being appointed unto man once to die, and after that the judgment. Then she realized he wasn't looking for theology, but something else entirely. She knelt at the same spot and told him the truest thing she knew.

"I don't know why people have to die, Son. I don't think death was what God wanted. But it sure was part of somebody's plan. I believe God is big enough and powerful enough to use it. There's more going on here than we can see."

Clyde had just looked at her with tears in his eyes. She'd hugged him and cried with him, and the more questions he asked, the tighter she held on. The words drifted high above the trees and blew with the wind. She could still feel his hug there at the gravestone.

"I never thought of myself growing older," she said to her husband and looked at the wrinkled skin of her weathered hands. "I tried to carry on and just head into life. And now four decades have passed like a strong wind. I've tried to learn the lessons God has taught me."

She pulled herself up and brushed the grass away from her knees. "I'm sorry, Leo. I wish I could go back and try again. I wish I had another chance. But it's okay now. You rest easy. I'll be seeing you soon, I expect."

She lingered a few moments, the memories flooding back, then took the long walk to the car and heard voices in the distance. A couple argued about thirty yards away. Clara couldn't hear the words, couldn't tell what the argument was about, but she wanted to shake them and point at the stones and tell them they were fighting the wrong battle. Tell them to see the real enemy. And that victories didn't come by accident, they came with strategy and mobilized resources.

The couple got in their car and drove away, and Clara shuffled back to hers and climbed in, suddenly out of breath. "If I didn't know better, I'd think this cemetery gets bigger and longer every time I come," she muttered to herself.

She could hear Leo laugh, that bittersweet echo across the years.

CHAPTER 1

✦ ✦ ✦

Elizabeth Jordan noticed everything wrong with the house she was selling before she ever knocked on the front door. She saw flaws in the landscaping and cracks in the driveway and a problem with the drainage of the roof near the garage. Just before she knocked three times, she saw chipping paint on a windowsill. This was her job. Presentation was everything. You had only one chance to make a first impression with a potential buyer.

She saw her reflection in a window and straightened her shoulders, tugging on her dark jacket. She had her hair back, which accentuated her strong face. Prominent nose, high forehead, and chocolaty skin. Elizabeth had a lineage she could trace back over 150 years. She had taken a trip with her husband and infant daughter ten years earlier to a plantation in the Deep South where her great-great-great-grandmother had lived. The little shack had been rebuilt, along with other slave quarters on the property, and the owners had searched the country for any relatives. Just walking inside made her feel like she was touching the heart of her ancestors, and she fought back tears as she imagined their lives. She'd held her daughter close and thanked God for the perseverance of her people, their legacy, and the opportunities she had that they could never imagine.

Elizabeth waited until the door opened, then smiled at the slightly younger woman before her. Melissa Tabor held a box of household items and struggled to maintain the cell phone balanced on her shoulder. Her mouth rounded into an O.

"Mom, I gotta go," she said into the phone.

Elizabeth smiled, patiently waiting.

Over her shoulder, Melissa said, "Jason and David, get rid of the ball and help me with these boxes!"

Elizabeth wanted to reach out and help her but had to duck as a kickball flew past her head. It bounced harmlessly in the yard behind her and she laughed.

"Oh, I am so sorry," Melissa said. "You must be Elizabeth Jordan."

"I am. And you're Melissa?"

The box nearly fell as Melissa shook hands with Elizabeth. "Yes. I'm sorry. We just started packing."

"No problem. Can I help you with that?"

A man with a briefcase and a work folder slipped past them. "Honey, I gotta be in Knoxville at two. But I finished the closet." He held up a stuffed bear and dropped it into the box. "That was in the refrigerator."

He passed Elizabeth on the front step and stopped, pointing at her. "Real estate agent," he said, sounding proud of himself. Not a name but a title he put on her. She was someone to put in a pigeonhole in his head.

Elizabeth smiled and pointed back. "Software rep."

"How did you know that?" he said, his eyes wide.

"It's on that folder you're holding in your hand." She was just as good at categorizing and commentating. She had to work at the connecting with others. Especially with her husband.

He looked at the folder and nodded with a knowing chuckle as if impressed by her observational powers. "I would love to stay but I have to leave. My wife can answer everything about the house. We realize it's a disaster and we've agreed to blame it on our kids." He glanced at Melissa. "So I'll call you tonight."

"Love you," Melissa said, still holding the box.

With that he was gone, down the walk to the car. He passed the kickball and didn't seem to notice.

"I understand," Elizabeth said. "My husband does the same thing. Pharmaceuticals."

"Oh," Melissa said. "Does he get tired of the travel?"

"He doesn't seem to. I think he likes being able to drive

and clear his head, you know? Instead of being cooped up in an office all day."

"While you're showing houses and dealing with people in big transitions."

Elizabeth stepped inside and noticed twelve things that would have to change if they were to make a sale. More first impressions. But she wouldn't list them all at the moment because she also saw something in Melissa's face that was close to panic.

"You know, they say that outside of death and divorce, moving is the most stressful change you go through." She put a hand on the woman's shoulder. "And this is probably not the first time you've moved in the past few years."

Melissa shook her head. "These are the same boxes we used last time."

Elizabeth nodded and saw missing paint on a ding in the wall but tried to focus. "You're going to get through this."

Right then a boy with spiked blond hair ran down the stairs, followed closely by another waving a tennis racket. Both were about the same age as Elizabeth's daughter and had enough energy to light a small city for a year. Who needed power plants and windmills when you had adolescent boys?

Melissa sighed. "Are you sure about that?"

✦ ✦ ✦

Tony Jordan had begun the day in an upscale suites hotel in Raleigh. He was up early, working out in the weight room alone—he loved the quiet, and most people on the road didn't work out at 5 a.m. Then he showered and dressed and had a bowl of fruit and some juice in the breakfast area. Other travelers hurried through, eating donuts or waffles or sugary cereal. He needed to stay fit and keep the edge so he could stay on his game, and his health was a big part of that. He'd always believed that if you had your health, you had everything.

Tony looked in the mirror as he headed out the door. His close-cropped hair was just the right length. The shirt and tie were crisp and hugged his running-back neck, strong and wide. His mustache was tightly trimmed above his upper lip, a goatee on his chin. He looked good. Confident. To tune up for the meeting later, he flashed a smile and stuck out a hand and said, "Hey, Mr. Barnes."

As an African American, he'd always felt like he was one step behind most of his white coworkers and competitors. Not because he lacked skill or ability or eloquence, but simply because of his skin color. Whether that was reality or not, he couldn't tell. How could he crawl inside the mind of someone meeting him for the first time? But he had felt the questioning looks, the split-second hesitation of someone who shook his hand the first time. He'd even felt it from his bosses at Brightwell, especially Tom Bennett, one of the vice presidents. Tony saw him as part of the old-boy network. Another white guy who knew somebody who knew somebody else and had eased into management, working his way a little too quickly up the ladder. Tony had tried to impress the man with his sales ability, his easygoing demeanor—the attitude that said, *I got this. Trust me.* But Tom was a hard sell, and Tony couldn't help but wonder if his skin color had something to do with it.

Accepting the reality he perceived, Tony vowed he would simply work harder, push harder, and live up to every expectation. But in the back of his mind he felt this unseen hurdle wasn't fair. Other people with a lighter skin color didn't have to deal with it, so why should he?

The hurdle in front of him today was Holcomb. There was no getting around the difficulty of the sale. But what was an easy sale? Even the quick ones took time and preparation and knowing and seeing. This was his secret—the intangibles. Remembering names. Remembering details about the customer's life. Things like the Ping driver he had in the trunk.

Calvin Barnes was going to salivate when Tony handed him that driver, as well he should. It had set Tony back a few hundred, but it was a small price to pay for the look on his boss's face when he heard Tony had sealed the deal.

The boardroom was tastefully decorated, the smell of leather permeating the hallway as he walked in and put his sample case on the redwood table. Calvin Barnes—who did not like to be called Calvin—would walk through the door and shake Tony's hand, so the driver needed to lean against the chair to Tony's left, out of view. He placed it there, then moved it into the chair and let the grip stick out over the back. When he heard voices down the hallway, he put the driver back on the floor. He needed to be more subtle.

Mr. Barnes walked in with another man—a familiar face, but for a moment Tony froze, unable to remember the man's name. He tried to relax, to recall the name using his mnemonic device. He'd pictured the man standing in a huge landfill with a John Deere hat on. Dearing. That was the last name. But he couldn't remember why he was standing in a land—

"Tony, you remember—"

"Phil Dearing," Tony said, extending a hand. "Good to see you again."

The man looked stunned, then smiled as he shook Tony's hand.

Mr. Barnes threw his head back and laughed. "You just won me twenty bucks. I told you he'd remember, Phil." His eyes fell on the golf club. "And what have we here?"

"That's the one I was talking about, Mr. Barnes," Tony said. "I'll be shocked if it doesn't add at least thirty yards to every drive. Your job is to make sure they're straight down the middle."

Mr. Barnes picked up the driver and held it. He was a scratch golfer who played three times a week and had designs on retiring to Florida. An extra thirty yards on his drives meant Barnes could exploit his short game, which meant that seventy-two for eighteen holes could come down to a seventy. Maybe lower on a good day.

"The weight is just perfect, Tony. And the balance is phenomenal."

Tony watched him hold the club and was certain he had the sale even before he opened his case. When they'd signed the papers and cared for the legal parts of the transaction, Tony stood. He knew he cut an impressive figure in his suit and tie and athletic build.

"I need to get you back on the course and work on that putting of yours," Mr. Barnes said.

"Maybe next time I'm through," Tony said, smiling.

"You don't mind coming all the way out here—even this early?"

"No, I do not. I enjoy the drive."

"Well, we're excited to do business with you, Tony," Mr. Barnes said. "Tell Coleman I said hello."

"I'll do it."

"Oh, and thanks for the new driver."

"Hey, you enjoy it, okay?" Tony shook hands with them. "Gentlemen, we'll be in touch."

He walked out of the room almost floating. There was no feeling like making a sale. As he neared the elevators, he could hear Calvin Barnes crowing about his new driver and how much he wanted to take the afternoon off and play the back nine at the nearest country club. While he waited, Tony checked his phone for anything he'd missed during the meeting, when he made a point of keeping it in his pocket. This was another thing he always tried to do. Value clients enough to make them the central focus. Never make your clients feel like there is anyone on the planet more important than them. They are your priority. Every. Time.

A young woman walked down a white staircase before him, carrying a leather folder and smiling. He put his phone away and smiled back.

"I see you made the sale," she said.

He nodded confidently. "Of course."

"I'm impressed. Most guys run out with their tail between their legs."

Tony extended a hand. "I'm Tony Jordan."

"Veronica Drake," she said, shaking with him. Her hand was warm and soft. "I work for Mr. Barnes. I'll be your contact for the purchase."

She handed him her card and brushed his hand slightly. Nothing overt, but he felt something click with her touch. Veronica was vivacious and slim, and Tony imagined them together at some restaurant talking. Then he imagined them by romantic firelight, Veronica leaning toward him, her lips moist and pleading. All this happened in a second as he stared at her business card.

"Well, Veronica Drake, I guess I'll be seeing you again when I return in two weeks."

"I'll look forward to it," she said, and the way she smiled made him think she meant it.

She walked away and he turned and watched her a little too intently.

As he waited for the elevator, his phone beeped and he looked at the screen.

Bank Notice: Transfer.

Here he was with the biggest sale in months, something he'd worked on and planned intricately, and right at the apex of his elation at the sale, he'd been given another smackdown by his wife.

"Elizabeth, you're killing me," he whispered.

✦　✦　✦

Elizabeth sat on the white ottoman at the foot of her bed rubbing her feet. The time with Melissa had been good—she'd been able to make a list of all the repairs and staging decisions that had to be done. The two boys hadn't made things easier, but children always had a way of complicating home sales. It was something you just needed to work with and hope you could navigate.

It had been a long day, with another meeting in the afternoon and then getting home before Danielle arrived from her last day of school. By the time she sat down, Elizabeth was exhausted and ready to curl up and sleep, but there was more to be done. There was always more to be done.

"Mom?"

Elizabeth couldn't move. "I'm in here, Danielle."

Her ten-year-old daughter walked in carrying something. She had grown several inches in the last year, her thin, long body sprouting up like a weed. She wore a cute purple headband that highlighted her face. Elizabeth could see her father there—that bright smile, eyes full of life. Except her eyes were a little downcast.

"Here's my last report card. I still got one C."

Elizabeth took it and looked it over as Danielle sat and shrugged off her backpack.

"Oh, baby. You have an A in everything else. One C in math is not that bad. But you get a break for the summer, right?"

Danielle leaned forward and her face betrayed something. She sniffed and then reacted like the room was full of ammonia. "Is that your feet?"

Elizabeth self-consciously pulled her foot away. "I'm sorry, baby. I ran out of foot powder."

"That smells terrible."

"I know, Danielle. I just needed to take my shoes off for a minute."

Her daughter stared at her mother's feet like they were toxic waste. "That's, like, awful," she said, repulsed.

"Well, don't just sit there looking at them. Why don't you give me a hand and rub them right there?"

"Ewwww, no way!"

Elizabeth laughed. "Girl, go set the table for dinner. When your daddy gets home, you can show him your report card, okay?"

Danielle took her report card into the kitchen, and Elizabeth was alone again. The odor hadn't been a problem until a few years earlier, and the foot powder seemed to take care of it. But maybe she was kidding herself. Maybe the odor was the sign of some deeper problem.

What was she thinking? Some disease? Some problem

with her liver that leaked out the pores of her feet? She had a friend, Missy, who was constantly looking online at various aches and pains and connecting them with her own symptoms. One day she'd be worried about a skin problem and conclude she had melanoma. The next day a headache would be self-diagnosed as a tumor. Elizabeth vowed she would not become a hypochondriac. She just had stinky feet.

She picked up one of her flats and sniffed. There'd been a cheese served at the hotel where she and Tony had honeymooned that smelled just like that. She dropped the shoe. Funny how a smell could trigger her brain to think about something that happened sixteen years earlier.

She ran her hand over the comforter and thought about that first night together. All the anticipation. All the excitement. She hadn't slept in two days and the wedding had been a blur. When her head hit the pillow in the honeymoon suite, she was just gone. Tony had been upset, and what red-blooded American male wouldn't be? But what red-blooded American females needed was a little understanding, a little grace.

She had made up for her honeymoon drowsiness the next day, but it was something they had to talk through. Tony had talked a lot in the year they had dated and been engaged, but not long after the *I do*s, something got his tongue and the river of words slowed to a drip. She wished she could find the valve or tell where to place the plunger to get him unclogged.

They didn't have a bad marriage. It wasn't like those celebrities on TV who went from one relationship to the next or the couple down the street who threw things onto the lawn after every argument. She and Tony had produced a beautiful daughter and they had stable careers. Yes, he was a little aloof and they'd grown apart, but she was sure that drift wouldn't last forever. It couldn't.

Elizabeth put her shoes away, as far back into the closet as she could, then went to the kitchen to start dinner. She filled a pot with water, put it on the stove, and dumped in the spaghetti. The water came to a slow boil, and she stirred the tomato sauce in a pan next to it.

Elizabeth watched the spaghetti, feeling something happening, something boiling inside her. A stirring she couldn't put her finger on. Call it restlessness or longing. Call it fear. Maybe this was all she could hope for. Maybe this was as good as marriage got. Or life, for that matter. Maybe they were destined to go separate ways and occasionally meet in the middle. But she had a nagging feeling that she was missing something. That their marriage could be more than two people with a nice house who rarely spent time together.

Elizabeth was busy with the salad and Danielle was putting napkins next to each plate at the table when the garage door began its hideous sound—a clacking that had gotten louder in the past year. If Elizabeth had been trying to sell their own house, she'd have suggested they get it looked at by her garage door guy. But Tony was content to let it clack and clamor.

Like their marriage.

"I just heard him pull in, Danielle."

"Will he be mad about my C?" Danielle said. The look in her eyes made Elizabeth wonder. She wanted to march out to the garage and tell Tony to affirm their daughter, say something positive, look at how full the glass was and not see the one little thing that was less than perfect.

"I already told you, baby. Getting a C is not that bad. It's okay."

She said it to convince not just Danielle, but also herself. Because she knew her husband wouldn't feel the same.

Miss Clara

✦ ✦ ✦

Clara was in her war room, as she called it, when she got the distinct impression that her life was about to change. It was a sense that she was about to do something drastic, but she had no clue what it was or why she should do it. Skydiving? She chuckled. At her age the ground was already too far away. Find some homeless woman down on the corner by the grocery and give her a sandwich? She had done that the day before.

Clara knew that prayer could easily become a list of things for God to do. Just run through the gamut of wants, needs, or things hoped for and put an *amen* at the end. Any way you sliced it, she thought, it was selfish. At the core of every human heart was someone who wanted to please herself, she believed, and that truth fought against the power of prayer.

Prayer, at its most basic level, was surrender. Like Jesus in the garden, saying, "Not My will, but Yours, be done." The ironic thing was, when a person surrendered their will, they got God's, and then they received what they were really looking for all along. This was what she believed.

Earlier in her life, she had looked at prayer as talking to God and telling Him things. It was like crawling up in the lap of a daddy and explaining your aches and pains and disappointments. But after a while, she discovered the listening part of prayer, the allowing of God's Holy Spirit to move and help her recall things and desire things she hadn't requested.

In her war room, the little closet on the second floor of her home, something began to stir. There was no audible voice, no mysterious letters sticking out at her from the word jumble in the morning paper. It was simply a sense that God was moving, pushing her from her comfort zone. She had no idea what that meant, and the more she prayed and asked God what the feeling was, the more quiet the Almighty seemed to get.

"Whatever You want to do, Lord, I'm willing to go with You. Just lead the way."

And then she waited.

CHAPTER 2

✦ ✦ ✦

Tony pulled into the garage and turned off the ignition. He hit the remote and watched the garage door inch its way down behind him. He had flipped through stations on his way home, trying to subdue the anger with some song on an oldies station, but instead he heard a conversation on a sports talk program about another football player accused of doping. The player had also had a public conflict with his wife. Everywhere Tony looked, he was being brought back to his situation with Elizabeth. Why did she have to do that with their money? Why did she spend . . . ?

He had switched off the radio and stewed as he drove the familiar streets of Concord, North Carolina. It was funny how he could get in the groove of his thoughts and not remember making turns or passing familiar landmarks. Such was life on the road.

He loved Elizabeth. He had always loved her. But he didn't like her right now and couldn't remember the last time the two had spent an evening together without getting into an argument. Maybe this was what married life became. Maybe this was the rut you got into and had to stay in the rest of your life. But he hadn't signed up for this.

As the garage door shut, Tony grabbed his satchel, and the business card Veronica had given him fell to the floor. He picked it up, pulled out his phone, and flipped to the app where he kept important names and numbers he needed to remember. This would record the information and any notes on his phone, but he could also access it from any device. He held the card to his nose and smelled a slight hint of Veronica's perfume that lingered. She was so delicate—slim and vibrant and younger. And interested. She'd given him the distinct impression that she was interested. It had been a long time since he'd felt that from anyone. Especially Elizabeth.

He put the card in his satchel and took a deep breath. He was not going to yell. He was not going to fly off the handle. He was not going to be "somewhere else," as Elizabeth often accused him. He would be there for Danielle and his wife. But before he could be there, he needed to set the money thing straight. If he got that out of the way, he'd be fine. He could go on with life and not feel so . . . tight, so constricted.

He walked inside and was greeted by the familiar smell of cooking spaghetti. He'd come to hate spaghetti because it was a symbol of their marriage. Something quick and easy to get on the table. Couldn't Elizabeth learn to cook something else?

Danielle greeted him with a hopeful look. She was holding something in front of her. "Hey, Daddy."

"Hey, Danielle." He wanted to sound warmer but there were things on his mind. Tony put his satchel on the counter and turned to Elizabeth.

"I got my last report card. And I made all As except for one C."

"So I just got a notification that you moved five thousand dollars from our savings into your checking account," Tony said, ignoring Danielle.

Elizabeth stopped dipping salad into the three bowls on the counter and glanced at him like some frightened child. Danielle was silent.

He stared at Elizabeth, his voice stern. "That better not be so you can prop up your sister again."

And with that, her back raised up. He'd tried to hold back, but five thousand dollars—and the history with her sister—sent him over the edge.

"You just gave that much money to your family last month," Elizabeth said. "And my sister needs it more than your parents."

"My parents are elderly," Tony said, his heart rate rising.

"Your sister married a bum, and I'm not supporting some-one who's too lazy to work."

"Darren is not a bum. He's just having a hard time find-ing a job."

"Liz, he is a bum! I can't even remember the last time he had a job."

Elizabeth's face tightened as she glanced at Danielle. He noticed his daughter walking away from them, the piece of paper on the island. What had she said? A report card?

The effect on Elizabeth was instant. She de-escalated quickly, tossing a shaming look at him. "Can we talk about this later?"

Tony stood firm. "No, we'll talk about it now. Because if you want to give them what you make, that's fine. But you're not giving them my money."

"Your money?" That brought out the fangs. "The last time I checked, we both put money into that account."

"And the last time *I* checked, I make about four times what you do. So you don't move a cent out of that account without asking me first."

So much for keeping his cool. So much for "being there." Tony kicked himself for exploding, but they were too far into the dance now to turn back. And she had to hear the truth, once and for all, about their finances.

Elizabeth looked away for a moment, and he felt the old wound reopen. He had heard early in marriage that once children came along, a wife turned her heart to the kids and a husband turned his heart to his work. He'd told himself that wouldn't happen with them. He wouldn't let it happen. She wouldn't let it happen. But here they were.

"Can we please just eat dinner?" Elizabeth said in a measured tone, like she was trying to talk a nervous home buyer down off the ledge after he looked at the interest of a thirty-year mortgage.

Tony glanced at the table, the plates and napkins, the salad and spaghetti, and he couldn't take it. There was something inside that wouldn't let him just sit down and bite his tongue and ask Danielle about her grades or anything else because of that five thousand dollars. For crying out loud, five thousand dollars!

"You know what? Go ahead," he said, picking up his jacket and satchel. "I'm going to the gym."

Elizabeth watched Tony turn his back to her and walk toward the bedroom. She wanted to scream at him. She wanted to run out and jump in her car and go to the gym herself. Why couldn't she be the one to run away? But running from their problems didn't help anything. She wanted to stand toe-to-toe and argue until he heard her, finally *heard* what she was saying instead of accusing and walking away. That was what he always did and it infuriated her. Just ended the conversation like he was slamming the door on an aluminum siding salesman.

The thing that had kept her from exploding was the sight of Danielle. She had stood there looking at her report card. All those As and all she could do was stare at the C. No wonder. Danielle had been nervous about her father's reaction—but he didn't react. He hardly acknowledged her presence, let alone her concern. Why couldn't he see what he was doing to her? Any person with half a heart could see it.

Elizabeth smelled something acrid, some disturbance in the cooking force, and looked at the oven. A tuft of smoke belched from the vent and her heart sank. She opened the oven door and pulled out the rolls that were supposed to look all buttery and brown on top but were as black as charcoal. She picked one up with prongs and inspected it.

"Well, I burned the rolls," she said, more to herself than anyone else. She tossed the roll in the trash and then threw the whole batch out.

"It's okay, Mom."

"Yeah, I know," she said. She dished out the spaghetti and sauce for Danielle, put her salad bowl beside it, and went to the bedroom to talk with Tony.

"Look, if you'll just come and eat with us—"

"I can't," he snapped. "This has wrapped me up all day. As soon as I got the notification . . . I can't believe we're going through this again! Of all days!"

"Of all days?" she said.

"I made a sale today. A big one. The one I've been angling for. I mean, it was the best feeling to seal that deal and shake that guy's hand. And then I get the news that you've—"

"Tony, please—Danielle needs to hear you say it's okay. That she's okay."

"I'll talk to her later," he said. "I'll tell her that later. And I don't need you telling me what I have to do. I have a relationship with my daughter, okay? You don't have to get between us like this."

"I'm not getting between you, I'm trying to help you understand!"

He grabbed his gym bag and stormed out of the room. The door to the garage slammed like thunder. And then she heard the familiar clacking and the sound of Tony's car pulling away.

Tony drove fast to the gym and stretched out while waiting for a pickup game—and then he was off, dribbling and moving the ball up court as fast as he could. He was aggressive, going for the basket each time he touched the ball, driving to find an open lane. When one closed, he'd pull back and look for another. On defense he went for steals, fouled hard, and worked up a good sweat at the expense of his opponents, mostly slower white guys. It felt good to be on the court, to be in a game he could control instead of something he couldn't.

They were at game point, going to twenty, of the third matchup when his lifelong friend Michael called for the ball at the corner. The defense shifted slightly and Tony shook his head. Finally he got him the ball and Michael dribbled near the top of the key and signaled. Tony nodded and followed Michael down the lane.

It was poetry in motion. Everything slowed as Michael elevated and laid the ball off the glass. Tony jumped, took the ball, and jammed it through the net.

"Ball game!" Michael shouted.

Every player on the court and those waiting whooped and yelled at the move. Tony was surrounded by teammates who slapped his back and gave him high fives. His opponents even congratulated him.

"That was sick," one said.

"Let's run it back again," someone said behind him.

"Nah," Tony said. "I gotta go, man."

"Come on, one more game."

"We just beat you three times." Tony glanced at the bleachers and saw two fresh players waiting. "Let these guys play."

"All right. Jump in, fellas."

Tony sat on the bleachers and wiped his face with a towel. His muscles were loose now and a lot of the stress from home was gone. The five thousand dollars still hung over him and stung his gut, but he had calmed somewhat about it.

Michael sat next to him and gave him a slack-jawed look. "You all right, dog?"

"Yeah," Tony said. "Why?"

"You looked like you played a little mad tonight."

Michael was a good player, quick and able to see the whole court. But he didn't have the killer instinct.

"So? It just means I play better," Tony said.

"Better means ball hog? Dude, I can't get a pass from you. It'd be easier to baptize a cat."

"I just needed to blow off a little steam, okay?"

"Well, I hope you're done."

Tony smiled. Michael was right, but he was also jealous. There were some who had it and some who didn't. On the court and in life.

"Anyway, it's cool, man," Michael said. "We all gotta do that sometime."

Tony could tell Michael was opening the door to talk about *why* he needed to blow off steam, and part of him wanted to go there. But he thought better of it, especially with somebody from church. The stuff about his family, his marriage—all of that was best kept to himself. And there were other things beneath the surface, steam rising from different places in his life he couldn't let escape. Not with somebody like Michael. Not with anybody, really.

"Yo, see you in church, right?" Michael said.

"Maybe."

"Maybe means no."

Which was true. A maybe in a sale meant no. You kept pushing until you got a yes. But church didn't hold much interest for Tony. He saw it as a necessary evil. Something that tied up his Sunday mornings but was good for the family, good for his marriage, and supposedly good for his soul. Networking. He made contacts there and kept his image intact.

It was just that church had become a guilt trip. He felt bad when he was there, as if something was off-kilter down in his heart, and sitting in the pew looking at all the people with their lives together—perfect kids and perfect marriages—pointed out how much he didn't have. But when he didn't go, he got the glare from Elizabeth.

"Hey, Tony, you gotta hit me one," a player from the other team said as he was leaving.

"Come on, man, I gotta go," Tony said, smiling.

The guy stuck his thumb over his shoulder to indicate the players behind him. "Dude, I just told all these guys. Just one."

He knew what the guy was talking about and it had nothing to do with basketball. He wanted to tell them he was tired. He wanted to just walk out. But everybody was turned now. He was onstage.

Tony tossed his gym bag and towel to the floor and looked at the players as if to say, *Watch this carefully. I'm only doing it once.* He braced himself, tightened the muscles in his legs, and let the memory work. From a standing position he jumped, flipped in the air, and landed perfectly on his feet with his arms tucked into his body.

The new guys stood with their mouths open. The ones who'd seen it before clapped and cheered.

"I told you!" the player yelled.

Michael shook his head and Tony grabbed his stuff.

As he reached the door, Ernie Timms came into the gym flipping through a stack of pages. He was a thin man with wisps of hair he tried to comb over, but that wasn't working for him. He'd been the director of the community center for a few years and things weren't going well. It always seemed like there was some crisis they were trying to avert with funds or programs.

"What's up, Ernie?" Tony said, noticing the man seemed a bit flustered.

"Hey, Tony. Do you know how long you guys reserved the gym tonight?"

"I think it was till nine thirty," Tony said. "Why?"

Ernie frowned. "Oh, boy. I think we've double-booked it. Okay, so . . . okay. Thanks."

Clueless. The guy was always walking around in some kind of daze. Tony was determined not to be like Ernie.

Miss Clara

✦ ✦ ✦

Clara was in the produce aisle at Harris Teeter, trying to choose the right size tomato, when Clyde dropped the bomb. Her son took her shopping each week and spent time with her in this humdrum duty. She was fine driving herself, of course, but it seemed to make Clyde feel like he was doing something for her, plus she got to spend time with him.

After she had gotten past seventy, visits to the doctor increased—they wanted her to come in every whipstitch. And investment people wanted to sell her some new policy, and the retirement home people practically camped out on her front steps. But she didn't expect the latest offer to come from her son.

"What would you think of coming to live with us, Mama?" Clyde said.

Clara found a soft spot she didn't like on the tomato and put it back. "Now why in the world would I want to do a thing like that?"

"Well, my guess is you won't want to right away. But Sarah and I have been talking about it. Praying about it."

She looked up at him. She could remember holding him on her lap, reading a story, kneeling down beside him. Then came the years she spent on her knees because she was concerned how he might turn out. Those years were long gone.

"With everything you've got on your plate, you're praying about me coming to live with you?"

Clyde inspected the tomato now. "Maybe this isn't the right place to bring it up."

"What are you so worried is going to happen to me?" Clara said. "You only live four blocks away."

"Mama, that old house and all those stairs—it concerns us. What if something happened? What if you fell? You won't keep that cell phone with you like we've asked."

"Do you want to see me do a handstand? Is that it? Here, hold my dress down while I—"

"Mama, stop it."

"What will it take to prove to you that I can handle living alone?"

"I know you love that house. I know your treasures are there."

"My treasure is in heaven, and if I could go there and not be a burden to anyone, I'd hitch the wagon right now."

"And if that's what God wanted, He would have taken you a long time ago. He apparently has things for you to accomplish down here."

Clara looked at Clyde squarely, a little twitch in her own eyes. "Don't you think I've lived long enough to have the right to live where I want? Haven't I done enough to deserve that?"

"You have, Mama. And you deserve a lot more. I'm just asking you to consider it for our sake. We don't want anything to happen—"

"Nothing is going to happen to me," she said, scrunching her face into a frown. "I'm not like some old codger who can't get around. You stop worrying about me."

He pushed the cart away from her to the bread aisle. For some reason every grocery store she had ever shopped at put the bread and milk on opposite ends of the universe. Produce and meat were separated too.

She followed him, toddling along until she caught up and put the tomato in the cart. She could tell this conversation was weighing on him.

"You want that raisin bread you always get?" Clyde said.

"Forget the raisin bread and turn around here and talk to me," Clara said, grabbing for a loaf and checking the stale date. "Now what's going on in that head of yours?"

"You know we did some work on the garage and put in a little apartment on the back."

"You said you were going to rent that out for extra income. Maybe take in somebody who needed help."

He bobbed his head. "Well, that was partially true. Sarah and I were kind of hoping we might be able to convince you to move in."

"That's what you were thinking all along?" she said. "That's the craziest thing I've heard in my life. What am I supposed to do with my house?"

"Sell it, Mama. The house prices are good right now. You'd have a nest egg."

"Nest egg," she said, like the words left a bad taste in her mouth. "My Social Security and your father's life insurance and pension are all I need."

"All it's going to take is one fall down those stairs—"

"Now there you go again," she said, interrupting. "You don't think I know how to use the handrail?"

"Excuse me," a younger woman said. She had a fussy baby in a car seat in the middle of her cart. "I just need a loaf of whole wheat."

"Grab her a fresh one from up there, Clyde, and check the stale date," Clara said. "This is my son. He thinks I should come live with him because I'm getting old and feeble."

Clyde shook his head as he grabbed the bread. "I didn't say that."

"Do I look old and feeble to you?" Clara said to the young woman.

"Mama, this lady doesn't want to get into the middle of our problems."

CHRIS FABRY

The young mother smiled and thanked Clyde for the bread. "No, ma'am. You look quite healthy."

"See there. A mother knows." Clara waved a hand. She peeked over the edge of the car seat. "My, would you look at that beautiful baby."

The mother told Clara the child's name, and the sight of the old woman seemed to calm the child.

"I'm going to add this little one to my prayer list, if you don't mind," she said.

"I wouldn't mind at all. You can pray for my husband, too." The woman said it with some sadness in her voice.

"Well, I might as well throw in the whole lot of you. What's your name?"

Clara spent the next few minutes learning the woman's name and where she lived. Clara told her about her church and pulled Clyde into the conversation. When the young mother left, she seemed to walk with a lighter step.

"Have you ever met a stranger, Mama?" Clyde said.

"I expect I have at some point," Clara said. She led Clyde to the dairy aisle for some low-fat cottage cheese. When she got there, she turned to him. "I know you care about me, Son. And I didn't know you were going to all the trouble of that apartment for me, so I'm flattered. When the Lord tells me it's time to move . . ." She stopped, thinking about the feeling she'd had in her war room. "I can keep the cell phone with me if it would make you feel better."

Clyde looked at the floor and inspected the tile. When he looked up, there was a mist in his eyes, and Clara could swear she saw a hint of Leo in his face—the same kindness and gentleness leaking through.

"It's about your granddaughter. Hallie is having a rough time."

"I pray for that girl every day."

"I know you do."

"I've asked her to come over and talk with me. I'm just down the street."

"And I wish she would, but she stays in her room most of the time. We've tried everything. Sarah and I were thinking if you lived with us, maybe your being closer would . . . I don't know."

She put a hand on his arm. "All that important stuff you do with the city, all those decisions—and a teenage girl will wear you out."

Clyde nodded. "I'd rather deal with a teamsters' contract than try to figure out my daughter."

"What makes you think she would come see me if I moved in?"

"She loves you, Mama. She always has. I think if you were there, it might be different. All we need is a crack in the door, just a little light. You know?"

The suspicious side of Clara thought this might be a ruse to pluck at her heartstrings. But when she saw the pain on her son's face, she knew it wasn't. "And you've been praying I'd come live with you because of Hallie?"

"I'd be lying if I said it was only that. We want you to be safe and not alone. And we don't want to force you or coerce you. But I got the impression the other day . . . and Sarah agreed. Both of us want this."

Clara searched his eyes and saw what she was looking for. It was there, underneath all the layers. Love. That's why he was bringing all of this up. She had to focus on that and not the bad feeling she had of being moved to the side of life's road. Even if this wasn't what he meant, it was the way she felt.

When they checked out, she saw the young mother ahead of them and waved at her and her baby.

"You'd have your privacy," Clyde said, picking up a magazine and leafing through it. "We wouldn't bother you a bit."

Clara stared at him. "Where do you get this stubborn streak? It must come from your father's side of the family."

Clyde laughed and shook his head.

After her things were put away at home and Clyde had left, Clara headed upstairs and at the top stopped and wobbled, the room spinning. She reached out just in time to grab the handrail to steady herself. What if she had fallen? She could see Clyde looking down at her in some hospital room and a doctor suggesting a hip replacement.

When she made it into her war room, she knelt and poured out her heart.

"Lord, if You want me to move, I'll obey You. You know that. But You can't want me to leave all these memories. There are too many answers to prayer in this room. We do some good work together here. Why would I need to . . . ?"

The questions mounted, one on top of another, until all she could hear was her own voice crying out. And then a wave of peace washed over her and told her it wasn't where she lived that mattered, but that she was walking with Him.

She began to sing softly, an old song. "'Every day with Jesus is sweeter than the day before.'" Tears came to her eyes and she nodded and shook her hands together.

"Father, I wanted to grow old in this house. I wanted to live here till the end. You know how much of my heart is wrapped up in the life I've lived here."

Then she was back to asking why and it felt like wrestling. But in the end she knew she was wrestling with her own will. She had a loving son and daughter-in-law. She had a granddaughter who loved her. But change was hard, especially for someone who had defined "home" as one spot on the planet for so many decades.

"Lord, if You're going with me, I don't want to be anywhere else. I want to walk with You wherever You lead. So if this is Your plan, You must have some assignment for me. Maybe it's Hallie. Maybe it's someone else. I'm going to trust You. I'm going to follow You. That's what I'm going to do, just follow You, and if this is a mistake, You stop me."

She stayed on her knees, hoping to hear some booming voice that didn't come.

"All right then," Clara said, standing. She gingerly walked down the stairs to the kitchen, where she still had the yellow pages stuffed into a drawer by the silverware. You could find anything you wanted on the Internet, but she liked the notes she'd scribbled beside the plumbers and electricians who had helped her through the years. She hand-copied notes from previous phone books into the new ones that came but she'd never had to turn to the realty section. How did you go about choosing such a thing?

"Now if I'm going to work with someone, Lord," she said aloud, "I might as well work with somebody who follows You so I can bless them with the commission."

Her mind whirred and spun like a hard drive. Maybe God wanted to use her in someone's life who didn't know Jesus. Maybe God wanted her to work with someone who had no religion at all or who was caught in some kind of lie about Him.

Clara looked over the pages, the catchy phrases that realty companies used to draw people in, and she thought about prayer. Of course. Everything came back to the topic. Most people made it more complicated than it really was, she thought. They looked for a formula or a mathematical equation. And believed that if you didn't do every step right, you didn't get what you were praying for. She knew nothing could be further from the truth because prayer was about relationship. Prayer was talking and listening and being excited to spend time with someone who loves you.

She turned the page and felt like putting a finger down and letting that be the determining factor—wherever her finger landed. Then the doorbell rang. Maybe it was God bringing a Realtor to her without her even calling!

She opened the door and saw the young man before her and realized she'd forgotten the appointment she had made. She searched her mind for his name until it came.

"It's Justin, right?"

"Yes, ma'am. My mom said you needed some help with yard work."

"That's a fact," she said. "Now you come on in here and let me pour you a glass of lemonade and we'll talk about terms and conditions."

The teenage boy didn't seem to understand, but he came inside anyway.

"Your mother says you're fifteen. Is that right?"

"Yes, ma'am."

"I like the way you talk. You're showing respect, and that's good." She poured a glass of lemonade and set it before him, thinking of the conversation she'd had with his mother the day before. The worry she had as a single mom who couldn't spend as much time with him as she wanted. All the bad choices a young person could make these days.

"I have two rules," she said. "Take pride in yourself and in the job you do."

"Ma'am?"

"I want you to do a good, thorough job on my yard. No skimping or shortcuts. You don't try to race around and see how fast you can get it done so you can do something else. You take your time and take pride in how this yard looks when you walk away from it."

"Yes, ma'am," Justin said. "I can do that."

"The Bible says whatever you do, do it to the glory of God. Whatever you put your hand to, do it with all your heart."

"Yes, ma'am. But what do you mean about taking pride in myself?"

"The way you dress. The way you stand up straight and look people in the eye. I can tell your mother has done a good job. I want you to keep that up—along with those pants. A man wears his pants around his waist, not sagging down to his knees."

Justin couldn't stifle a smile, and Clara knew this was the way you changed the world. You first let God change you. And pretty soon He brought somebody else along and if you were attentive enough to listen and hungry enough, He would bring others who wanted to not only see a change, but live change.

Clara showed Justin the yard and the hard-to-get places with the mower. When she finished, she asked, "You don't know any good Realtors, do you?"

"No, ma'am. But the next-door neighbors just sold their house and they seemed to like them."

"What was the company?"

"The sign had a number and then rocks, I think. No, stones. That's what it said. Twelve Stone."

Clara nodded, thanked him, and told him to come back the next day to start work. She found the listing for Twelve Stone Realty and called, finally reaching a woman named

Elizabeth Jordan. She sounded young and pleasant. Easy to work with.

"Now I'm not sure when I want to sell, but I need somebody to help walk me through it."

"I would be more than happy to help you, Ms. Williams," Elizabeth said. "I'll give you my cell number so you can reach me anytime."

CHAPTER 3

✦ ✦ ✦

Elizabeth got up early Sunday morning and went for a walk to clear her head and heart. The blowup with Tony a few days earlier still hung over her. The distrust he felt about her sister and brother-in-law was like a knife in her side. But the strain in their relationship didn't seem to bother Tony at all. He was just as stoic and stubborn as ever. His running off to the gym and grabbing something to eat rather than eating with them told a lot. He was like a little boy who couldn't deal with issues. Things simply had to go his way or he'd take his toys and play somewhere else.

Elizabeth got the uneasy feeling that there might be something else going on with him, bigger than the money struggles or their constant bickering. Bigger than the communication problems and the way he'd get antsy and snap at them. But what could it be?

She walked past the finely manicured lawn of a man in their church. Carl was always tinkering with the lawn mower or string trimmer, spraying weeds or digging out a new flowerbed for his wife. The brick house looked like some Thomas Kinkade painting, everything clipped and in its place. A lantern hung over the mailbox. Even the sidewalk in front of their place somehow looked better. Did people ever have a perfect marriage? Was her family the only one that went through this kind of pain?

She woke Danielle when she returned but decided not to disturb Tony. She wasn't going to nag him, wasn't going to remind him what day it was and that they needed to leave by 8:45 to make it on time for church. But to her surprise, he was already up and in the shower.

They didn't talk as they drove, mainly because Tony flipped on the radio to a sports station counting down to the big game that afternoon. He didn't ask what she wanted to listen to. He didn't speak to Danielle about her report card. He just drove and reacted to the sports news.

At church, Elizabeth sat with an arm around Danielle and listened to the pastor speak about a passage in the Gospel of Matthew. She was having a hard time concentrating on the message because all she could think about was Tony. He had absolutely no compassion, no understanding of her or Danielle. He was upset about the money and hadn't even asked about her sister. Cynthia was going through a really hard time and Elizabeth wanted to be there for her. But Tony stood between them. He was obsessed with getting ahead and getting enough in the bank, when he knew good and well that there would never be "enough." The more he made, the more he needed to make. And any withdrawal, no matter how necessary or compassionate, was looked at as a personal affront to him.

"Jesus gives us the cure for anxiety in this passage," the pastor said. "He tells us to look at the birds of the air and the way they go about life. Now I don't know about you, but I've never seen a stressed-out bird, except for ones in cartoons."

The congregation laughed, and the pastor transitioned into a story from his childhood about how stressed his mother would get when they went on vacation. His father planned the route of the trip with pinpoint accuracy, and if anything went wrong, he got flustered and angry. The two of them together made a volatile mix and provided anything but relaxation. "Vacations in our home were things you needed a vacation from."

Elizabeth glanced at Danielle and smiled. Her daughter was only ten, but she already had an open heart to the things of God. She paid close attention as the pastor talked about God knowing every human heart and having a plan for each of us.

"God can't be finagled into doing what we want Him to do. The favor of God can't be bought, traded, or manipulated," the man continued. "So if you think putting on your Sunday best and throwing a halfhearted smile across your face impresses God, you are deceiving yourself. And we all know we can deceive ourselves. You and I cannot manipulate the hand of God. He looks for those that seek Him with their whole heart, and He does incredible things in their lives. So it all comes down to this. Either we truly seek Him, or we don't."

Elizabeth heard the door open behind them and saw a young woman walk past them to an open seat nearby. She wasn't bothered that the woman had come in late or that she had distracted her from the message. She was just a teenager and the length of her skirt and the amount of cleavage she showed were a little too revealing for Elizabeth's tastes, but that wasn't what bothered her either. The thing that galled Elizabeth was that Tony watched the young lady walk past with the concentration of an archaeologist studying a newly found artifact. She kept expecting him to look away but he didn't. His eyes followed every movement until she sat. And then he looked some more. Elizabeth couldn't shake the sense that Tony was on the hunt. But that was preposterous. Tony would never . . .

After the service she slipped into the restroom and gathered herself, then walked toward their car. A woman approached and stopped her, introducing herself as a mom of one of Danielle's classmates at school. She apologized for keeping her.

"It's no problem," Elizabeth said. "What's on your mind?"

"I've been looking for an opportunity to ask you something."

"What about?"

"I know you're a Realtor and I've always been fascinated with real estate. I'd really like to get my license, but I'm not sure about the process."

Elizabeth answered her questions and suggested a book she had read before she entered the realty world. One of her colleagues was also giving a class at the local library. She handed the woman a card and told her to get in touch with anything else she wanted to know.

"Maybe we can have coffee at some point?" the woman said.

"That would be great," Elizabeth said, knowing that time for "coffee" was nonexistent in her busy schedule. She smiled politely and gave the woman a hug.

"So who was that lady you were talking with in the parking lot?" Tony asked as they drove home.

Elizabeth kept her eyes straight ahead. "She's interested in being a real estate agent. Why?"

"I could tell you had your professional voice on," he said. She glanced at him and he gave her a smirk.

"Are you saying I do something you don't do?"

"When I come to church, I'm just being myself," he said.

Steam didn't shoot out of her ears, but she could feel her heart rate quicken and her face flush. "I guess you were just being yourself while you were checking out that young girl who walked past us."

She regretted saying it as soon as it was out of her mouth. She regretted saying it in front of Danielle and not in private. She regretted putting her in the middle of one of their disputes again. But she didn't regret letting him know what she had clearly seen.

"You better watch that tone, Liz," Tony said, his voice a little too flat and unemotional.

Before she could answer, her phone rang. She stared at him a moment and in her peripheral vision saw Danielle shift uncomfortably.

"Elizabeth Jordan," she said, answering with her "professional voice." Tony raised an eyebrow.

"Elizabeth, this is Clara Williams. I spoke with you about my house."

"Yes, Ms. Williams, how are you?"

"I'm well, thank you for asking. I've made my decision to move ahead with the sale. And I'm calling to see if you could come by in the morning and take a look at the place."

Elizabeth checked her schedule on her phone. "Yes, I can see the house at 10 a.m. tomorrow."

"That's perfect. It'll give me a chance to spruce the place up a bit."

"Very good. I look forward to it."

"See you then."

"Bravo," Tony said sarcastically when the call ended.

Elizabeth set her jaw and willed herself not to respond.

She turned and saw Danielle putting in her earphones. Better to listen to music than hear her parents fight again.

Tony turned on the radio for the latest sports report.

✦ ✦ ✦

Tony put up his feet that afternoon and watched the game. He couldn't believe Elizabeth had seen him looking at the young lady in church. He didn't even realize he had been staring at her—that was a natural thing for guys, he was sure. Just checking out the beauty of creation.

Danielle said it was time for lunch, and he came to the table to grab some food. One look at Elizabeth told him she was upset. He shook his head, turned off the TV with the remote, and sat, pulling out his phone to watch the score. There were a couple of text messages he hadn't seen, one from Calvin Barnes at Holcomb.

I've never hit a ball this far in my life. Thanks, Tony!

Tony smiled, picturing the old guy swinging that big club.

Elizabeth broke the silence between them. "Danielle, I have to meet a client in the morning, so I'm going to drop you off early at the community center, okay?"

"Okay. Can we pick up Jennifer on the way?"

"Sure, if it's okay with her mother," Elizabeth said.

Tony often felt on the outside looking in at his daughter's life, and this was a good example. "Who's Jennifer?"

"She's on my double Dutch team," Danielle said softly, looking at her food.

He held his phone away for a moment and cocked his head. "I thought you were playing basketball."

"I wanted to jump rope again."

Jump rope? he thought. That wasn't what they'd agreed she would do.

"Tony, you should go see her practice tomorrow," Elizabeth said quickly, stepping into the uncertain space between them. "She's really very good."

He shook his head, trying to process the new information along with his schedule. "I'm out of town this week."

Elizabeth held her fork pointing down, her face bewildered. "When were you going to tell me?"

"I just did," Tony said matter-of-factly. This was how it always started. She wanted to know everything going on in his head. Every little thing. Like he could remember to tell her everything.

The frustration showed on Elizabeth's face. She put her fork down and sat back. "Tony, I know you're the company's top salesman, but in order for this family to function, we have to communicate. I thought you'd be here this week."

Slow and measured, he prepared his response, like a tennis player hitting a topspin forehand to her weak side. "Well, if you want to continue to live in this house, I have to make sales. And that means being flexible." He waited for her comeback. But she let the ball hit and bounce to the fence, saying nothing, which unnerved him.

He took a sip of his tea and turned to Danielle. "Aren't

you a little too old to be jumping rope?" He meant well with the question. He was trying to encourage her to excel at one thing instead of bouncing from one to another, and with her height and coordination, basketball was clearly what she should go for.

Danielle's face fell. She looked at her plate and then at her mother. Elizabeth's lips were tight and she shook her head slightly, a signal a teammate would give. Just another indication that he was on one side of the net and they were on the other.

"May I be excused, please?"

"Yes," Elizabeth said. "I'll put this in the fridge for you to eat later."

Danielle left and Tony watched Elizabeth empty the table. Finally he couldn't take it any longer and threw his hands up. "Hey, all I was doing was finding out about our daughter. Why did she quit basketball?"

"She wants to jump rope, Tony," Elizabeth said. "It's good exercise. She made a good friend in Jennifer, who you obviously don't care enough about to know."

"What are you talking about? Do you know how many things I have to keep in my head, how many plates I have to keep spinning to keep things going around here? So I don't know about one of her friends. Is that a federal offense now?"

She turned her back to him. He brought his dish over to the sink and she told him to just leave it. "I'll do these."

It was a demand, not an offer. She wanted him to leave.

So he did. He went back to the television and watched the game.

Elizabeth put in a load of laundry and organized her closet—anything to stay busy and out of Tony's path. When she got like this, she didn't even want to look at him. She was upset at the way he had treated Danielle and the stare he'd given the girl in church, like she was a piece of meat, and all the other things that had happened in the past few months piled up like wet towels and flopped around in the drum of her heart.

She sat on the bed facing her bookshelf and spotted a book on marriage. She had bought so many of these, thinking they were a good investment. She'd learned new communication techniques and ways to show respect. She'd even read books on intimacy by pastors and counselors who promised the best sex ever, but no matter how they couched the subject, the pages always made her feel inadequate, like she was the problem. She'd set out to discover Tony's love language but found that his was an unknown tongue and there was no translator available.

Elizabeth stood and retreated to her office, the spare bedroom upstairs. Pulling up the information about the Williams house she would see the next day, she looked through the homes in the area that had recently sold. This was part of the advance work she did to make sure they could come up with a good asking price that wouldn't be too high or too low. The home was in a nice neighborhood and the comps came out favorably, given what the housing market had been like in the past few months.

This was part of what she loved about her job—she was not in the business of selling houses, but was matching people with homes. You could run numbers all day, calculate square feet and bedrooms and fluctuating mortgage rates, but these were not the equations of life. What she loved was matching up a person, a family, with a dwelling where life would work, where they would fit and thrive and settle in and believe that they were finally *home*. Conversely, she loved being able to give a seller freedom, an ability to fly, whether they were moving because of a job change or downsizing or because of a death or divorce.

She put together the listing documents in a package to give Clara Williams. She didn't intend to get the listing contract signed at their first meeting. She'd do a good walk-through of the property and go over the contract details. If Ms. Williams was as old as she sounded on the phone, she probably would have a lot of questions about what to expect. And from the information she pulled up online, Ms. Williams had been in the same house for decades. Why did she want to move? A fall? The death of her husband? Maybe pressure from family members?

Every house was a story, a mystery to be solved. Every house had quirks and idiosyncrasies, and if you looked closely enough, you could figure out things about the people who'd lived there. She'd learned a lot selling houses. Sometimes she learned a little too much.

Elizabeth spotted a home online that a client had bid on a year earlier—a small three-bedroom bungalow that was still on the market at a reduced price. The deal had fallen through at the last minute because the buyer got cold feet. How many times had that happened in the past year? All that work, the multiple showings, the time, the mileage, getting the contract signed—all wasted because the buyer decided it wasn't the right time. Or that the backyard didn't have enough room. Or that the sun would be in their eyes while they drank coffee in the morning—seriously, one buyer backed away from a deal because the kitchen was too sunny three months of the year. But the frustration was part of the attraction. She never knew where a client might lead her, what they might put her through, or if she would ever get paid for the work she was doing. It was a matter of faith, a relinquishing of rights. Elizabeth resisted the urge to be upset with some client who backed away. How many times had she felt the same way? Yes, it was hard not to get paid for the searches and the time and energy expended, but she told herself that she would never regret treating people kindly and respectfully as they tried to make the biggest financial decision of their lives.

She didn't believe in overloading sellers with fancy flyers and printouts that would just be thrown away. Other Realtors believed that inundating sellers with information was the best way to go—more was better. But Elizabeth believed in simplicity. Someone selling a house wanted to know two things: how much their house was worth and how much it would cost to sell it. In other words, when everything was over, how much money could they keep? Those seemed like fair questions that deserved straight answers, so she always shot straight with her clients.

She looked at her watch, transferred the laundry to the dryer, and walked through the kitchen, spotting Tony simultaneously on his phone and watching a game. He glanced up at her and she tried hard not to frown or react negatively.

"Hey," she said.

He grabbed the remote and muted the announcers. "Hey."

"I didn't mean to snap about your traveling. It just kind of surprised me."

"I should have said something earlier," he muttered. "I can see your side. But I don't want to feel guilty for working. I don't want to have you come down on me because I'm trying to provide."

"I'm not against you providing, Tony." She wanted to push back, but something told her to let it go. Move on. Let the questions flop like the wet clothes and focus on something else.

"So where you headed?" she said.

"Asheville. There's a doctor at a medical center who's interested in one of our products. It's not as exciting as selling houses, of course, but it pays the bills."

What did he mean by that, "not as exciting as selling houses"? Was he dissing her chosen profession? She couldn't look at him without becoming suspicious or hurt, and there was a growing knot in her stomach that Tony had been right earlier. If she wanted to stay here, in the house she loved, she had to acquiesce, just go along with him.

The longer she stood there, with him glancing at the screen to check the next play, the bigger the knot grew.

CHAPTER 4

✦ ✦ ✦

Elizabeth watched Tony jump into his clothes and head to the garage Monday morning. This was his pattern of late— no breakfast, not even coffee to start the day. He would never let Danielle run on empty like that, but he did it all the time. At least when he was at home.

"Aren't you going to eat?" Elizabeth said.

"No time. I'll grab something on the road to Asheville. See you later."

Elizabeth woke Danielle and drove her and her friend Jennifer to the community center later in the morning. She reminded Danielle about her meeting and said she and Jennifer should wait at the center until Elizabeth returned at noon. The girls seemed excited to wait there after practice together.

Elizabeth pulled up to Ms. Williams's house and saw a teenage boy with lawn clippers and a wheelbarrow standing in the lawn at the front. He was as tall as she was, thin, sweaty from his work, and carried garden gloves in his back pocket. An old woman counted out some money to pay him and he was off.

The first thing Elizabeth thought when she saw the house was that it would sell quickly. It was in a great part of town. It had mature trees and a manicured and well-maintained lawn. The American flag hanging at the front stairs was a gorgeous touch. There were mostly older homes in the neighborhood. Elizabeth picked out the spot on the lawn that would be best for the Twelve Stone Realty sign.

As Elizabeth got out of the car, she heard Ms. Williams say, "Tell your mama I said hello, and I'll see you next week."

"Yes, ma'am. Thank you."

The boy was off with a grin as broad as the street, clutching the money and the wheelbarrow handles.

"Ms. Williams?"

"That's me," the woman said. "You must be Elizabeth."

She had an accent that was Southern, through and through. And a way of holding her mouth when she talked that looked like she was trying to keep marbles from escaping. Elizabeth shook hands and tried to be gentle, in case the woman suffered from arthritis, but Ms. Williams squeezed her hand like she was juicing a lemon. She asked Elizabeth to call her Clara, then invited her inside to show her the house.

She walked with a hopping gait, throwing out her elbows as she stepped lively up the concrete stairs. She wore a teal sweater over a pink shirt and black pants. Her hair had gone gray long ago, but there were glimpses of the original color there.

As soon as they walked inside, Elizabeth felt a warmth. She stopped in the foyer, looking at the sitting room on her left and the study on her right. She could see her reflection in the hardwood floor. Everything was neat and tidy, though the furniture was a bit aged and the carpet, where there was carpet, looked a little worn. It had been lived in—that was to be sure—but there was no sign of neglect and her first impression was that the home reflected a sense of class—it had a regal feeling.

"I've got to put the coffeepot on. Can I get you something?"

"Oh no, thank you. I had mine at home. This is a beautiful house."

"I think so too," Clara said from the kitchen. "Built in 1905. And I've lived here almost fifty years. Leo added that sunporch in the back all by himself."

Elizabeth surveyed the front rooms, then found a picture on the wall of a much-younger Clara standing beside a man in a military uniform. She guessed from the age of the photo that it was sometime in the late 1960s or early

1970s. There were other photos of him alone and two eagles of different sizes mounted on the wall.

"Oh, this must be Leo," Elizabeth said.

Clara walked around the corner and beamed at the photo. "That's Leo. We were married for fourteen years before he died. He had just been promoted to captain before that picture was taken. He was so handsome in that uniform. He's fine, ain't he?"

Clara chuckled and Elizabeth felt warmed by the old woman's voice. Words like *before* came out *befoe*.

"Yes, we wanted five or six children, but the Lord only gave us Clyde." Clara gave her a wide-eyed look. "'Cause he was all I could handle."

Elizabeth smiled. She liked the old woman already. And that was half the battle of a real estate transaction. Liking the people you worked with was a huge plus. She was going to have such satisfaction in getting the asking price for this place.

Clara turned to the sitting room and pointed at the ceiling. "You see that big crack over there on the wall? That was Clyde."

She led Elizabeth into the room, which was flooded with light. A sofa and chairs were flanked by old lamps that gave an antique feel.

"This is my third-favorite place. It's my sitting room."

"What do you do in here?" Elizabeth said.

"Mainly sit," Clara said a little sadly, tossing her head to the side.

Elizabeth stifled a smile. If she was trying to be funny, the woman's timing was impeccable, but Elizabeth wasn't sure. She didn't want to offend her by laughing.

"Well, come on in here," Clara said, leaving like an early train. "Let me show you the dining room."

Elizabeth followed into an even-brighter room with pale-green walls and a large wooden table and chairs. There were candlesticks on the fireplace mantel and a delicate centerpiece on the table.

"Now this is my second-favorite place," Clara said, looking around. "I love this room."

"This is beautiful. And I love this fireplace."

Clara ran her hands across the tops of the wooden chairs as if she were replaying the past like she would a piano. "I've got a lot of good memories in here. Yes, I do. Lot of good talks happened in here." She said *here* like *heeyuh*. "Lot of laughter. And a few tears, too." She looked at Elizabeth as though she was trying to say more.

Elizabeth wondered what the memories were, if they were of her husband, her son—or more. It was hard to tell. She watched the old woman with a sense of awe at her easygoing way. There were some people in the world who, when you first met them, made you feel welcome, made you feel like you'd known them all your life. Clara seemed like one of those people.

Elizabeth followed the woman as she slowly navigated the stairs to the second floor. The staircase felt narrow, like in many of the older homes she had sold in the past few years.

"The kitchen needs some fresh paint, but it's still in pretty good shape." She slowed at the landing and grabbed one of the huge finials on the railing. Her breath became a little shorter the more she climbed. "Now this is why I'm moving in with Clyde a few blocks away. Whoo. It's getting harder to negotiate these stairs."

Elizabeth made notes about the house on her phone as they moved from one bedroom to the next. She noticed two wigs on Clara's dresser but didn't ask about them. There were also an ample amount of crosses and other Christian symbols throughout the home, not tacky but tastefully used.

"Okay, so three bedrooms and two full baths. Do you mind if I take some pictures?"

"Go ahead, that's fine." Clara stood with her hands behind her like a sentinel. Then she leaned forward. "Oh, you've got one of those smartphones. I've been meaning to get me one of those. Can't do nothing with mine but call folks. Must be a dumb phone." She leaned on the railing and waited for Elizabeth to finish.

Clara offered to pull the stairs down from the hall ceiling to get access to the attic, but Elizabeth said that wouldn't be necessary. When they were finished upstairs, the two made their way back down to the kitchen.

Elizabeth turned and offered a hand to the woman as she came to the last few steps. "You got it?"

"I do," Clara said. "They say if you live in a house with stairs, you'll live longer. So I should make it to 180."

Elizabeth stopped at a large frame in the hallway. At the top of the frame were the words *Answered Prayers*. Inside were several small pictures of people with dates and captions scrawled to commemorate events through the years. She studied the photos and faces. Martin Luther King Jr. was there. Faded photographs of families.

"This is fascinating, Miss Clara."

The old woman stood shoulder to shoulder with her. "That's my Wall of Remembrance. And when things aren't going so well, I look back on it and I'm reminded that God is still in control."

She said *God* like it was a two-syllable word, elongating the *o* as if out of reverence.

Clara crossed her arms. "It encourages me."

Elizabeth scanned more of the pictures. "I sure could use some of that," she whispered. As soon as the words were out of her mouth, she regretted them. She tried hard not to let her personal life into the business relationships she had with clients. This was about them, not her. But something in the house and the photos and the demeanor of the old woman made her want to open up.

Miss Clara turned to her and stared.

"Oh, I'm sorry. So, I've got a few questions about utilities and then we should probably talk about the asking price."

"All right," Clara said.

It took a while for Clara to find her utility bills and some other information. Elizabeth plugged in the numbers and thought about showing her the comparisons in the area, then glanced at her phone. She needed to get back to the office before she picked up Danielle and Jennifer. It felt like she'd been with Miss Clara for only an hour but it had been longer.

"Do you have a number in mind that you'd like to get for your house?"

"Isn't that your job?"

"Yes, it is, but sometimes a homeowner has a good handle on what to ask. I don't want to throw out a number that's way below what you think the property is worth."

The woman chewed at her lip for a moment. "I'm sure you'll come up with something fair."

Elizabeth smiled. "Let me look over the comps again before we decide. Would that be okay?"

Clara dipped her head. "That would be fine. I've been in this place a long time and I paid the mortgage off on it years ago."

They walked to the front door. "Okay, so I think I got everything that I need for now. So nice to meet you, Miss Clara. Listen, if you're available tomorrow, I'd like to come by and show you some comparisons in the area."

"Well, why don't you come by for coffee tomorrow morning and we'll talk about it then? Say, ten o'clock."

Elizabeth checked her phone and thought through her schedule. Tony popped into her mind. He would be out of town. What about Danielle? "Okay, yeah, I can do that. I'll see you at ten."

She started to walk to her car, but something bothered

her. In all the conversation she'd missed an important bit of information. From the top step she turned back. "By the way, what's your most favorite room?"

Clara smiled and Elizabeth could swear the woman's eyes twinkled. "I'll tell you tomorrow."

Elizabeth smiled back at her. "And I'll look forward to tomorrow."

Tony made it to Asheville in time to stop for some coffee and a breakfast bagel. He ate in his car in the parking lot, listening to a morning zoo show on the radio to fill the silence. Something the pastor had said the day before in his message made him uneasy. *"God looks for those that seek Him with their whole heart."* That stuck in his craw. Plus the part about people deceiving themselves. There were lots of people who were probably doing that, but he wasn't one of them.

He turned up the radio a little louder and finished his breakfast, then drove to the Asheville Medical Center about the time it opened for business hours. He lifted the hatch of his black Tahoe and pulled out the box of medical samples tucked away. He opened the case of Predizim, took two boxes from the package of eight, and set them aside, then rearranged the remaining boxes. He glanced around to make sure no one had seen him, then put the two boxes in his leather bag. He grabbed the case of Predizim, closed the hatch, and walked toward the building, taking out his phone.

"Starts with an *L*," he said to himself. "Lorna . . . no. Leslie . . . ?" He went to the Asheville listing and found the list of contacts and smiled when he saw he had remembered the letter correctly.

The receptionist was pretty and young and had a killer smile.

"Lindsay Thomas, how are you?" Tony said, turning on the charm.

"I'm fine," Lindsay stammered. "Mr. . . ."

"Tony Jordan. We met a few months ago. I came to see Dr. Morris."

"That's right," she said, blushing. "I can't believe you remembered my name."

"I like the name Lindsay, so it was easy."

More white teeth showing. She picked up the phone. "Let me see if I can get him for you."

Tony smiled and leaned a little closer, close enough to smell Lindsay's perfume.

✦ ✦ ✦

Elizabeth arrived at Twelve Stone Realty and finished the process of entering Clara's house into the multiple listing service. She met with Mandy and Lisa, who were talking about the latest scuttlebutt in town—the city manager who had taken charge of some dilapidated old homes and blighted areas in the city and turned things around.

"We need more leaders like C. W. Williams," Mandy said. "I'd vote for that man for president."

Elizabeth brought up Miss Clara's property, showed them the comps in the area and the asking price she'd been working on, but their conversation quickly turned to more personal matters. This was what generally happened at work. One or more would start talking personal issues and they would be off down that road until a phone call interrupted one of them.

Mandy was a managing partner of the firm. She was always dressed well and prided herself in making Twelve Stone one of the top firms in the region. No detail escaped her on contracts, and she only hired those who passed her checklist.

Lisa was one of those—she had been working at the firm two years before Elizabeth had signed on. She was younger than Mandy but cared for all the details that Mandy didn't have time for. The three of them worked as a team, though they had their moments of disagreement.

Mandy scrolled through some listings on her laptop as Elizabeth steered them back to the Williams property. Lisa took notes and asked good questions.

"Is she motivated to sell?" Lisa said.

"I think she'll sit tight for the right offer," Elizabeth said. "She owns the house outright."

"Where's she moving?" Mandy said.

"In with her son. He evidently lives pretty close to her."

Mandy glanced at Lisa and something passed between them. The two seemed to sense something was wrong with Elizabeth. Was it the look on her face? They'd asked when

Elizabeth walked in, and she'd said it had been a tough weekend at home but tried to leave it at that.

"Would you please just tell us what's going on at home?" Mandy said. "Your face says you've been through a tragedy."

Elizabeth sighed and spilled the story about Tony and their less-than-stellar conversations. Lisa sat a little closer to the edge of her chair and bore down on the truth that the main contention rested on the money Elizabeth wanted to give her sister.

"I knew it," Lisa said. "It always comes back to money."

"Oh, but it's deeper than that," Mandy said. "The money is a surface issue."

"We've gone around and around over this," Elizabeth said. "My sister and her husband have gone through a tough time and I think they deserve the help."

"And what does Tony say?" Mandy said.

"He says Cynthia married a bum."

"Is he a bum?" Lisa said. "Because there are bums out there."

"Let's not bring your personal life into this," Mandy said to Lisa, smiling at the jab.

Lisa rolled her eyes and looked at Elizabeth. "So what did you do? You transferred the money to your sister's account, right?"

"No, I took it from savings to checking. I was going to write her a check, but the way Tony reacted, I think I need to transfer it back."

"And what are you supposed to do about your sister?" Mandy said.

Elizabeth sighed. "I don't know what to do. Darren is having a hard time finding a job. But Tony has judged him as unfit. And he thinks it's my sister's fault. Can you even believe that?"

"Well, if my man said that to me, I'd be angry too," Mandy said. "We don't fight much anymore. After thirty-one years of stalemates, it just is not worth it."

"Oh, I wouldn't put up with it," Lisa said. "His money became your money the minute he said, 'I do.' So I'd give it to my sister anyway." She paused. "I don't even like my sister."

Mandy looked up from her laptop. "Just be careful, Elizabeth. You do not want World War III to break out in your home."

"No, I don't. But there are days, Mandy. There are days. . . ."

Mandy gave her a sympathetic look.

Elizabeth didn't have the heart to tell them about what had happened in church and the sick feeling she had about Tony's ogling the young lady who passed them. She pushed the memory down and told herself it was just one time. One little slip. There was no pattern there. She should just move on. Stop thinking about it.

"It's hard to submit to a man like that," Elizabeth said.

"You know what my mama used to say to me?" Mandy

said. "She used to say that submission is sometimes learning to duck so God can hit your husband."

Elizabeth laughed, but the pain was still there. "It's tough being a woman."

"You got that right," Mandy said.

Elizabeth looked at her watch. "I need to pick up Danielle and her friend at the community center. You guys okay without me?"

"We'll get along," Mandy said. "The question is, what's going to happen between you and Tony when he gets home?"

Lindsay let Tony through the door that led to Dr. Morris's office. He thanked her and watched her walk away. She had called ahead to a nurse who met him and led him to the samples closet.

"You can just use the third shelf down," she said when she unlocked the door. "Leave the door open and I'll come back and get it later."

He found the samples closet full, but there was a space in front where the literature and his business card could go. He pulled the Predizim boxes out of the case and placed them on the shelf. If he had left them in the case, it would have been easy to see there were bottles missing, but this way no one could tell. And what doctor was going to check whether they had been given six bottles or eight?

"You must be Mr. Jordan?" Dr. Morris said as Tony passed.

Tony smiled and shook the older man's hand. He had gray hair and was balding.

"Dr. Morris, yes, I'm Tony Jordan. Brightwell Pharmaceuticals. We met last March."

"I remember. How are you?"

"I'm doing fine. I saw your write-up on new stimulants and you showed interest in Predizim, so I just left you a case in the samples closet."

Dr. Morris smiled. "Oh, fantastic. I appreciate that."

"It's no problem. You'll easily find them. It's the third shelf, blue caps. What I need you to do, though, is just sign this receipt to show that I left them with you." He held out his digital device and the doctor signed the screen with a finger. "Now, Dr. Morris, if you need any more, you just let me know and I'd be glad to bring some over."

"Thank you, Tony. We'll try them out."

Tony shook hands with the man and smiled. "Sounds good. We'll see you again." He turned to leave and said over his shoulder, "And I'll be looking forward to that next article."

The man laughed and thanked him, and Tony quickly walked to his car.

✦ ✦ ✦

Tony pulled into a scenic overlook and took a picture with his phone. The view was amazing, the rolling mountains and trees coalescing in perfect symmetry with the low-hanging clouds. It looked like a postcard. He spent so much time driving from point A to point B that he rarely stopped to actually appreciate the beauty of nature. He rarely slowed down, period.

The view made him feel small, the way you feel when comparing yourself to something vast like the ocean. Perhaps that was why artists came to places like this, to record themselves in comparison with that which can't truly be captured on canvas or through a lens.

The pastor had talked about people's lives being like a vapor, here today and gone tomorrow. And even though Tony was still young, there was a sense of the years passing by too quickly. Danielle had been a baby just last week, it seemed. Now she was ten. Tomorrow she'd be getting married.

When they married, he and Elizabeth had both been happy, starting out on a journey together and moving in the same direction. But somehow, the journey had brought them to a place where neither was happy and he felt like they were moving in separate directions, pulled apart at the seams. Wasn't life supposed to be about happiness? Wasn't life too short to argue all the time? It was clear that they were at odds about so much, not just the situation with Elizabeth's sister. Elizabeth picked at him over such little things, things that hadn't bothered her early on but now seemed so big to her.

He stared at his phone, then pulled out the business card Veronica Drake had given him. Seeing Lindsay at the medical center had reminded him how many fish there were in the sea, so to speak. And while he wouldn't cheat on his wife, just dipping his toe in the water felt good, exciting.

He looked out at the expanse before him. There was beauty in the world and he was missing it. If he didn't take advantage of it, his window of opportunity would close. He dialed her number and heard it ring, then her voice mail answered. "This is Veronica Drake. Please leave a message."

He put a smile in his voice as he spoke. "Veronica, this is Tony Jordan. We met a few days ago after I met with Mr. Barnes. Hey, listen, I'll be coming through town next week and I was wondering if you could recommend a couple of nice restaurants. Feel free to call me back at this number. Take care."

Tony ended the call and drove away, looking out at the beauty of the vista. In the distance, just pushing toward the range of mountains, were ominous, dark clouds.

Miss Clara

✦ ✦ ✦

As soon as Clara met Elizabeth Jordan, she'd known this was the person God had brought. Elizabeth was beautiful, prim and proper, well-dressed, competent, and in control. She looked like she'd just stepped off the pages of *Success Journal,* if there was such a thing.

But Clara could sense Elizabeth was wearing a mask. It was nothing people could see on the surface, but something deeper.

God did not talk to Clara about people she met for the first time. In fact, people who played the "God told me" card annoyed her. She believed you got into trouble when God became your personal genie who wanted everything in life to turn out the way *you* wanted it to and spoke to you every moment of the day.

She did believe, however, from the minute Elizabeth set foot in her house, that God had brought her for a reason. Clara didn't know why or what was happening in her heart, her family, or her marriage. But she had enough faith to not have to know any of that.

Clara added Elizabeth's name to a list on the wall of her closet and asked God to help her see what Elizabeth needed most. "Lord, help me say the right amount. Not too much, not too little. Draw her to Yourself through me, if that's Your will. And make me a faithful witness for You because, Lord, You have been faithful to me."

At the end of the prayer, Clara asked God to help her sell her house. She had almost forgotten that part. But she'd found that's what God would do to her soul—He would take the things that felt so big and show what was really important.

"O Lord, You know I have a big mouth. But You can use anything that's surrendered to You."

Life was best at the point of surrender. It was there that she saw God do His special work. And it was that surrender Clara hoped to see in Elizabeth.

That evening she called Clyde and they talked about the weather and Clyde's work for the city and some big decision he had to make and what Sarah was into. At the end of the conversation she said, "Now what color carpet did you put into that garage apartment you made?"

"Carpet?" Clyde said. "Why in the world would you want to know what color—?"

"Because I want to know if my curtains are going to clash with the color scheme."

Clyde paused a moment. "Mama, are you saying what I think you're saying?"

"I don't know what you think I'm saying, but there was a Realtor at the house this morning and I'm supposed to sign some papers tomorrow."

Clyde cackled and called Sarah to the phone. "You have to tell her what you just told me. She's not going to believe it unless it comes from you."

It was the happiest Clara had heard her son in a long time. And that made her feel warm all over.

CHAPTER 5

✦ ✦ ✦

Walking into Clara's house felt like coming home to
Elizabeth, in a way. The two of them sat in the dining
room as Clara waited for her coffee to finish percolating.
The smell of the fresh brew permeated the house. The
old woman sure loved her coffee.

Elizabeth put a folder in front of Clara. "I ran a sales
report from the area and wrote down a suggested asking
price for the house." She pushed the page across the table.

Clara picked it up, adjusted her head to see the writing clearly, and gave an "Um-hmm." Elizabeth let her read
and waited. It was important not to rush people who were
mulling contracts and legalese and especially the asking

price. Everything was standard, but older people in particular had a harder time with change and feeling like someone
was trying to fool them.

"Well, what do you think?" Elizabeth said after a few
moments.

More sounds from the woman's throat, but no words.
Studying the page like a surgeon looking over a chest
wound, Clara said, "What did you say your husband did
for a living?"

The question took Elizabeth aback. She thought the
woman would ask something about the house, how fast she
thought they could have an offer, how she'd come up with
that price.

Elizabeth quickly composed herself and answered,
"Well, we actually haven't talked about that, but he's a sales
rep for Brightwell Pharmaceuticals."

"Mmm-hmmm," Clara said, still glued to the pages.
"And where did you say you attended church?"

"We occasionally attend Riverdale Community."

"Uh-huh," Clara grunted positively, like she was pleased
to hear it. She looked up. "So you would say you know
the Lord?"

Elizabeth felt confused. Was this a counseling session or
were they trying to sell the woman's house? But she smiled
and put on a good face. "Yes, I would say I know the Lord."
When Clara didn't respond, Elizabeth leaned forward. "Do
you think the Lord is okay with this asking price?"

Clara ignored the question and it almost sounded like

she was humming some kind of holy tune to herself. "And you have children?"

Elizabeth was both annoyed and amused by the questions. She'd been through a lot of these meetings, but this was the first time she'd been grilled by anyone about her spiritual and personal life before signing off on the asking price.

"Miss Clara, my husband, Tony, and I have been married sixteen years. We have one daughter, her name is Danielle, and she's ten. She enjoys pop music and ice cream and jumping rope."

The woman's face lit from the glow of the new information. "Well, that's good to know," Clara said, nodding and smiling. Instead of being satisfied with the information and moving back to the contract, she doubled down on Elizabeth's spiritual life. "Now you say you attend church occasionally. Is that because your pastor only preaches occasionally?"

What had been amusing and a little cute coming from an older woman was moving toward offensive. Elizabeth took a breath and tried to choose her words carefully. She didn't want the sale to sour, but she had to draw a line in the sand. She had to be clear.

"Miss Clara, I really would like to help you sell your house. That's why I'm here. As far as my faith is concerned, I believe in God, just like most people. He's very important to me."

The woman dipped her head and with hands folded

gave a pained grunt. "Ummm." She rose from her chair, saying, "Let me get our coffee."

Elizabeth watched her move slowly past and wondered if that would be the end of the spiritual grilling.

From the kitchen, Clara's voice rose to carry through three rooms. "So if I asked you what your prayer life was like, would you say that it was hot or cold?"

Why in the world would the woman want to know about Elizabeth's prayer life? Clara kept stepping over the line Elizabeth had drawn. But she was sure Clara didn't mean to offend. She was amiable and kind. It was certainly easier to work with her than with some of the other clients who were hyper and asked Elizabeth to cut her commission in order to make the sale. Instead of placating, Elizabeth decided to answer truthfully. Just go with the flow.

Elizabeth spoke up so the older woman could hear, though she didn't seem to have any problems with her hearing. "I don't know that I would say it's hot. I mean, we're like most people. We have full schedules. We work. But I would consider myself a spiritual person. I'm not hot, but I'm not cold either. Just somewhere in the middle."

She felt proud of the answer. It was honest and forthright. She'd made clear that she was serious about spirituality—but not to the point of fanaticism. She hoped that would get the conversation going in the right direction.

Clara returned to the table with two cups. "I've got cream and sugar if you need it."

"Oh no, thank you. I like it black." Elizabeth took the cup as Clara sat. She took a sip and set the cup down again. "Miss Clara, you like your coffee room temperature?"

The woman cradled the mug in front of her. "No, baby, mine's hot." She blew across her mug and took a satisfying sip.

Elizabeth stared at her as if she were crazy, and then realized what the woman had done.

Clara leaned in closer and looked straight into Elizabeth's eyes. "Elizabeth, people drink their coffee hot or cold. But nobody likes it lukewarm. Not even the Lord."

Something ran through Elizabeth—a mix of embarrassment and humility, she guessed. She remembered something about a verse that said the Lord would spit you out of His mouth if you weren't hot or cold. It was a good word picture, but still a bit disconcerting.

"Point taken, Miss Clara. But why do you feel the need to examine my personal life?"

"Because I've been where you are." She said the words forcefully but kindly, like she knew what she was saying was hard but good. "And you don't have to step on the same land mines that I did. That's a waste of time."

Elizabeth felt the air go out of the room. What land mines had Clara stepped on? What did she know about Elizabeth's life?

Clara pointed at the paper. "And this asking price . . . is just fine."

She stood and moved toward the kitchen again. "Let

me get you a hot cup of coffee." She cackled as she walked. "I was a little sneaky the last time."

Elizabeth felt like she had whiplash. Clara had gone from her personal life back to the house without any signal. With the woman out of the room, Elizabeth had a chance to think. More curious now than hurt, she spoke up.

"What land mines do you think I may step on?"

"You tell me," Clara said. "Now, if there was one thing in your life that you could make better, what would it be?"

Such a good question. Like one of those things a seminar leader might throw out to a small group to get them talking, to get underneath the surface to something real.

"Just one?" Elizabeth said, smiling. "I'd probably have to say my marriage. If there's one thing we do well, it's fight."

Clara returned to the room, put the hot coffee mug down, and sat. "No. I don't think you do."

"I'm sorry?"

"Just because you argue a lot doesn't mean that you fight well. Every couple has some friction every now and then, but I'll bet that you never feel like you've won after you've had an argument with your husband."

Clara was exactly right. No matter how certain Elizabeth was about some issue that came up, no matter how many zingers she got in at Tony's expense, even if she felt like she was 100 percent right and he was 100 percent wrong, she never felt good after the argument. There was always a sense of loss after a confrontation. She sat back and thought about the argument over Cynthia and the money she'd moved to the checking account.

"Can I ask you how much you pray for your husband?" Clara said.

Prayed for Tony? She gave the woman a nervous look. In that moment she was unguarded and exposed, as if her whole life were being put under some Clara Williams microscope.

"Well, very little," Elizabeth finally said.

Clara looked at her tenderly, her eyes full of something close to empathy. She placed a hand on Elizabeth's and leaned forward. "Elizabeth, I think it's time to show you my favorite place in this house."

Elizabeth followed her up the staircase to the bedroom at the top. Clara swung her arms to give herself momentum when she reached the landing and her breathing became a bit labored. The bedroom was small, with a twin bed nicely made and a picture of a young man on the nightstand. Miss Clara's footsteps made the hardwood sag. She entered the room, opened the small closet door, and switched on the overhead light. Elizabeth peered inside what appeared to be an empty closet except for the small chair in the corner. There were no clothes or items stored above, no ironing board or umbrellas. Just a pillow, the chair, a Bible, and notes taped to the walls.

"Now this is where I do my fighting."

"A closet," Elizabeth said.

"I call this my war room."

Elizabeth stepped inside and felt a sense of peace waft over her. She glanced at the pieces of paper taped to the walls, the neat handwriting spelling out names and phrases. Some pages with verses of Scripture on them. Others had pictures on note cards. Some of the notes looked like they had been there for years.

"So you wrote prayers for each area of your life?"

"A prayer strategy. Yes. I used to do what you and your husband are doing, but it got me nowhere. Then I started really studying what the Scriptures say, and God showed me that it wasn't my job to do the heavy lifting. No. That was something that only He could do. It was my job to seek Him, to trust Him, and to stand on His Word."

It was like stepping into some holy place, a shrine of sorts, and pulling back the curtain that separated the everyday from the holy.

Elizabeth walked out of the closet, her arms crossed, and turned. "Miss Clara, I've never seen anything like this. And I admire it, I really do. It's just that I don't have time to pray that much every day."

"But you apparently have time to fight losing battles with your husband."

The woman could be brutal. But she was right. They frittered away their relationship with angry words that led to bitterness and distance. Elizabeth looked down, not knowing how to respond, how to cut to the heart with the insight of this old woman.

Clara spoke up again, her voice filled with passion.

"Elizabeth, if you'll give me one hour a week, I can teach you how to fight the right way, with the right weapons."

Elizabeth didn't answer. She just stood there in thought, looking at Clara. Then she led the way down the stairs, holding on to the banister to steady herself. She gathered her purse and the documents and walked out the front door, thanking Clara for the coffee.

On the porch, she turned. "Since you're good with the asking price, I'll go ahead and list the house," Elizabeth said. "I'd like to think about our other discussion."

The old woman's face was etched with concern. "Elizabeth, please forgive me for being so direct. I see in you a warrior that needs to be awakened. But I will respect whatever decision you make."

"Thank you, Miss Clara. I hope you have a good day."

"You too."

Elizabeth got in her car and drove away, but she couldn't help looking back at the woman on her porch, the flag flying above her. She looked like some kind of soldier on duty, watching the walls of the fort. Elizabeth couldn't shake the image of her war room, as she'd called it. And the fact that she'd seen her own name on one of the notes taped to the wall.

Elizabeth went to the office and made a few calls, then had a showing on the other side of town. By the time she got home, she was exhausted, and not just physically. The time at Clara's house had taken something from her. She sat on

the end of the bed, unable to change into more comfortable clothes, deep in thought. Her cell buzzed and she
checked the message. It was Jennifer's mom confirming
that Elizabeth was home. She texted back, I'm here.

Elizabeth rubbed her foot and stared at the wall, a sort
of spiritual and emotional paralysis setting in. Funny how
a few words from an old woman could press so deeply
against a person's heart, against her soul. She glanced at
her Bible on the shelf, a study Bible that had rarely been
studied. So much information in there, so much content
that sat unattended.

She heard the front door open and Danielle and
Jennifer walk in. Jennifer's mom had promised to drop
them off so they could practice jumping rope.

"If they do that stunt in the competition, they'll win,"
Danielle said.

"Hey, why don't you ask your dad about helping us get
uniforms?"

"He's not here. It's not like he would care anyway."

"Can you ask your mom? My mom already gave part
of the money."

"She's not here. She's out selling houses. Come on, we
can go to my room."

Elizabeth went to greet them, but the two were upstairs
already, on to some other conversation.

"So I told my dad that he could jump with us, and he
totally started laughing," Jennifer said. "He said he would

only do it if Mom did it with him, which of course she would never do."

Elizabeth followed up the stairs, drawn to the innocence in their voices.

"So they, like, start talking about doing the worst routine ever," Jennifer continued, "like in a funny way, and she starts laughing so hard her face turns bright red, then she just starts squeaking 'cause she can't breathe . . . It was hilarious!"

Both girls giggled. As Elizabeth reached Danielle's door, she stopped. Her daughter was lying on her stomach and cradling a stuffed panda. Jennifer was sitting up on the bed beside her.

"I wish I lived at your house," Danielle said. "Whenever my parents are together, they just fight."

The words stung. No, they were a stab in the heart. The pain was immediate, and Elizabeth wanted to lash out at Danielle for saying such a thing. For exposing their family like that. And then she realized her daughter was just telling the truth. She was sharing feelings with a friend that she couldn't share with her own parents.

Elizabeth wanted to retreat down the stairs, but Danielle saw her and Jennifer looked as well. There was an awkward moment of silence, and then, like any good mother would do, Elizabeth filled it by changing the subject.

"Jennifer, how's your family?"

The girl's face flushed. "Fine."

What was she supposed to say? *"We're all happy and*

laughing and have such good relationships compared with you, Mrs. Jordan"?

"Would you like to stay for dinner? You're welcome to eat with us."

"Okay," Jennifer said tentatively. The two of them looked like they'd been caught jumping on satin sheets with muddy shoes.

"Okay, I'm going to go change," Elizabeth said. "I'll call you girls down in a few minutes."

She made sandwiches and dished some potato salad onto their plates. The girls arrived quieter than usual. There was a lot of tinkling silverware and sighing around the table. The girls didn't speak and Elizabeth didn't see the need to jabber. You could spread the awkwardness on a piece of bread and still have some left over for breakfast the next morning.

Elizabeth couldn't get Clara's voice out of her head. And the revelation about how Danielle felt about their family only pressed harder at her heart.

After Jennifer's mother picked her up and Danielle got ready for bed, Elizabeth walked into her daughter's room and sat on the bed, slowly speaking the question she was afraid to ask.

"Danielle, you know we love you, right?"

The response was less than reassuring, just a silent nod.

"That wasn't very convincing."

"Well, I think you love me a little bit."

"A little bit?" Elizabeth said. "Danielle, you are my

daughter. You're the most important thing in the whole world to me. You've got to believe that."

Danielle stared back at her and came up with a question of her own. "What's my team name?"

Clara's questions had been enough for one day. Now here was another that seized her heart because she wasn't sure of the answer. "Umm . . . the Firecrackers."

"That was last year," Danielle said. Her voice began to choke with emotion as she continued. "What are our colors?"

Elizabeth thought a moment, straining to remember something she didn't know, hadn't noticed. She felt like a deer in double Dutch headlights.

"What jump rope trick did I just learn to do? Who's my new coach?"

Bewilderment turned to embarrassment as Danielle's eyes filled with tears. She sniffed and her chin puckered. "What award did I win last week on my team?"

Elizabeth looked through blurry eyes now, stunned. "You won an award last week?" She cradled her daughter's chin in one hand. "Danielle, I'm sorry. I'm so sorry." Then she reached out with both hands. "I'm so sorry."

Danielle leaned forward and Elizabeth hugged her and rubbed her back, apologizing over and over. Somehow her emotion helped calm her daughter.

Later, she thought about what had happened at that vulnerable moment for both of them. She had seen her daughter's tears and hadn't dismissed them or tried to explain herself. She had simply entered Danielle's world and validated her feelings instead of pushing them aside. Wasn't that what she was looking for with Tony? She wanted him to change, wanted them to move to the same page in life, but the first step was *seeing*. The first step was looking at the situation for what it was, not for what she wanted it to be.

As she finished straightening the house, the phone rang and she looked at the caller ID. It was Tony. She took a deep breath and immediately thought of Clara's closet. "Oh, Lord, help me not light into him."

He asked how she was doing and Elizabeth couldn't hold back the emotion about what she had learned, how she wasn't as connected with Danielle as she wanted to be.

"You think that just because I don't know the color of her uniforms I'm a bad father?"

Elizabeth stepped onto the back deck and closed the door. "Tony, *I* didn't know the color of her uniform. This is not about you."

"I'm busting my rear out here trying to provide for us, Elizabeth."

"I know that, and I appreciate you providing—"

"I don't need you tearing me down every time I check in."

"I'm not trying to tear you down."

"Yes, you are. Why are you telling me this about Danielle? It's because you think I need to step up, right? I need to do things just like you're doing."

"No, don't you see? I've missed Danielle too. I haven't

shown her the love I wanted to." She told him about the conversation she'd overheard between Danielle and Jennifer. "So if you think I'm trying to make you feel guilty, it shows how far apart we are."

"Right. What you're saying is, if I cared more about Danielle, and if I cared more about your sister—"

"This is not about Cynthia—don't turn it into that. Listen to me. Your daughter feels pushed to the back corner of our lives. She needs our attention. She needs to know she's loved."

"It always comes back to me being a bad father, doesn't it? I don't need this."

"I'm not calling you a bad father. This is a wake-up call for both of us."

Silence on the other end of the line.

"Tony?"

Elizabeth looked at the phone and saw a blank, flashing screen. He'd hung up on her. She wanted to punch something. She wanted to throw the phone all the way to Charlotte. She wanted the pain to be gone, and as she walked back inside, she slammed the door behind her.

It was hopeless. Her marriage was hopeless. Tony was hopeless. And she had no power to change anything.

✦ ✦ ✦

Tony hung up the phone and cursed. He didn't need constant drama. Every conversation dragged him down. Every day was more guilt heaped on him like trash in a Dumpster.

There was only so much a man could take. Only so much guilt could be piled up before something collapsed.

He went to the hotel bar, ordered a drink, and watched a game. He wanted enough alcohol to take the edge off and help him sleep. Just enough to quiet the voices in his head. He wasn't hooked on anything. He hadn't let it go that far.

He thought of Danielle. That girl had real talent, real athleticism. If anyone had reason to complain, it was him. Elizabeth should have insisted she stay with basketball. She was comfortable dribbling, and she saw the court, just like he could. The girl could get a scholarship when she graduated, there was no question. Was there a college in the country that gave you a full ride for jumping rope?

He shook his head. Elizabeth didn't think practically or logically. She wanted Danielle to feel affirmed. She wanted her to be emotionally healthy. Well, when you got in the real world, you got affirmation by doing a good job. The money and bonuses came when you landed the deal, not when you *felt good*. He should have put his foot down. He should have made Danielle stay in basketball.

The more he thought, the more upset he became, and he ordered another drink. He pulled out his phone and hit the Redial button, then thought better of it. He knew what would happen. Elizabeth would yell at him. He would yell at her. And the drama would escalate.

He didn't want any more drama. He'd worked hard to *not* have drama messing up his life. So he hit the Sleep button on his phone and turned his attention back to the game.

Miss Clara

✦ ✦ ✦

Clara watched Elizabeth leave and prayed she hadn't come on too strong. Elizabeth's face said it all. The mask was still there, tightly in place, but there were cracks and fissures showing. Clara asked that God would simply use their conversation and the tepid coffee to melt the young lady's heart.

Clara believed with all her heart that God worked all things together for good to those who loved Him and were called according to His purpose. But she did not believe that everything that happened was good. The world was fallen and there was sin in every heart. But God's grace was bigger.

The other truth she believed, from a life of experiencing it, was that for real change to happen deep in the soul, God tended to make people miserable rather than happy. He brought them to the end of themselves and showed them how powerless they were in order to show them how powerful He was. The children of Israel didn't push back the Red Sea. They didn't knock down the walls of Jericho. It was only when they were at the end of their rope and had to depend on someone bigger that they saw God work mightily. It was the same with each follower of Jesus.

She wanted to pray that God would restore Elizabeth's marriage and turn her husband's heart around and that everything would be fixed overnight. Immediate healing was easier to pray for than a transplant because a transplant takes time and someone else has to die. But the more Clara spoke with the Lord about the situation, the more she understood Elizabeth's life was probably going to get worse before it got better. And the issue wasn't just Elizabeth's husband. It was Elizabeth herself.

It wasn't an easy prayer, asking God to break someone's heart, asking God to bring people you cared about to the end of themselves. But before she prayed, Clara thanked God that He was big enough to do all that and big enough to bring praise to Himself in the process. She was sure He was going to do that somehow, though she wasn't sure how.

As she prayed, the tears came—tears for a daughter with parents who spent more time fighting than loving. Tears for

Elizabeth, who wanted to love the family God had given her. Tears for her husband, who seemed to have lost his way.

Clara ended her prayer thanking God for His power to change and His power to provide hope. "There is hope for everybody, Lord, no matter how far they've strayed. I know it better than anyone."

CHAPTER 6

✦ ✦ ✦

Elizabeth stood at Clara's house and knocked, checking her face in one of the windowpanes on the door. She heard shuffling in the front room, then the door opened and Clara stood smiling, her eyes showing more than words could tell.

"Well, good morning," she said.

The woman hugged Elizabeth as she entered, and Elizabeth felt warmth spread through her. Clara poured them both a cup of coffee. How she loved that coffee.

"I'll take mine a little warmer today," Elizabeth said.

Clara chuckled. "You know why I did that yesterday, right?"

"I caught the biblical reference. And I looked it up before bed last night. Book of Revelation, right?"

Clara nodded.

"I've been to church more often than you think."

Clara sat and looked into Elizabeth's eyes. "Do you want to talk about the house first or what's really on your heart?"

Elizabeth felt a deep ache inside, sitting here with this older woman. "I'm struggling with being a professional, with you as my client. I don't want to burden you with my personal life, but . . ."

"But your heart is breaking and you don't know where to turn. Go ahead. Clara can handle a little unprofessional conversation." The old woman smiled and patted her hand.

"Well, it's Tony," Elizabeth said, and she was off on a tirade about how he'd acted and the things he'd said and how he wasn't the father to Danielle that he should be.

"I can see it in Danielle's face when he comes home. And he's on his phone or watching TV. She's starved for his attention and her heart is just breaking and I was so unaware. Tony, he's *completely* unaware. That man is running out of time, Miss Clara. He's off in his own world being top salesman somewhere while his daughter is growing more calloused to him every day. He shows no interest in anybody but himself. And I'll tell you another thing. I don't have proof of this, but if he's not getting it from me, he's got to be getting it from somebody. He makes all these little flirtatious comments to other young women that just . . ."

Clara held up a hand and Elizabeth stopped midsentence.

"Elizabeth, just so I know. How much of the one hour we got together today are you gonna spend whining about your husband, and how much are we gonna spend on what the Lord can do about it?"

Elizabeth felt her face grow warm. "I'm sorry, Miss Clara. I just get so wound up the more I think about it."

"Your thoughts about your husband are almost entirely negative, aren't they?"

Elizabeth digested the question and realized she was right. But there was a reason she was negative. Tony really did act that way toward her and Danielle. "He acts like an enemy to me," she said.

Clara leaned forward. "See, you're fighting the wrong enemy. Your husband certainly has issues, but he's not your enemy."

Elizabeth searched the woman's eyes for some clue, some understanding of what she was saying.

"When I fought against my husband," Clara continued, "I was fighting against my own marriage and my family. I tried for years to fix Leo, but I couldn't do it."

"Well, I've gotten nowhere with Tony."

"'Cause it's not your job! Who said it was your responsibility to fix Tony? It's your job to love him, to respect him, and to pray for the man. God knows he needs it." She raised her voice to a falsetto. "And men don't like it when their woman's always trying to fix them."

Elizabeth chewed on that thought. If it wasn't her job,

who was going to do the fixing? Somebody sure needed to step in. . . .

"Elizabeth, you got to plead with God so that He can do what only He can do, and then you got to get out of the way and *let Him do it*."

Elizabeth's mind whirled. It was a helpless feeling not to try to change Tony. She had done it for years and the problems had only gotten worse. Now she could tell she was being drawn to answers born out of a life tested by time and circumstances. She felt the emotion welling and choked out the words "I don't even know where to start."

Clara handed a leather-covered journal to her. "You'll find some of my favorite Scriptures in there. They were my battle plan to pray for my family. You can start with that."

Elizabeth opened the journal to the beginning and saw pages filled with writing.

"You're going to see that there are some verses I wrote out and made personal, plugged in names in different spots. I poured out my heart in those pages. You get your own journal and find your own war room."

Elizabeth held the journal to her chest. "The house . . . I need to get the yard sign up and . . . so many details."

Clara leaned forward. "This house is going to sell in God's good timing. He's preparing the right person to come along. I believe that with all my heart. But this is more important, Elizabeth. Focus on the battle ahead. And I'll be right there with you."

When Elizabeth reached home, she went to her room, passed through the sink area, and opened her closet door. The space would certainly be secluded, but it was much too small and claustrophobic. She had so many clothes, so many shoes. She gave up on the idea and sat at her desk to read through some of the verses Clara had written down. She wasn't sure of the translation the woman used, but the words seemed to jump off the page at her. She quickly opened her own journal and like a scribe began to copy.

> If we confess our sins, He is faithful and righteous to forgive us our sins and to cleanse us from all unrighteousness.
> —1 JOHN 1:9

> The Lord is near all who call out to Him, all who call out to Him with integrity.
> —PSALM 145:18

> Rejoice always! Pray constantly. Give thanks in everything, for this is God's will for you in Christ Jesus.
> —1 THESSALONIANS 5:16-18

As she read, she could hear Clara's voice in her head, the way she said "God" so reverently and with a sense of awe. She would have emphasized the words *cleanse* and *always* and *constantly*.

Elizabeth came to Jeremiah 33:3, which nearly took her breath away.

> Call to Me and I will answer you and tell you great
> and incomprehensible things you do not know.

That's exactly what Elizabeth wanted. She wanted to know more about God, like Clara. She wanted to experience Him and talk with Him and have God speak to her. Her main concern was Tony, of course—that was the number one request, but she sensed there was more going on inside her than just wanting Tony to shape up. God was drawing her; it was clear to her now.

When she came to Matthew 6:6, it all seemed to come together.

> But when you pray, go into your private room, shut
> your door, and pray to your Father who is in secret.
> And your Father who sees in secret will reward you.

Elizabeth looked at her closet again. There was something about that sacred space Clara had, a place where she was all alone, could shut the door and silence the rest of the world. And the walls. She could put up reminders in there. Of course God could hear her anywhere she prayed, but if she truly committed to a space like that, if she went to the trouble to clear it out and get on her knees, maybe God would see that and reward a willing heart.

She got up from the desk and walked into the closet, pushing the clothes hangers apart. She turned to the opposite wall and taped her list there, then knelt and looked at it. There were shoes in boxes stacked up before her, so she closed her eyes and began.

"Dear Lord, I don't know how to do this. I mean, I know You want me to pray. You want me to spend time with You. And I'm going to bring my requests to You now."

Her knees ached already. She sat back and crossed her legs in front of her.

"Lord, You know that Tony is not the man I want him to be. He's not the man You want him to be. So I'm putting him right at the top here."

Her legs started aching. Maybe if she found something to sit on. She retrieved a sturdy storage box with a lid and sat on it, closing her eyes and continuing.

"You know, O God, that he's angry and doesn't pay much attention to Danielle and me. He's hurt her little heart so badly."

She tipped back and almost hit her head against the built-in dresser behind her, so she sat forward and crossed her legs. She looked at the prayer list again. Where was she? Still on Tony.

Maybe if she brought in the white chair with arms, it would be easier. Yes, that would help. Something with a strong back to it. She put the box away and got the chair and set it next to the prayer list and sat.

She wasn't sure if she needed to start over again or not.

Did God want her to just jump in or did she need to ramp up? Clara had said something about beginning with praise to God rather than just rattling off a list.

"Lord, thanks for this chair. And the house You've provided for us. Thank You for my daughter and what You've taught me through her." She paused a moment. "Thank You that You brought Tony and me together, Lord. I don't think I've thought about that for a while. I believe You did bring us together all those years ago."

Just the thought of thanking God for Tony was foreign to her, but there it was. It slipped out like a compliment she hadn't intended for someone who didn't deserve it. Maybe spending time with God like this would really help. She began to have a little hope, but then her backside started to grow numb from the hard seat, so she returned the white chair and found a bean bag in Danielle's closet that she didn't use anymore, plopped it on her closet floor, and sank into the beans.

"Lord, thank You for Jesus, for salvation, for the fact that I can be forgiven because of His sacrifice for me. . . ."

She glanced at the shoes in front of her. There was the pair she'd been looking for to go with that black dress. She picked up the shoe and studied it. Shoes held so many stories. She remembered the store where she'd seen this one. She and her friend Missy had been shopping that day and stumbled onto this cute little boutique. These shoes had called to Elizabeth, just whispered her name until she walked down the aisle and found them and tried them on.

She held the shoe close and sniffed. What an awful smell. She really needed to do something about her foot odor. Maybe if she got online and looked that up, she could find some kind of natural remedy like rubbing orange peels on everything. She had heard of one remedy that was also used after a skunk had sprayed a dog, something about tomato sauce and . . .

Elizabeth glanced back at the prayer list. Where had her mind run? Why was it so hard to stick with the task at hand? She should put her feet up there on the list, but healing them seemed almost as far-fetched as healing her relationship with Tony.

She was amazed at how easily distracted she could be when praying. As soon as she began her conversation with God, something else would creep in. She thought of all the things left undone around the house and things at work. Bills that needed paying, the grocery list she should add to. When she managed to push those thoughts aside, she became hungry and there was no pushing that aside. She crept to the kitchen, listening to Danielle and Jennifer practicing jump rope in the front yard, then retreated again with her snacks.

The front door opened. She heard Danielle and Jennifer in the kitchen talking.

One of the drawbacks of this particular closet was that she could hear just about anything going on in the house. Maybe if she added some music? No, she wasn't going that direction. Clara didn't need music to pray. Did she need a sound track in order to get close to God?

"My parents said you could spend the night if your mom was okay with it. We can jump in the pool too."

"Let me go ask her," Danielle said.

Elizabeth's stomach tightened. She had hoped to keep her war room a secret, but only a few minutes after she had finished setting it up, footsteps padded into the room.

"Mom?"

Elizabeth closed her eyes and spoke as if being in her closet were a natural thing. "I'm in here, Danielle."

The door opened slowly and there was Danielle staring at her and the nearly empty soda bottle and the opened bag of tortilla chips. Danielle's face told everything.

"Mom, are you okay?" her daughter finally said.

"Yes. What do you need?" She crunched another chip, sitting back on the bean bag chair.

"Why are you eating chips in the closet?"

The tortilla got stuck somewhere in her throat and Elizabeth swallowed hard. "I'm just having some private time, okay?"

The look on the girl's face was priceless, but Elizabeth kept up the appearance that this was perfectly normal.

"Okay," Danielle said, sounding unsure. "Jennifer wanted to know if I could spend the night. I already did my chores, and it's okay with her parents."

That last part came out a little whiny, but Elizabeth

decided to let that go. "All right, but I want you home by lunch tomorrow."

"Yes, ma'am."

Elizabeth crunched another chip, speaking with her mouth full as Danielle turned to leave. "And, Danielle, don't tell anybody I was eating chips in this closet."

Her daughter nodded, then said over her shoulder, "Don't tell anyone my mom was eating chips in the closet, okay?"

Elizabeth sat up, mortified. "Who are you talking to?"

"Jennifer," she said, deadpan.

Elizabeth sighed. "Jennifer?"

Jennifer stood beside Danielle now, her arms crossed in front of her and a sheepish look on her face. "Yes, ma'am?"

Elizabeth put the bag of chips beside her on the floor. She'd had no idea the girl was there listening. "I'm asking you not to tell anyone I was eating chips in my closet."

Jennifer nodded. "Okay."

"Thank you."

The two stood there looking at her. Then Jennifer got a curious look on her face. "What's that smell?"

"That would be my shoes, Jennifer," Elizabeth said quickly, firmly. "And if you girls would kindly shut the door, you won't have to smell them anymore."

Danielle closed the door slowly, the hinges creaking. That was another thing Elizabeth had to do. Oil those hinges.

Elizabeth heard Jennifer whisper as they left, "Is she not allowed to eat chips?"

"I can have all the chips I want," Elizabeth said loudly. "This is my house!"

She sighed and studied her list. Prayer was a lot more difficult than she thought. And it was a full-time job to hang on to your pride when you were downing a bag of tortilla chips in your war room.

Tony walked down the hall of the Brightwell corporate offices in Charlotte. It was an elegant complex with the best furniture, the best-dressed workers, and a bright future. He spotted a corner office and smiled. If things kept going the way they had been, he would make his home here someday, with a parking space in front as well.

Coleman Young's secretary, Julia, welcomed him and showed him into the office. She was an older woman with graying hair and dark glasses that framed a kind face. She always seemed to have a smile. Kind but competent and jealous for her boss's welfare.

"Coleman's expecting you, and Tom's in there too," she said.

"Thanks for the heads-up," he said.

She laughed. "You're welcome."

Coleman was in his late forties, Tony guessed, with thinning salt-and-pepper hair and a neatly trimmed beard. His office sitting area looked out over the city, a view you could expect for the president of such a successful company. Tony buttoned his top button as Coleman rose to meet him. Tom Bennett, one of a long line of Brightwell vice presidents, was slower to rise.

"Tony! How's my favorite rep?" Coleman said with a smile.

"I'm real good. How are you doing?" Tony said, shaking his hand firmly.

A glint in the man's eye. "Heard we got the Holcomb account."

It felt good to hear his boss say the words. Seeing his face light up was icing on the cake. "Yes, we did."

"That's fantastic! You did it again."

"I appreciate that—thank you."

"Even Tom was impressed, and you know that's hard to do."

Tony hadn't interacted much with Tom Bennett. The man's demeanor was less than cordial and a little on the suspicious side. He was thin and wiry and always seemed a bit irritable. Was he prejudiced or just an introvert? Who knew? Frankly, Tony didn't care. He just tried to steer clear of Tom as much as he could and keep selling, keep moving up the ladder at Brightwell.

Tom shook his hand and said, "Good work." It was half-hearted at best. The handshake seemed like an obligation.

"Thank you."

"Look, I know you're on your way home, but we just wanted to say thanks. And you've got a nice bonus check coming your way."

Tony couldn't hold back the smile. "I like that."

"Yeah, you do!" Coleman said, reaching out a hand again. "How's Elizabeth?"

"She's good."

"Tell her I said hello."

"I'll do it," Tony said.

"Good to see you," Coleman said, turning back to Tom.

It was a brief encounter, one of a very few he'd had with the president of the company, but Tony could have floated to the car. It was the best feeling to land a deal and then have people at the company hear about his exploits. The drive home should have felt like a victory lap. It should have been his best day ever. But the prospect of seeing Elizabeth weighed on him. He didn't want to go through the bickering and nagging he was sure he'd get when he walked in the door. And he didn't want to tell her about the account and bonus. She'd just use it as another excuse to give money to her sister.

The only thing worse than Elizabeth's nagging was what he *wasn't* receiving. At the start of their marriage, Tony and Elizabeth had what he would call an equal desire for each other. She would initiate some romantic evening with the suggestion of a movie and dinner and everything that came after it. He couldn't wait to get home from work to be with her, explore everything about her. She was a beautiful woman, inside and out.

But something had changed when Danielle was born. Elizabeth had become more guarded, and because of their work schedules they spent more time apart. Instead of that

daily distance bringing them together when he returned, it
kept them isolated. Tony couldn't remember the last time
they had been intimate. Was it a month ago? Two months?

He pulled into the garage and chewed on the inside
of his cheek from the tension he felt. No wonder he was
looking for action elsewhere. He knew it wasn't right. He
knew he'd made a vow to be faithful. But if it happened, it
was her fault. She had pushed him away in so many ways.
She had told him he wasn't living up to her expectations.
Couple that with all the fighting over money and how to
raise Danielle and it was a miracle the two were still in the
same house.

The more he thought about it as he had driven home,
the more his stomach tied in knots, and as he turned off
the ignition and hit the garage door button, he didn't even
want to go inside. What new complaint would she have?
What was the latest thing he had done to scar his daughter?
He was sure he'd hear about it at dinner. That and how
much money her sister needed.

Elizabeth had entered her closet committed to prayer and
exited committed to tackling her foot odor. That was the
danger of spending time with God—most of the time
you found something else to do. And if she couldn't have
success at prayer, at least she could accomplish something
practical. She lined up a dozen pairs of shoes, found her
foot spray, and began dealing with each one.

The phone rang and she recognized her sister's number. It wasn't long until Cynthia got to the crux of the matter: her husband. She complained about their situation, just like Elizabeth had complained to Clara about Tony. The financial pressure they were constantly under was overwhelming. Cynthia had tried to motivate Darren, but nothing was happening.

"Cynthia, it's not going to do you any good to fight about it. You can't get the job for him."

"Don't you think I know that?"

Elizabeth tried to calm herself. "Well, is he trying at all? Is he sending out résumés or making calls? Anything?"

"I think so. He leaves in the morning and comes back at night but I don't know where he's been or what he's done. It's just so hard, Elizabeth."

"I know," she said with as much compassion as she could muster. She spurted some more foot powder in a shoe and set it down.

"This is not easy for him either," Cynthia said.

The words struck a nerve. "Well, I'm sorry, but he's making it hard not just on you but everybody around you."

"So you're saying you're not going to help. Is that it?"

"No, I'm not saying we won't help. We're still talking about it, okay?"

Elizabeth heard a noise behind her and turned to see Tony leafing through the mail on the kitchen counter. Seeing him there while Cynthia was on the line sent her spirits crashing. He already thought she spent every

CHRIS FABRY

minute on the phone with her sister. He had to walk in at just this moment.

"Listen, Tony just got home. I need to call you later."

"All right, Sis. Thanks for talking. Love you."

"I love you too," Elizabeth said.

Tony studied each letter like it was a draft notice. She hung up and took a breath and tried to engage with him. Something safe. Like work, perhaps.

"How was your trip?"

Head down, scowling at the mail. "It was good. I take it that was your sister."

"Yep. It was."

"Darren getting a job?"

"Not yet."

"'Not yet' as in he's trying? Or 'not yet' as in he's still sittin' on the couch playing video games?"

How quickly the tide of conversation ran onto the beach of conflict. "Tony, what he does is not Cynthia's fault. She just needs one month's rent and a car payment. I think we should at least do that."

Tony's face hardened. "Cynthia married a loser. Okay? That was her choice when everybody told her not to. It *is* her fault."

Elizabeth stood and faced him. He approached from the kitchen—the power in her voice finally calling him from his corner. Like two fighters ready to begin the bout, they sized each other up.

"Tony, she cannot control him. She's got a job, but it's

119

not enough. Listen, I'm not asking for five thousand dollars anymore. I'm asking for one month's rent and a car payment."

"And next month you'll be askin' for the same thing, Liz. So the answer is still no." Tony turned his head, scowling again. "And what is that smell in here?"

Elizabeth looked away, half in frustration and half from embarrassment. She felt like a little girl again. Back in her house with her father criticizing her. Tony had the same tone of voice her dad had when she needed new clothes or brought home a bad grade.

"I'm putting powder in my shoes," she said.

He glanced at the line of shoes in front of the couch. She thought he might apologize or console her. Tell her it was all right or that it wasn't her fault or that she didn't have to do that for his sake.

Tony just looked at the shoes like they were dead fish and said, "Well, can't you do that outside?"

Defeated, deflated, and crushed, she said, "Yes." Then she thought of Cynthia. She thought of her voice on the phone and how lonely and sad she sounded. She would give it one more try with him.

"Tony, if you won't do it for her, do it for me."

It was an open invitation for him to express some semblance of love. It was her being vulnerable—like a deer running into a meadow with a big red target on its side, ready for the kill.

Tony's face grew even harder. "No."

And with that, he turned and walked into the bedroom, leaving Elizabeth alone with her thoughts and her shoes. She knew she and Tony were far apart. She knew there wasn't much hope for their relationship. It had been so long since he had lovingly touched her or said anything positive. At that moment, with her eyes watering and her heart breaking, she realized there was nothing she could do to bring down that wall. No amount of parading around it and shouting would bring it down. No amount of holding up a staff would part the waters of their flooded relationship.

She picked up as many shoes as she could and carried them to the back door and tossed them onto the deck. She made another trip for the rest, slammed the door behind her, and stood on the deck staring into the distance, arms folded. She was tired of the battle, weary of the war. She was tired of seeing Danielle live under the weight of all this. There had to be another way. There had to be something better for all three of them.

Miss Clara

✦ ✦ ✦

Over the years people discovered Clara was a prayer warrior. They would slip her a piece of paper with someone's name scrawled on it or whisper something about a family member during the offertory. Clara felt honored when that happened. But the practice also saddened her because she knew some thought she had a special "in" with God. There was nothing she did in her prayer closet that others couldn't do. There was no answer to prayer she snatched from God's hand because she was so crafty. The power she had was available to all.

The question had come up in one of her Friday gatherings with her girlfriends. They were down to four regular members of a club that had never officially been formed. Cecilia Jones, Eula Pennington, and Tressa Gower were women who had crossed Clara's path years earlier and had stuck by her—and she them—through several decades. They had been through the deaths of spouses, children, and pets, as well as a divorce, several miscarriages, and two lawsuits. All four of the women were believers, though sometimes there seemed to be a little antagonism at how sure Clara was about everything she believed.

"Do you think there's more power in lots of people praying about something?" Cecilia said to the group. She looked out the corner of her eye at Clara as if baiting her to jump into the fray first.

This was how one of the group started a free-for-all— she just threw out a question or an idea and watched the others respond. Cecilia was particularly good about goading Clara, but on this one, Clara held back.

"I think the more people who pray about something, the more chance God has of hearing," Tressa said. "What was that book a few years ago, had all those angels fighting in it? You read what was going on with people and then what happened with the angels when people started praying?"

Tressa said the title of the book and Cecilia remembered the author. All of them nodded in recognition.

"I think it's like that," Tressa continued. "The more you pray, the more you get other people to pray, it just piles up on a scale somewhere in heaven. And God listens. The persistent widow—she kept knocking at the door of the judge. Remember that parable?"

Eula Pennington put her coffee mug down. "I don't think God can be moved like that." She said the word *God* with an extra "duh" on the end, as if it were more reverent to add another syllable to the Almighty's name. "It's not how many times you pray something or how many people you get praying, it's whether or not you're asking something that's in God's will."

Clara nodded at that and the ladies around the table seemed to agree. But Cecilia wasn't finished. "So does that mean there's no reason for a prayer chain? If a whole congregation prays about something, it's no different from one person praying?"

"'The effectual fervent prayer of a righteous man availeth much,'" Eula said. She was a King James adherent, though she tolerated the RSV and NASB.

"So that means if you're holy enough, God will hear your prayers? Is that it?" Cecilia said.

"Nobody is holy but God," Eula said. "The rest of us are sinners standing in the need of prayer."

"You got that right," Tressa said.

Cecilia leaned forward. "Clara, you're being awful quiet."

Clara took a sip of coffee. "Having lots of people pray about something doesn't force God to listen or act. God knows everything. Prayer is not informing Him because He already knows what we need and why we're crying out."

"So why pray at all?" Cecilia said.

Clara held up a hand. "Now you asked me to answer you and I'm trying to do that."

Cecilia smiled and sat back, also raising a hand as if the floor was Clara's.

"God does hear what we pray. You don't need a megaphone or a million people to get His attention. But the point of prayer is not to get what we want. Prayer changes the person who prays. You take the parent who prays that a child will get on the straight and narrow. You know I've been there with Clyde. We've all been heartsick about something or other regarding our kids. But what I've found is this. Whenever I was worried about Clyde, God was doing something in me. He wanted to turn my heart around as much if not more so than my son's. God helped me trust Him in greater ways than I ever thought possible because of that boy and what he dragged me through."

"And he dragged you through a lot," Tressa said.

"Mmm-hmmm," Eula agreed.

"So what about my question?" Cecilia said, dissatisfied with the answer.

"There's not more power in a lot of people praying because the power comes from God and not the people. But what happens when many pray for the same thing is an opportunity for God's glory. Everything comes back to the glory of God. Everything in history, the purpose of our lives, is the glory of God. Every breath we take."

"But isn't it selfish of God to want glory?" Cecilia said. "That's the opposite of humility."

Clara could tell her friend was poking her now, prodding her to get to something below the surface. "Let me tell you something. Is it wrong for the person who deserves it to get credit? God made everything. He fashioned the little baby in its mother's womb and set the stars in place. He put a plan in motion to redeem us, to showcase His love and goodness and mercy on the cross so that all glory would go to the One to whom it belongs. Glory that goes to anybody or anything else is a sham. And you put an *e* on that and it becomes a shame. That's what the world has come to by giving glory to people who can catch a ball or twist on a stage."

Cecilia smiled and Clara knew this was her intent, to get her involved enough to come up with what the group called a "Clara-ism."

"So, Clara, tell us what happens when a group begins to pray about the same thing," Cecilia said.

"Well, first of all, more people know about the need. More people get involved in bringing a person or a situation before God. He doesn't need to be reminded because He knows everything. But He wants us to participate in people's lives and the things going on around us. He wants us to partner with Him in His plan to draw people to Himself. So the end result of a lot of people praying about the same thing is increased glory to God. That's the way it works. When we pray, we participate in what God is doing. He gets the glory, and we get the privilege of walking with

Him, and in that process we are changed. And guess what happens from that change? He gets the glory."

"How do you figure that?" Eula said.

"Philippians 2. Paul talks about having the same mind that Jesus had. He didn't have to come here and give up His life. He didn't have to be obedient and die on a cross. But He humbled Himself. And look at what happens at the end of that passage. God raises him up to the place of highest honor and gives Him the name above every other name. Every knee is going to bow, every tongue will declare that Jesus Christ is Lord—now get this—to the *glory of God the Father*. The whole point of the work of Jesus, the whole reason for His sinless life, the reason for the miracles and raising Him from the dead was the *glory* of God."

"Praise Jesus!" Tressa said.

"That's good," Eula said.

"You know it," Cecilia said.

"Wrap your heart around that the next time you go through a struggle," Clara said. "The goal of prayer is not to change God's mind about what you want. The goal of prayer is to change your own heart, to want what He wants, to the glory of God."

CHAPTER 7

✦ ✦ ✦

Tony was headed to the gym anyway, so he took Michael's invitation to meet him at the workout room. Michael climbed on the stationary bike while Tony did pull-ups. It felt good to work up a sweat and try to forget the conflict at home. To build muscle, he knew he needed to push himself, to feel the burn and the pain. Too bad his marriage hadn't been like that. There was plenty of pain but little building.

Their conversation turned to work and Tony revealed what had happened the day before. Not to brag, but to bring Michael up to speed.

"You got another bonus? Man, I went into the wrong line of work."

Tony spoke through his reps. "I couldn't have been a paramedic."

"You got that right, bro."

"And you're too calm to be a salesman."

Michael laughed. "Yeah, but could you imagine if I got a bonus every time I saved somebody's life? Check it out. Heimlich, two hundred dollars. CPR? Four hundred. And I'd get a thousand if they're ugly."

Tony laughed as he moved over to the rack of dumbbells. He loved Michael's dry humor and the stories about the people he encountered as an EMT.

"Remember that one lady who had swallowed garlic and she choked and I had to give her mouth-to-mouth? That should have been a Hawaiian vacation."

Tony began curling twenty-five-pound weights. "I couldn't have done it."

"Yeah, you could do it. You're not going to let somebody just die in front of you while you eat your salad."

"I don't do CPR, Mike. I'd just call 911."

"That's just cold. You'd just let somebody die? What if it was your wife?"

Tony put the weights on his thighs and held them there. What if Elizabeth were choking and needed help? What if she needed CPR? *She would probably tell me I wasn't pushing on her chest right,* he thought.

Michael stopped pedaling and got a sad look on his face. "Hold on, bro, what's that?"

"What's what?" Tony said, continuing his routine.

"What's up with you and Liz?"

Tony strained through another set of reps. "Nothing."

"Nothing? Look at you getting all tight. You got extra veins popping out that weren't even there before. Dude, what's going on with your marriage?"

Tony didn't like sharing the hard stuff with anybody, especially someone like Michael, who was pretty much perfect. But he was so close to the falls with Elizabeth, he knew he would have to explain sooner or later, so he let the water carry him over.

"Mike, I'm just tired of her, okay? All right, I said it. I don't need her nagging me all the time. I'm just tired of her junk."

Michael was fully focused now. The stationary bike had stopped. "Her junk? Dude, you married her, junk and all. It's not like some sort of buffet where you get to pick and choose what you want. You get all of her." He paused and let the next sentence sink in. "And you'd better not have somebody on the side."

Tony let the weights stretch his arms out. How in the world did Michael come up with that? Was he following him around? Was it that clear?

"So you're trying to do CPR on my personal life now?" It was defensive, but Tony had to at least put up a good front. What was he supposed to say—*I am looking for someone?*

Michael resumed his workout. "Yeah, I'm a paramedic. But I'm also a Christian. Which means I help people . . . while I'm helping people."

"Mike, we've been friends a long time, but some things are none of your business."

"True, and since we've been friends a long time, I'm not going to just watch your marriage die. So if it's bleeding, I'm not gonna keep eating my salad."

Tony dropped the weights and stood straight, grabbing his gym bag. He looked at Michael with a sly smile and with a little sarcasm said, "I'll see you in church."

Michael called after him as he walked away, "Need to see the church in you, bro."

Tony kept walking, not wanting to respond. He didn't need Michael's guilt. He hit the door and walked through the atrium of the community center, passing the reception-ist at the front. She was one of Elizabeth's friends. What was her name? He nodded at her and felt coldness from her as he passed. He wondered what Elizabeth had said to her about him, about their marriage.

As he got in the car and drove away, he thought of several comebacks for Michael. Questions that could push him to the edge of his belief in God. The Almighty had created marriage to be happy and vibrant. Wasn't that what He wanted for His children? Well, Tony wasn't happy and neither was Elizabeth. In fact, Tony was one of the major reasons Elizabeth wasn't happy at all. And she was the main reason he heard fingernails on the blackboard of life when he walked into the house. The loving thing, the kind thing would be for the two of them to go their separate ways. It would be hard, but in the end, it would lead to happiness.

What about Danielle? Michael's voice said in his head.

She wouldn't understand. She was too young to get it. But Tony would be in her life, on weekends, at special events. Birthdays and graduations. He might be an even better dad from a distance than he was sleeping in the same house. And he would finally be out from under all the weight of obligation. Obligation to listen to the nagging and feel like a jerk. That's how Elizabeth treated him. Instead of respecting him and being grateful for what he'd provided, how hard he worked, she only looked at him as a glass half-full. He would be happy living apart from them and that would spill over to Danielle, so she would be better off in the end.

The loving thing to do here was to make a decision. Elizabeth wanted him to be the leader in the home, so that's what he'd do. Just like in the gym, short-term pain led to long-term gain. They would endure the questions from family and friends and move forward on the journey to a happy life.

As Tony hit the garage door opener, he once again thought of Veronica Drake from Holcomb. Maybe he should get back there sooner than planned to go over some details of their deal. Maybe have dinner. Maybe stay overnight. After all, he thought, it was never too early to think about your own happiness.

Elizabeth had never tried to sell the house of anyone who seemed more interested in her life than in the sale. Clara wanted to know more about her relationship with Tony, more about Danielle, more about their whole family situation. When Elizabeth had a free afternoon, she told Danielle they would go to the park downtown together and she could jump rope or feed the pigeons. Then she got the idea of inviting Clara and the woman didn't have to think twice about it.

"That would be lovely," she said. "I'll be ready when you get here."

Danielle was a little nervous about meeting one of Elizabeth's clients, but as soon as they pulled up to Clara's house, the old woman doted on Danielle and talked to her like she was her own grandchild. They drove to the park downtown and ate sandwiches on a bench. Danielle had to show Clara what she could do with the jump rope and the woman seemed amazed.

"When you said you jumped rope, I thought you just jumped rope. But look at you, girl! You're faster than my coffee grinder! That's amazing!"

Danielle ate up the attention more than she did the sandwich. And then she gave the crust and crumbs to the squirrels and birds nearby.

"She is really something," Clara said. "I can see you in that little girl."

Elizabeth smiled. "I wish I had her energy."

Clara laughed. "You've told me a lot about her, but seeing you two together, well, it helps me pray better—more informed."

"What do you mean?"

"I've found that God honors the specifics. You can pray for Him to bless this person and be so generic that you make God yawn. Or you can pray arrow prayers that get to the heart of what that other person is going through. Do you see what I mean?"

Elizabeth nodded. "I've been trying to be as specific as I can with God. Sometimes I lose hope that He's hearing me."

"Well, He heard what somebody prayed about that young thing," Clara said, nodding at Danielle. "This was a treat for me, Elizabeth. I enjoy coming here. And your daughter is precious."

"She is. There are days I wish she had a brother or sister. We were just too busy chasing our careers. I don't know that that was a wise thing to do."

"You don't enjoy your job?"

"There are days I do. I sold a house this morning, so that was good. I'd just rather have a good marriage than more money."

Clara looked tenderly at her as Danielle ran up to them.

"Mom, can we get some ice cream? They sell it right over there." She pointed to an ice cream shop nearby.

Elizabeth turned to the older woman. "Miss Clara, would you like some ice cream?"

"I'll tell you what," Clara said to Danielle. "If you go get the ice cream and let your mother walk me to the car, I'll pay for it."

"Oh, no, no, no. I'm paying for it," Elizabeth said.

The old woman dug in her purse. "And rob me of a blessing? I'm paying, we're all eating. I'll take two scoops of butter pecan, please. In a cup." She handed Danielle a twenty-dollar bill.

"I'll have one scoop of cookies and cream," Elizabeth said. "And stay right there because we're going to pull the car around and pick you up at the entrance."

"Okay," Danielle said, beaming. "Can I have strawberry sherbet with gummy worms and chocolate syrup on top?"

The combination turned Elizabeth's stomach, but she gave her daughter a nod. Clara laughed as the girl walked away and they watched her carefully cross the street.

"So what does a normal week for you look like?" Elizabeth said as they made the slow walk toward her car.

"Well, my son drops in for an hour or two during the week. I go grocery shopping, an occasional doctor's visit. I go to church service and midweek prayer meeting. Every now and then I drive to the cemetery to tend to Leo's grave. And my girlfriends and I get together on Friday afternoon for coffee. Other than that, I read a lot and spend time with Jesus."

They neared the end of the alley where Elizabeth had parked the car.

"I used to spend so much time with my girlfriends, before my job became—"

"Hey!" a young man shouted, jumping out at them and clicking open a knife. He was white, wore a baseball cap backward, and had crazy-looking eyes. "Give me your money right now!"

By pure instinct, Elizabeth moved close to Clara to protect her. Both were startled by the man and took a step backward. Elizabeth wanted to steady Clara and make sure she didn't fall. She thought of Danielle and was glad she wasn't with them. She'd always heard in a situation like this you should give the person robbing you what they wanted so no one got hurt.

"Did you hear me? Both of you, give it to me now!"

Elizabeth held out a hand to calm him. "Okay, okay, we'll give you our money. Just please put the knife down."

"Do it, and do it now," the robber said, holding the knife at eye level.

Elizabeth opened her purse. It had happened so quickly. How could she not have seen him hiding? Shaking, she prayed the young man didn't attack them. She prayed they would both just survive.

Then she heard a voice, strong and determined, next to her.

"No. You put that knife down right now. In the name of Jesus." Not a hint of fear. Not a smidgen of nerves. Just a clear, strong voice that reverberated through the alley.

The robber stared at Clara, then looked at Elizabeth. He seemed confused but still angry. He glanced down the alley and then back at them, finally lowering the knife.

"Miss Clara, just give him your money. It's not worth it."

But Clara would not be moved. She stood defiant as

the robber glanced away, unable to hold her gaze. After a moment, his face changed and he seemed to panic. He took two steps to the side and ran past them toward the street.

Elizabeth pulled out her cell phone and dialed 911. They found Danielle, the ice cream melting as she walked toward them.

"What happened?" Danielle said, seeing the fear on her mother's face.

"We just had a run-in with a troubled young man back in the alley," Clara said. "Did you get my butter pecan?"

Elizabeth shook her head at her friend and they waited until a squad car arrived. Two officers listened to their story.

"And you believe he was early twenties?" one officer said.

"Yeah, maybe twenty-five," Elizabeth said.

Clara spooned the ice cream like she was ravenously hungry.

"So let me get this straight," the second officer said. "He was pointing a knife at you, and you told him to put it down in Jesus' name."

Clara nodded and stretched out a hand. "Right. Now when you write that down, don't you leave out Jesus. People are always leaving Jesus out. That's one of the reasons we're in the mess we're in." She went back to her ice cream and finished off the cup.

The officers glanced at each other as if they didn't know how to respond.

"You know, what concerns me is that you could have easily been killed."

"Well, I know a lot of people would have probably given him their money. I understand that. But that's their decision."

As the officers wrote information for the report, Clara leaned closer to Elizabeth and Danielle on the bench where they sat. "Are you not eating your ice cream, Elizabeth?"

"No. I'm not hungry anymore."

"Let me help you out with that." Clara reached for the cup. "No reason to waste perfectly good ice cream."

The officers stared at Clara as she dug into the cookies and cream.

After the police report had been completed, Elizabeth drove Clara home. The woman invited both of them inside, and Elizabeth called Tony to let him know what had happened.

When he answered, he sounded preoccupied. She knew he was on another trip and was probably heading into a meeting. She spoke anyway.

"I don't mean to bother you. I just thought you'd want to know I was held up today."

"Held up?"

"As in robbed. The guy had a knife."

"Whoa! Where were you?"

Elizabeth told him. She paced on Clara's front porch, Danielle sitting in the swing alone with a book on her lap.

"Yeah, that's not the best part of town. Did he take anything?"

"No."

"Good."

That was it? That's all he could ask about?

"What's wrong?" Tony said. "You're okay, right?"

"Yes, we're fine, but you could show a little more concern, Tony."

"Hey, there's nothing I could do. I'm over here in—"

"I know there's nothing you could have done about it," she interrupted him. "I'm just saying I was scared. And to think, Danielle could've been with us."

"I'm sure it was scary. But calm down. You're okay."

"Well, I just thought you'd want to know."

"I do want to know. But it's over now, Liz."

"Fine. Okay. We'll talk later. Bye."

The insensitivity. The callous feeling. It oozed through the phone line. Did Tony even care? Had he ever cared?

She ended the call, wanting to throw the phone through a window. But taking a deep breath, she turned to her daughter. "Danielle, can you read your book while I go talk with Miss Clara?"

"Can I text Jennifer on your phone?" Danielle said, her face suddenly brightening.

Elizabeth thought a moment. "Okay, but not too long. I want you to read, okay?"

"Yes, ma'am."

Clara was waiting in her sitting room with paper and pen.

Elizabeth sat across from her. "I'm sorry. I just thought I should call Tony."

"I understand."

"You would think he would be more alarmed, but he kept saying that since we were all okay, I should just calm down."

The woman scowled, her lips moving and head wagging from side to side. "I'm having trouble calming down myself."

"Really? You seemed calm earlier."

"Yeah, but I got a huge sugar rush from all that ice cream. I feel like I could run around the block a few times." Clara picked up her elbows and pretended to jog like an Olympic athlete.

Elizabeth smiled. The old woman was full of surprises. Elizabeth learned something new about her with every meeting.

"Oh, while we're on the subject of Tony," Clara said, "I have something for you to do." She handed Elizabeth a legal pad and a pen.

"What's that?"

"I want you to write down everything you can think of that he's done wrong."

She shook her head and frowned. "Miss Clara, if I did that, I'd be writing a long time."

"Then just write down the highlights. I'll be back to check on you in a little while."

Clara walked out and Elizabeth was left with the paper and her thoughts. She fought back the resentment, the childish feeling of being controlled and pushed into doing something she didn't want to do. Instead, she did what she was asked.

Forgot our anniversary last year.

Puts his work over his family.

Has said no to a pet in the house.

Interrupts me when I try to share my feelings.

Walks away during arguments.

Looks at other women.

Doesn't lead his family spiritually.

Once she started, it was like a flood. Instead of trying to list things in chronological order, she wrote them as they came—and sometimes they came so fast she just jotted down words so she wouldn't lose the thought. She covered the first page and went to the next, and the more she wrote, the more things came to her. There were some struggles she couldn't write because they were too intimate, so she put *unmentionable*. She was just getting momentum on the list when Clara returned and sat.

"That's almost three pages."

"And I could write more, but you'll get the gist of it when you read it."

"Actually, I'm not gonna read it."

Elizabeth cocked her head at Clara, confused. The whole point was to tell her what Tony did wrong, wasn't it?

Clara leaned forward. "My question to you is this. In light of all these wrongs, does God still love Tony?"

Elizabeth thought about the question. The theological answer was that God loved everyone. With regret in her voice, she said, "We both know He does."

"Do you?"

Elizabeth tried not to look away, tried to stay right with Miss Clara. Tried not to laugh. "Now you're meddlin'."

Clara smiled and waited. Elizabeth thought that this was what love often did, smile and wait.

"There is love in my heart for Tony, but it's buried under a lot of frustration." *Buried.* That was the right word. Their relationship had been buried long ago, and though there was no stone above, she could only imagine the bones wasting away under the cold dirt.

Clara nodded. "So he needs grace."

"Grace? I don't know that he deserves grace."

Another penetrating look. "Do you deserve grace?"

Suddenly Elizabeth felt exposed. This old woman knew how to get rid of a teenage robber with a knife. She also knew how to cut to the heart with a question.

"Miss Clara, you have a habit of backing me up in a corner and making me squirm."

"I felt the same way. But the question still remains. Do you deserve grace?"

Elizabeth looked at the pages filled with all the words she had written about Tony. She wondered what he would write if he had the same chance.

"The Bible says, 'There is no one righteous, not even

one.' So really, none of us deserves grace. But we all still want God's forgiveness."

It was all Elizabeth's Sunday school lessons rolled into one. God had been an important subject to Elizabeth her whole life, but the way Clara put it made it sound like He wasn't a subject, He was everything. *Grace* had been a nice word in her vocabulary that she used to talk about God, but Clara was using it personally, pulling her toward the truth.

"Elizabeth, it comes down to this: Jesus shed His blood on the cross. He died for you, even when you did not deserve it. And He rose from the grave and offers forgiveness and salvation for anyone who turns to Him. But the Bible also says that we can't ask Him to forgive us while refusing to forgive others."

Elizabeth nodded. "I know, Miss Clara, but that's just so hard to do."

"Yes, it is! Yes, it is! But that's where grace comes in! He gives us grace, and He helps us give it to others. Even when they don't deserve it. We all deserve judgment, and that is what a holy God gives us when we don't repent and believe in His Son. I had to forgive Leo for some things, and it wasn't easy. But it freed me."

Freedom. That was a word Elizabeth wanted so desperately, and it finally seemed to her that they went well together. *Grace. Freedom.* There were surely more good words to come after those.

"Elizabeth, there's not room for both you and God on

the throne of your heart. It's either Him or you. You need
to step down. Now, if you want victory, you're gonna have
to first surrender."

Elizabeth pushed the thought away. "But, Miss Clara,
do I just back off and choose to forgive and let him walk all
over me?"

"I think you'll find that when you let Him, God is a
good defense attorney. Trust it to Him. And then you can
turn your focus to the real enemy."

"The real enemy?"

"The one that wants to remain hidden. The one that
wants to distract you, deceive you, and divide you from the
Lord and from your husband. That's how he works. Satan
comes to steal, kill, and destroy. And he is stealing your joy,
killing your faith, and trying to destroy your family."

The old woman was fiery now, like an old-time preacher
just getting wound up and ready to pound the pulpit. "If
I were you, I would get my heart right with God. And you
need to do your fightin' in prayer. You need to kick the real
enemy out of your home with the Word of God."

So many of Elizabeth's conversations through the day
were just words and concepts thrown back and forth.
She really didn't listen to much of it carefully. Like music
played in the background to set a mood, conversations
were the same thing. But this one was more than a conversation, more than just a few concepts thrown out between
two people. She stared at Clara with a laser focus.

"It's time for you to fight, Elizabeth. It's time for you to fight for your marriage! It's time for you to fight the real enemy. It's time for you to take off the gloves and do it."

Elizabeth felt a strength coming, a resolve. With an understanding of grace came a freedom to love she'd never experienced. She glanced at Clara's Bible. She'd always thought of it as a book filled with stories. Lessons and tales of people who succeeded against great odds. But if Clara was right, it wasn't just a storybook. It was a manual of warfare. It was a path toward deep forgiveness and love from God that could empower her to forgive and love others.

Something came alive as she sat there. Something was reborn. And for the first time in a long time, Elizabeth found something she'd lost. Hope. Hope for herself. Hope for Tony and Danielle that things could be different. Hope for her family.

She put a hand on the old woman's shoulder and Clara hugged her. "You think about what I've said here."

"I will," Elizabeth said in a daze. She brushed away tears all the way home and was glad Danielle didn't ask questions.

CHAPTER 8

✦ ✦ ✦

Tony stared at his phone. What he had heard from Elizabeth shook him. His wife had been assaulted. She had been in grave danger, or so she said. Elizabeth had always been a little dramatic, though. Maybe it had just been a person living on the street and she thought he had a knife. Maybe the guy just wanted a bottle and asked for change.

He walked back into Veronica Drake's office. He never took phone calls during a meeting, but he'd happened to see that Elizabeth was on the line and felt a pang of guilt that made him step out to take it.

"Sorry about that," he said.

"It's okay," Veronica said. "Sounded like it was important."

Her voice was as sweet as a honeycomb. And the

package wasn't hard to look at either. She had a seductive smile and a knockout figure. She treated Tony like he was the most important person on the planet, getting him coffee and making time for him in her busy schedule.

"The important thing here is your company getting exactly what it needs from Brightwell Pharmaceuticals," he said. "On time. Period. Now, where were we?"

She flipped through the papers on her desk. "We have a signed contract, the shipment date, the payment schedule." She looked up at him and bit her lower lip. "I have your personal cell number so I can contact you anytime I need to. I think we're good."

He put both hands on the desk and leaned over the papers but instead looked into her eyes. Veronica was a beautiful woman. And her eyes said something that reached to his core.

"We haven't talked about you," he said.

"Me?"

"I'm in sales, of course, but I see part of my work for Brightwell as a coach."

"A coach?" Veronica said, dipping her head, her eyes twinkling.

Tony sat on the edge of his seat. "It's my sports background. Everything in life is being part of a team. Getting people to move in the same direction."

"You mean, everything is a competition?" she said. "Isn't that what sales is all about? Isn't that what makes you good at what you do?"

He smiled. "There's nothing wrong with competition. It actually can bring out the best in a person. You strive to become everything you can be. And as you become the best, you bring others along on that journey."

Veronica leaned back in her chair, her fingers interlaced under her chin. "Tell me more, Coach Jordan."

"Well, as a coach, I try to do more listening than talking. I find out the person's hopes and dreams. For example, how long have you been at Holcomb?"

Veronica told him and offered information about her personal life. He followed up, asking about her romantic relationships. "A gorgeous person like you surely has had some kind of long-term relationship."

She stifled a smile and blushed. "I've had boyfriends, if that's what you mean. But I'm waiting on the right one to come along."

"Now that is wise. A lot of people don't wait for the right one. They jump at the first one who says they love you. You're an intelligent, wise, beautiful young woman and I see a bright future for you."

"Does a coach do anything more than butter up his players?"

Tony laughed. "This is not buttering up, this is the truth. But teammates have to have a correct view of themselves. A realistic look at strengths and weaknesses."

She looked at her watch and crossed her arms. "Hmmm. Sounds like you're going to need more time to help me discover that. And I have another meeting in ten minutes."

"There's so much more we have to talk about," Tony said. "Why don't you give me the chance to continue this over dinner?"

Her eyes widened and she smiled. "You want to take me to dinner?"

He nodded. "There's a lot more to cover. Plus, it's on me. My service to the cause, and to thank you for being so easy to work with."

"Coach Jordan, is it a problem that you have a ring on your finger?"

He stared at the wedding band he wore. The only problem was that it was holding him back from really being happy. "My wife and I are having some struggles. In a long line of struggles."

"Well, maybe I can help you out, then. You know. Be a team player." Veronica looked at her schedule, then back at him. "All right. Dinner it is."

When she got home, Elizabeth went straight to her closet and, with resolve, tossed out the bean bag chair, moved her clothes to the spare room closet, then carried the boxes of shoes to the same.

She went to her desk and opened her Bible and Clara's journal. As she read, she could hear the woman's voice, her encouragement, her advice.

"There's no magic in the location you pray. But Scripture does say to go into your inner room and pray in secret,

and your heavenly Father who sees what is done in secret
will reward you. Get rid of any distractions, and focus your
heart and mind on Him. Acknowledge that He is God and
that you desperately need Him."

Clara had suggested Elizabeth find several prayers in the
Bible and meditate on them. One of the woman's favorites
was the prayer of King David at the end of his life.

"This is something you can memorize and keep going
back to time and again," Clara had said. "If you can't think
of what to pray or you run out of things to thank God for,
go to this one."

The prayer was in 1 Chronicles 29. As Elizabeth wrote
the words, she prayed them from her heart.

Yours, Lord, is the greatness and the power and
the glory and the splendor and the majesty, for
everything in the heavens and on earth belongs
to You. Yours, Lord, is the kingdom, and You are
exalted as head over all. Riches and honor come
from You, and You are the ruler of everything.
Power and might are in Your hand, and it is in Your
hand to make great and to give strength to all. Now
therefore, our God, we give You thanks and praise
Your glorious name.

Elizabeth thought that was a great way to start any
prayer, reminding herself who God was and immediately
praying that to Him.

Clara had also made a point to talk about confession. "Now, be grateful for your blessings, but lift your needs and requests to Him. If you've got something to confess, then confess it. Ask Him for forgiveness. Then choose to believe when He says that He loves you and will take care of you."

Elizabeth began to pray as she wrote and a new thought came. Instead of focusing on all the things Tony had done to wrong her, she wrote down the things she had done to hurt him. Once she began writing, the floodgates opened and the tears flowed and she saw the ways she had fallen short in her own heart. It was a lot easier to remember her husband's faults. Writing down her own gave her a sense of ownership, that she had to not just recognize the ways she had fallen short, but tell those things to God and ask Him to relieve her of the guilt and shame. She knew she'd have to apologize to Tony at some point too.

The funny thing was, through the tears and all that writing, there came with the exercise a sense of freedom, of relief and release to the discovery.

Clara had said to ask God for the truth. "Discover the truth about God, who He is, how He works, how much He loves. And then you'll uncover the truth about yourself, your sin, the ways you displease God. The truth about your life is always better to know, even if it hurts."

So Elizabeth asked God for the truth. She wrote down each true thing that came to her mind. And with each entry she made a request.

"Father, I confess that I have yelled and interrupted my husband so many times. I've been so angry at him, and I haven't really listened. Would You forgive me for my tone of voice and treating him unkindly? And would You create in me a heart that wants to respond to Tony out of love and respect and really wanting to hear him? Would You do that in my heart, Lord?"

"Then pray for the hearts of your husband, your daughter, and anyone else that the Lord brings to your mind," Clara had said. "And don't rush it. You take your time. Then you listen."

Listening to God. What a concept. What a radical thought, to pause long enough to actively listen for God to speak. Elizabeth knew it wasn't an audible voice she would hear, but that the process of reading the Bible and desiring for God to come alongside her would yield good things. That's what Clara had said, and the woman seemed to know what she was talking about.

She prepared three pieces of paper for the wall of her closet: one for Tony, one for Danielle, and one for herself. On Tony's she listed prayers for his work, his role as a father and as a husband, for his friendships, and for his heart. She asked that God would bring someone into his life who would tell him the truth.

Unite us in marriage, Father, and unite us as parents to do the very best thing for our daughter. Don't let the enemy tear us apart. Whatever You have to do in order to break me and him of our dependence on ourselves, would You make that happen? Would You bring us together in a way that causes us to cling to You no matter what? Bring us together so we can give You glory, just like Clara said.

She sat back and looked at what she had just written. Did she really mean that? Was she really ready to surrender? It looked good on paper, but how would it work in the real world?

And *would* it work? Would Tony respond? A little doubt crept in. Was she doing this just because some old woman had held out hope like a carrot on a string? Or was the feeling coming over her real? If Tony didn't change, if things got worse, would she stop believing? Stop praying?

She looked at the section of Clara's journal that held verses about doubt. One from Hebrews 11 stuck out to her, and she copied it down.

Without faith it is impossible to please God, for the one who draws near to Him must believe that He exists and rewards those who seek Him.

She closed her eyes and lifted her voice, whispering to the ceiling, "God, I want to have faith. I do believe You exist. I believe You reward people who seek You sincerely. And that's what I'm doing. With everything in me, I want to know You. And I ask You right now to give me the kind of faith I need to be the wife, the mother, the person You want me to be. Thank You that You answer cries of the heart like this. I want to do like Miss Clara says—I want to surrender every part of me to Your will, to Your kindness and mercy and grace. Put a spotlight on the areas where I've never given You control. And thank You for bringing this woman into my life. In Jesus' name, amen."

It felt like a victory. It felt like movement toward God and toward her family. It felt like Elizabeth was becoming whole instead of fractured in little pieces. And she began to see the ways God had already worked in her life. He had given her a family, and she rarely thanked Him for that. God had given her a job she enjoyed. The feeling of fulfillment when a family moved into their own home was amazing, and she thanked Him for the chance to make a living helping others. She thought of Mandy and Lisa in the office and clients who had been kind. She should start a page for them. Then she thought of the clients who had stiffed her. What would she do with the anger and hurt and resentment she felt for them? Well, God would have to deal with her on those people, and she was willing to open that door, as painful as it was.

After dinner with Danielle, Elizabeth returned to her closet and taped the three pages to the wall. As she did, her phone chimed with a text message. How was she going to handle the distraction of the phone with this new prayer life of hers? She figured Clara would tell her to silence it and check it afterward.

She glanced at the message and saw it was from her friend Missy. She had texted Elizabeth before about new shops in town. But this message said: Liz, this is Missy. I'm in Raleigh. Just saw Tony in a restaurant with a woman I didn't recognize. Somebody you know?

Elizabeth's heart stopped. She stared at the message, reading it again. Maybe her fears about Tony were true. Maybe the look he gave the girl in church was nothing compared to what he was doing on the road. Her legs felt wobbly, and she leaned against the shelf. She held the phone to her heart. It felt like a punch in the gut, all the air going out of her lungs and her mind spinning, like spiritual vertigo. She tried to gain her balance, tried to stop her mind from racing with possibilities.

While she had been praying for her husband, praying that God would work in his heart, confessing her own sins to God, Tony had been cheating. Panic rose up in her like a flood. She wanted to call him and tell him she knew exactly what he was doing. She'd seen the way some women retaliated, ruining lives and lashing out in anger, and the thought crossed her mind—she could make his life really uncomfortable. But when she put the phone down, she saw her Bible.

She picked up the leather-bound copy and sank to the floor with her back against the built-in chest of drawers. She stared at nothing, unable to focus, unable to think or breathe. Then she remembered her prayer. She had asked God to give her faith. She had surrendered herself to His keeping. Maybe this was her chance to walk with Him in a place too difficult to walk alone.

With full reliance on a power she knew didn't come from herself, she looked up and prayed, "God . . . I need You. I know I haven't prayed like I should. I know that I haven't followed You like I should. But I need You right now."

Alone in that closet, in that war room, her heart over-flowed and she let the fountain spill at the feet of God Himself.

The restaurant Veronica had suggested was pricey, but Tony thought the atmosphere was perfect. And so was she. She had worn a white, satiny dress and her hair fell over her shoulders. She was like a vision, her face lighting up the room. Though the place was crowded, it felt like it was just the two of them.

He smiled at her. "I want to thank you for meeting with me tonight. You've gone above and beyond the call."

"Thanks for suggesting it, Coach," she said.

He didn't think of his wife or his daughter. He didn't think of the promise he had made. Tony was simply in the moment—that was what he had learned about life. You had to be all there wherever you were, whether it was on the basketball court or on a sales call or at a restaurant with a beautiful girl who wasn't your wife. There was no one here to see him looking at her, and he took all of her in.

Their server arrived, a pretty young woman in her twenties with her hair pulled back. She brought water with lemon slices and said she'd give them a few minutes with the menus.

Veronica looked hers over. "It's a little expensive, isn't it?"

"Not for a valuable client," he said. "And you have to start believing that you're worth something nice like this."

"Really?"

"If you don't believe you're worth the best, others won't believe it either," Tony said. "Try whatever you'd like."

She glanced up at him and he could tell she was enjoying the attention. He was enjoying the attention too. And the view. There was something about this girl, something about the look in her eyes that signaled desire and intelligence and that she was a person who took what she wanted. She must have interpreted his signals already. Tony was interested in being more than her coach.

They ordered drinks and Tony got an appetizer for the two of them to split. He showed her the best way to eat the shrimp cocktail, pinching the tail so she got all of the meat.

"Are you my food coach too?" Veronica said.

"I'll be any kind of coach you want," Tony said, raising his eyebrows.

"That sounds dangerous," she said.

"Life is dangerous. It's full of choices. And it's too short not to enjoy yourself."

"Is that your philosophy of life? Just enjoy yourself?"

"My philosophy of life is to help others become winners. If you do that, you win too."

"That's the Coach Tony rule?"

"Veronica, I see a lot of potential in you. Obviously Holcomb does too, or you wouldn't have the position you have. And when I see someone with the kind of abilities and intelligence and charm that you have—"

"Charm?" she laughed. "Nobody has told me that in a long time. I thought charm was something for princesses in fairy tales."

"Charm is this innate quality that few people have. It puts a spell on those around them. It attracts others like bees are attracted to the flowers."

She took a sip of her drink and licked her lips. "There sure seems to be a lot of buzzing going on around here right now."

Tony laughed. Something inside tingled and he couldn't suppress it. Something that felt like it had died long ago was being reborn. And he couldn't wait to see how the evening progressed.

Elizabeth wrestled with God, with Tony, and with her own heart in the closet. "Lord, I've been so angry at Tony. And I am still so angry at him. But I don't want to lose my marriage. Lord, forgive me. Forgive me. I'm not his judge, You are. But I'm asking You, please."

She held her hands out in supplication, then balled

them into fists. "Please, don't let him do this. Take over. Please take over. Take my heart and take all this anger. Help him love me again. And help me love him."

An image flashed through her mind. Tony at dinner. Then Tony in a car with another woman, driving toward a hotel. Was it from God? Was it true? She blinked and pushed the image away.

"If he's doing something wrong, don't let him get away with it. Stand in his way. I'm asking You, please, to help me."

Tears again, and she wanted to shrivel into a ball and roll into a corner. She wanted everything gone, all the conflict in her life, her marriage. Her heart raced, the room pressed in, and she knew the only way forward was with God. But it seemed like such a narrow path ahead.

As she wept, she spoke to God silently. *I don't understand this, Lord. I feel like I've come back to You and asked You to help, and now You bring this up. Are You punishing me?*

She felt the tears roll down her cheeks. She wanted to bang on the wall and reach out for someone's hand, but there was no one there.

The truth.

She didn't hear an audible voice, just an impression in her mind. *The truth.* She had prayed for the truth about herself, about God. She wanted to deal with truth and not what she could imagine. Clara had said, *"The truth about your life is always better to know, even if it hurts."* Wasn't there something in the Bible about the truth setting you free? She was sure Jesus had said that. It probably didn't mean knowing the truth about your husband out with another woman—surely that couldn't set you free—but still, knowing the truth was better than living in the dark. Living with truth was much better than living with what you hoped life was like. Knowing the truth about your diagnosis or bank account or marriage was better than believing something that wasn't true.

Oh, Lord, I'm scared, Elizabeth prayed. *I'm frightened. There's the truth. But if this message about Tony is right, if he's seeing someone else and this is where we are, thank You for showing me. As hard as it is to take, thank You for letting me see the truth now rather than finding it out down the road. But I don't know what to do.*

She let those words echo in her heart. *I don't know what to do.*

That wasn't true. She did know what to do. She could pick up right where she had left off on her list. She looked at the words on the pages on the wall and something stood out to her, something Clara had copied down from her Bible.

A thief comes only to steal and to kill and to destroy. I have come so that they may have life and have it in abundance.

Tony probably thought that running after another relationship would bring him life. Someone prettier or younger would make him happy. But the truth was it

161

would only lead to death, the death of their marriage. He was probably as tired of all the fighting and bickering as Elizabeth was. How could he buy into that lie?

She looked at the wall and read the next verse aloud. "'But the Lord is faithful; He will strengthen and guard you from the evil one.'"

The Lord is faithful. *The Lord will* strengthen. *He will* guard you.

She focused on those words and her heart felt lighter somehow. God had seen what was happening. He knew her need. And He knew that Tony was headed down a path he'd regret the rest of his life, if what she feared was true.

She put her hand against the wall and looked at the next verse she had copied.

Submit to God. But resist the Devil, and he will flee from you.

She repeated the verse and wiped away her tears as a feeling rushed through her. Call it fire or resolve or determination—no matter the term, it rose up and so did she, finally understanding. If she submitted to God, which she had done, asking Him to take control of her life, then she could resist the devil. She was resisting the urge to move toward anger and bitterness or anything but God Himself, and she was standing up for her husband's heart, for the life of her family. If those things were true—and by faith she believed they were—the enemy had no recourse.

There was only one thing he could do. He had to leave. She wiped at new tears and stood, walking into the living room and staring as if there were unseen forces behind the scenes. She remembered what Clara had said to her before she had ever begun to study with her.

"I see in you a warrior that needs to be awakened."

Now, here Elizabeth stood, fully awake to the battle.

"I don't know where you are, devil," she said loudly, "but I know you can hear me." She looked at the stone fireplace and the furniture in the room. "You have played with my mind. And had your way long enough. No more! You are done!"

She walked into the kitchen, lights reflecting on the granite countertop. She glanced back from where she had just come. "Jesus is Lord of this house, and that means there's no place for you here anymore! So take your lies, your schemes and accusations, and get out! In Jesus' name!"

Elizabeth could hear Clara's voice echoing in her head—the way she would say those words. She opened the back door and walked onto the deck.

"You can't have my marriage, you can't have my daughter, and you sure can't have my man! This house is under new management, and that means you are out!"

She walked inside and slammed the door behind her. Then something clicked in her mind and she opened the door again and stepped outside.

"And another thing! I am so sick of you stealing my joy. But that's changing too. My joy doesn't come from my friends, it doesn't come from my job, it doesn't even come from my husband. My joy is found in Jesus, and just in case you forgot, He has already defeated you. So go back to hell where you belong and leave my family alone!"

Elizabeth slammed the door again and it felt like the exclamation point to her proclamation. She was finally taking control. No, that wasn't the truth. She was getting out of the way and letting God take control. She was going with Him, agreeing with Him instead of her enemy. No longer would she be ruled by fear or by the actions of anyone else.

As she walked back into the house, she glanced upstairs and saw Danielle looking at her with a puzzled stare. There was no way to explain this change, so she didn't try. She just kept moving, back to her closet, back to the war room. There was something urgent she had to say, something she needed to do on her knees.

She got to the closet and knelt, closing the door. "Father, I am asking You now to intercede for me. I don't know how any of this works. I don't know if You send angels or if Your Holy Spirit works this way. But I don't need to know how it works. I need to believe You can do what I'm asking. And I'm asking You in faith to stop my husband from doing something he's going to regret. Stop him somehow, Lord.

"If Tony is honoring You, bless him. But if he's doing something wrong, don't let him succeed. Stand in his way, Jesus."

She let the words drift toward heaven and realized something had changed. Something wonderful and assuring had come over her. It was more than a feeling—it was a deep-rooted conviction that she was no longer going through life alone. God was with her. Maybe He had been there all along and she hadn't noticed. But He was going to walk with her through all of this. And she couldn't wait to see what He was about to do.

CHAPTER 9

✦ ✦ ✦

Tony pushed his plate away and wiped his mouth with a napkin. The server asked if they'd like dessert and Veronica declined politely.

"Are you sure?" Tony said. "It's on me. We could share a crème brûlée."

Veronica smiled and shook her head. "I can't eat another bite. But you go ahead if you want."

"We'll take the check," Tony said and their server disappeared.

Veronica leaned forward. "You know what I'd really like right now?"

"Tell me."

"A glass of my favorite wine."

"Okay, we can do that," he said without hesitation. "What is it?"

"It's not here. It's at my apartment."

She gave him a look and Tony stared back. He'd thought he would start with dinner, get to know her better, and let things move forward at a measured pace. But her words were clear. She was ready.

Tony smiled. "Well, if it's your favorite, I'd like to try it."

"I think you'll like it."

The server reappeared and handed Tony the bill. "Here you are, sir. I hope you have a wonderful evening."

"Thank you," Veronica said. She glanced at Tony. "We will."

He got out his wallet, excited, like a high school kid who'd asked the prettiest girl in school to the prom and she had said yes. Not just to the prom but to the whole night. He couldn't wait until they got to Veronica's place. He couldn't wait to see what happened after a glass of wine.

Shifting in his seat, he felt his stomach gurgle. And it wasn't small, it felt like something major—a funny pain he hadn't experienced since a conference he'd gone to when he'd first joined the company. Several of the group had eaten some rubbery chicken at a banquet and they had all paid the price. But the food he'd just eaten was cooked to perfection. Surely he couldn't have food poisoning.

Tony signed the bill and added a generous tip. He thought maybe he was just nervous, butterflies and all that.

But as he put his credit card away, it felt like his stomach was about to do a backflip. The room swayed and spun like he was on an amusement park ride or he was looking at one of those sideshow mirrors that made your face too fat or too tall.

"Veronica, listen," Tony said, trying to act nonchalant as the pain intensified. "I need a minute, all right? I'll be right back."

She watched him get up. "Okay."

He walked into the bathroom and looked at himself in the mirror. *Are you really going to go through with this?* he thought. *There's a young lady waiting right now to take you home.*

As he looked at his reflection, his mind spinning, an image of Elizabeth flashed for a moment. He blinked, then saw Danielle. The pain in his stomach intensified and he ran water in the sink and splashed it on his face, groaning as he did. The churning heaved and suddenly he couldn't hold back. He hit the stall door and made it to the toilet just as the gurgle became a geyser.

Elizabeth was still on her knees, still praying. She couldn't stop knocking at heaven's door. There was a burden so heavy on her heart that she couldn't hold back. It felt like her whole being burned with conviction.

"Jesus, You are Lord. You can turn Tony's heart back to You. So whatever it takes, Lord. I trust You."

Tonight Elizabeth's mind didn't wander like other times in prayer. When she ran out of ways to ask God to reach Tony, she thanked God for things like Missy and her text message. "Lord, what are the odds that she would be at the same place as Tony? That she would see what she saw? You placed her there for a reason, and You let me know this information. I thank You for that and pray You would use it for Tony's good. I pray that You wouldn't punish him, if he's doing something wrong toward me and Danielle, but that You would enable him to make good choices. Help him turn to You. Don't let the enemy win a victory in his heart. Lord, do whatever You need to do in order to bring him to his senses."

There were no guarantees in prayer. She couldn't know if God would do something miraculous or if He even heard. But by faith she believed God not only heard but was working in Tony's heart at that very moment.

Tony had tried to leave the bathroom twice, only to have to retreat and endure another round of stomach clenching and the awful loss of that expensive dinner. He wondered if Veronica could hear him outside because the noise he made was anything but romantic. A man had come in, briefly, and exited when he heard Tony. He couldn't blame the guy.

As a child Tony had hated even the idea of throwing up. He'd felt the quiver in his stomach late one night in bed and ran down the hall to get his mother, then ran back to the bathroom, stuck his head out the door, and tossed his cookies on the carpet. That was a story his mother loved to tell, and when Danielle went to see her grandma, she always asked her to repeat it—and she and Elizabeth laughed and laughed. He had to admit it was a funny story, but the idea of getting that sick had terrified him as a child. Even as an adult, he did everything he could to avoid it, and when Danielle was ill, he let Elizabeth care for her in that department.

Tony came up for air and wiped his eyes. What in the world had happened? One minute he was fine and the next he was violently ill, like a tornado had hit his insides. He glanced at himself in the mirror. He looked like he'd gone several rounds with a prizefighter. He washed his face again and let the room stop spinning, then gathered himself and headed to the front of the restaurant.

Veronica was waiting by the door, a concerned look on her face. "You okay?"

His stomach did another flip. He needed to get to his car. If he could just get inside and sit, he might be okay.

"Veronica, I'm sorry, but I need to go back to my hotel room."

"Well, I can go with you."

"No, I mean, I'm not feeling well. I need to go lay down."

She gave him a pouty look. "Baby, I can take care of you."

If she'd heard him in the restroom, she wouldn't have been so keen to follow.

"No, it's okay. I'll call you later. But I need to go."

Tony walked outside slowly, the pavement spinning beneath him. He had to close his eyes as he neared the car and take a deep breath. He looked back at Veronica. She was heading to her car looking hurt and confused.

✦ ✦ ✦

Elizabeth wasn't sure how long she had been in her closet, but there came a point where she felt her job was done. She wanted to call Tony or text him and ask him who he was with. She wanted to call his hotel, if she could track it down, and see if they'd send someone to knock on his door.

Maybe just a text, she thought. Something like *Praying for you.* No, that would just be telling him she was checking up. She wanted to rely on God fully. And she wouldn't worry about this the whole night. She was putting it in God's hands. If Tony came to mind, she'd pray. Otherwise, she needed to keep moving forward. Do the things she was assigned to do.

Elizabeth washed her face and emptied the dryer, bringing the clothes basket to her room. As she dumped the clothes on the bed to fold, Danielle entered, already in her pajamas.

"What happened to your closet?" she said.

Elizabeth smiled and sat on the end of the bed, then motioned for Danielle to sit next to her. Danielle obliged. She was getting so big, so grown-up. They had only eight more years with her—no, less than that. She'd soon be off to college and then she'd meet some guy and get married and start a family.

"I'm doing something that I should have done a long time ago," Elizabeth said. "I'm learning how to pray and fight and trust."

Danielle looked as though she was trying to digest her mother's words. "By cleaning out your closet?"

"No. Well, yes. But no. I mean . . ." Elizabeth tried to think of the best way to help her daughter understand what she'd only come to understand herself. "It needed to be cleaned out, but that's not why I did it. I did it to fight in prayer."

A scrunched-up face. "You're fighting God?"

"No, I'm not. Well, sometimes I do fight God. But I shouldn't because He always wins. So I'm praying for God to fight for me, because I'm just sick of losing, but not against God. I need to lose against God."

She wasn't doing a very good job of explaining. She took another run at it.

"I'm sick of losing in other areas where I'm just fighting but I keep losing all the time. It's exhausting. So I'm learning how not to fight God and how to let Him fight for me so that we can all win. Does that make sense?"

Danielle frowned and gave her a look like her mind had been spun in a blender. "No."

"You know what?" Elizabeth said. "I don't make much sense when I'm tired."

"You must be really tired."

Elizabeth couldn't hold back a smile. "Let's just go get a late-night snack and I'll try it again, okay?"

Danielle hopped up and raced her to the kitchen. They made fruit smoothies, though Elizabeth put her foot down and refused to include gummy worms or chocolate syrup that late at night. While they cut up the bananas and added the frozen berries and yogurt and a little granola, Danielle said, "Is Dad on another trip?"

"Yes, he had to go to Raleigh."

"Why does he have to be gone so much?"

"It's part of the job. Comes with the territory of being a salesman."

"I wish he could be home more," Danielle said. "Sort of."

"What do you mean, sort of?"

"I like it when he's home, but I don't like it when you guys fight."

Elizabeth poured the smoothies into two glasses. It was such a thick concoction that the spoons stood straight up.

"I don't like it when we fight either. And I'm hoping that's going to change really soon."

"Is that the reason you emptied your closet?"

"Sort of."

"What do you mean, sort of?" Danielle said.

Elizabeth laughed. Such a bright girl. If she and Tony could only get their lives together, they could watch her grow together and be good models for her. They could show what reconciliation looked like.

"Danielle, I haven't been the mother I need to be to

you. I haven't been the wife I should be. I've nagged your father, I've tried to get him to see all the things he's done that are wrong, and I haven't seen a lot of the things I've done that are hurtful. So I asked God to forgive me. I asked Him to come in and clean out my heart, just like I did the closet."

Danielle focused on her smoothie as her mother spoke, swallowing spoonfuls of the cold creation as she listened.

"I'm going to apologize to your father when he comes home. But I guess I owe you an apology too."

Danielle looked up at her. "You want to apologize to me?"

Elizabeth smiled. "I'm so sorry, baby."

Her daughter's forehead wrinkled. "You didn't do anything wrong, Mama. You were right to be upset with Daddy. He yelled at you a lot."

"I was right to be upset for some of the things he's done, but I didn't handle those things well. I let my anger guide me. What I'm saying is, I want to love you and your father like God has loved me. He's been so good to all of us. And I want to show that love to you and your dad. Does that make sense?"

Danielle didn't respond. She just took another bite of smoothie, put the spoon down, and folded her arms on the table in front of her.

Part of being a good parent was knowing when to say something and what to say, Elizabeth thought. The hardest part of parenting was knowing when to say nothing and listen.

Finally Danielle looked up at her mother with something that looked like regret. "You're not the only one who needs to love that way."

"What do you mean, sweetie?"

"I haven't been the daughter I want to be either." Her chin quivered and her lips began to tremble.

Elizabeth took her daughter in her arms and held her tight as Danielle began to recite some of the things on her heart she had been holding in. Little things, stuff she'd said, things that had happened at school—they all just came spilling out there at the table, and Elizabeth stroked her head, letting her talk. As Danielle confessed the things she had held inside, Elizabeth closed her eyes and turned her face toward heaven and whispered, "Thank You, Jesus."

The two of them prayed together there at the table. They finished their smoothies and Danielle seemed like a weight had lifted from her.

"Could you help me do something?" Danielle said after they washed their dishes.

"It's getting late, sweetie. What is it?"

"Could you help me clean out my closet?"

The question made Elizabeth want to cry and shout at the same time. She wanted to call Clara right then and tell her they had another prayer warrior to add to the platoon.

"You know what I'm going to do?" Elizabeth said when they'd cleared a space in the girl's closet. "I'm going to order you a prayer journal just like Miss Clara has. Would you like that?"

Danielle's eyes widened and she gave her mother another hug.

✦ ✦ ✦

Tony awoke with a splitting headache and an ache in his stomach. He stumbled down the corridor to a vending machine and bought a soda to settle the turmoil in his gut.

He had ordered for Veronica last night and they'd both had the same meal. He wondered if she had gotten sick. A quick call could have solved the mystery, but he decided against it.

Had it been the food? Maybe he'd picked up a bug. You never knew, with all the germs floating around. Somebody with the flu could have used the same gas pump, or it could've been the person at the checkout line at the grocery store—plus, he'd shaken a hundred hands in the past few days.

Returning to his room, he watched the news and drank the soda. It seemed to calm him a little. He took a long, hot shower and got ready for the day. He checked his messages and the schedule on his phone. He wasn't super busy with sales calls, but there was enough to keep him on the road for a couple more days.

There was a text from Veronica. He checked the time and figured he'd been asleep when it came in the previous night. Sorry you didn't feel well. Hope you're better today. Are you staying in Raleigh? Call me.

He hit Reply. I must have caught a bug. Really sorry I ran off like that. I need to make it up to you.

He was about to hit Send when another pain hit him and he ran to the bathroom. Something was seriously messing with his insides. A few minutes later he returned to the phone and found a message from Danielle. She had used her mother's phone.

Love you, Daddy. Hope you have a good day. See you soon.

He smiled. His little girl was growing up. And something about the words made him think about her future. He'd grown up in a single-parent home, his father leaving and then divorcing his mother. He and his dad had a bit of a relationship now, but he'd always been closer to his mother. He had vowed he would never make a child of his go through that. Life was hard enough with two parents, especially ones who fought as much as he and Elizabeth did. Would Danielle be better off with the two of them together or apart? And how would she react to a new woman in his life? Someone like Veronica?

He scrolled back to the reply he had written and hit the Delete button. He would call Veronica later and explain.

The conflict he felt at home and the pull toward Veronica only led him to something else that was brewing, a cloud that hung over him. Something had grown in his heart and woke him at night and it was part of the reason he didn't like going to church or even talking with his friend Michael.

He'd promised himself a hundred times that he would stop stealing samples. He had done it by mistake the first time. A box of rather expensive medication had gotten stuck in the bottom of his sample case, and the doctor at the office had signed off on the number without even looking at the form. He just put his chicken scratch down and Tony was on his way. Later, when Tony inspected the case, he found the box. He told himself he'd return it to the doctor on the next trip, but one thing led to another and he found a guy who knew a guy and the hundred-dollar bill seemed like a good payoff. He'd been weighed down with financial struggles and the extra cash gave him a measure of comfort he didn't seem to have otherwise.

But the onetime incident turned into a second time that wasn't an accident, and everything seemed to escalate from there. He rationalized that the company was making so much money that they would never miss a few extra bottles of this or that. Plus, they weren't really paying him what he was worth, so this was his way of taking a little extra bonus. He was actually saving the company from having to pay him, and he was saving not having to pay taxes. And the government was getting more than it deserved, as far as he was concerned.

Tony checked out of the hotel, quickly walking past the breakfast buffet without a thought of eating anything. He drove to his first appointment at the medical center. It was a hub of activity, even this early in the morning. He opened his trunk, removed the samples he would present, and checking around the parking lot, set two aside for himself. He locked the car and walked inside, remembering the names of the receptionist and the doctor awaiting his delivery.

Miss Clara

✦ ✦ ✦

Clara had spoken forcefully to Elizabeth and with great conviction the day before, and that bothered her. In the middle of the night she'd gotten out of bed and slipped to the floor.

"Oh, Lord, that girl looked like a thirsty child standing by a fire hydrant. And she thinks I'm a spiritual giant, but You know how weak I am. How flawed I am.

"Prayer warrior," she whispered to herself, then chuckled. "You know I'm not that. I'm just somebody who's come to the end of herself and her ability to fix things."

There were things Clara had prayed about for decades that hadn't changed. That fact didn't stop her. There were people on her prayer list from the first time she had ever made one. She just moved the names from one worn-out, tearstained page to another and kept praying, kept begging God to intervene. Kept believing He was working.

Clara wanted to talk to Elizabeth about trusting in the Lord with all her heart, but there would be time for that. She knew trust was the essence of prayer. But how could she communicate that to someone just starting out? She wanted to tell Elizabeth that if you come to God with a good plan, you'll probably leave frustrated. The believer's job was to come to God with a surrendered heart. To come empty-handed every morning not to get what you wanted but to receive all of who He was and what *He* wanted *for* you.

Clara received a phone call from Cecilia in the morning. Someone who knew somebody at the police station had called someone else and the grapevine extended to Cecilia's house.

"What came over you, Clara? Why didn't you just give that man the money?"

"Honey, if you had been with me in my prayer time yesterday morning, you'd know why I stood up to him."

"What are you talking about now? Come on. Tell me."

"I was reading in Luke about the man of the tombs. You know, the man full of demons. The people in his town chained him up to keep him at bay. Jesus came along and found this man and spoke with authority. He told those demons their day was up. And they obeyed because He is the King of kings and Lord of lords. The power of Jesus is amazing."

"Clara, I hate to inform you, but you're not Jesus."

"I know that. But when that young man jumped out and held up his knife, I could see it in his eyes. He was just like that man of the tombs. I prayed one of those arrow prayers: 'Lord, show me what to do.' And the answer came—give him the name that's above every name. So I did it. And if he hadn't run off, I would have given him the Bible I keep in my purse."

"You could be stone-cold dead right now. You know that?"

"Mmm-hmm. You're right about that. But I'd rather speak the name of Jesus. And I've been praying that God would track that young man down and that he would hear the words of life."

"Remind me not to go downtown with you, girlfriend."

The two laughed, but Clara couldn't help but think of Elizabeth. She had chains on her heart. The enemy was after her and her family. But in those moments in Clara's living room, she'd seen a flicker of faith and known Elizabeth was about to unleash God's power on her family. This problem of theirs was an opportunity for God to work. But she knew that God sometimes let things get worse before they got better.

CHAPTER 10

* * *

Elizabeth felt a little hope seeping into her soul the next
day. She hadn't heard from Tony and wasn't sure God was
making any progress with him, but she had sold a house
to a young couple that reminded her a lot of Tony and her
when they were just starting out. Handing a family the
keys and walking through the front door with them was
the highlight of being a Realtor.

Danielle had thrown herself into her double Dutch
team and was working hard on conditioning and on several
tricks with their routine. Jennifer, Joy, and Samantha were
such talented girls, and the way the team worked together
was amazing. Elizabeth watched them from the bleachers

at the community center and cheered as they jumped. Several times Danielle looked up at her, smiling at having her mom alongside the court.

Any worthwhile endeavor, any desired goal or outcome, took teamwork. Danielle was learning valuable lessons about the importance of practice and tenacity in sticking with anything in life, just like Elizabeth was learning about prayer.

Elizabeth expected Tony home the next day, and she had prayed early this morning that God would allow her to speak kindly to him when she saw him, and that Tony would sense her love for him in the midst of their struggles. Not that she'd put up a false front, but that he would sense genuine love and understanding from her.

As she was putting some things away in Danielle's room later, she walked into her daughter's closet. She stopped as she saw two sheets of construction paper taped to the wall. One simply said, *Jesus Loves Me*, but it was the other that took her breath away. It was a prayer checklist with an empty box in front of each request. It read:

Dear God,

☐ Help my parents love each other again.

☐ Help me with my double Dutch routine.

☐ Sell Miss Clara's house to a good family.

☐ Show me how to love Jesus more.

☐ Give me ways to help others in need.

Elizabeth put a hand to her heart and smiled. God was already answering her prayers about Danielle. He was drawing her to Himself even with imperfect parents. No, God was actually *using* the difficulties they were facing to draw Danielle—and if He could do that with such a young person, He could do that with her.

"Lord, thank You," Elizabeth whispered. "Thank You for Your mercy and Your goodness. Thank You for answering. And help me focus on the things I can see You doing instead of the things I can't see."

There had been no movement on Clara's house, no showings, no phone calls, and only a few hits online. For the first time in her realty career, Elizabeth felt good about the lack of interest in her client's home. This meant she could spend more time with her friend and talk about life with two cups of coffee between them. She'd never enjoyed the sale of a home so much, and she wondered what would happen when Clara finally moved.

She drove to Clara's and the two sat on the front porch and talked about what had happened since they met yesterday. She told Clara about the progress she felt like she was making in her prayer life as she drew close to God. She really felt like He was drawing closer to her.

"But the amazing thing is what it's done for Danielle," Elizabeth said. "She asked questions. She started writing down her requests and some verses. I ordered a prayer journal for her—she has a war room of her own!"

The joy on Clara's face nearly glowed. "See, you're already influencing your daughter. This can change everything for her!"

Elizabeth smiled. "I admit, when I first started praying in there, ten minutes seemed like an eternity. Now I have a hard time even wanting to leave."

"And those times will get sweeter. It's like anything else you learn to love. The more you move into it, the more you'll desire it. God loves to be chased, Elizabeth. And when we do that, He loves to show up in unexpected ways. He says in the Word, 'You will seek Me and find Me when you search for Me with all your heart.'"

"Well, I'm seeking. For me. For Danielle. And especially for Tony."

"I'm praying for Tony too. The Word says, where two or more are gathered in His name, He's there with them. So I say, let's just gang up on Tony."

Clara leaned in and held out her hands. Elizabeth took them and they bowed and began to pray.

"Lord Jesus, I thank You for bringing this young lady into my life," Clara said. "I thank You that You are over all our problems and that You are the answer. You're not just the one with solutions, You *are* the solution. Thank You for Your Holy Spirit. Thank You for Your blood that washes us whiter than snow. Thank You for moving into our lives and drawing us to Yourself."

Elizabeth picked up and continued the prayer. After a few moments, she turned her attention to Tony. "Lord, I

know Tony is not my biggest problem. I know that I have
my own issues, and thank You for showing me those. I
thank You for the kind way You've peeled back those layers.
But I do pray for Tony. I ask You to do whatever You need
to do in order to draw him closer to You."

"That's right, Lord," Clara said, almost interrupting.
"I agree with my sister! I believe You're doing something
powerful. And I ask You to keep moving, keep waking him
up to himself and to You. And give my sister the ability to
walk through that with him because, Lord, I've never seen a
man wake up who hasn't gone through something hard. So
do Your work, do it in Your timing, and help us to be faithful while You work."

Elizabeth got Danielle in bed and fell asleep reading
another chapter in her marriage book.

She dreamed that the three of them—Tony, Danielle,
and Elizabeth—were riding in a car over a rickety bridge
with no guardrails. The bridge was icy and when the back
fishtailed, the car plunged into the frigid waters. Elizabeth
managed to pull Danielle from the backseat and get her to
safety, but when she tried to rescue Tony, she couldn't get
to him. He gasped for air, trapped inside the sinking car.

She awakened, her heart beating wildly, the book still
in her hands. Was it some kind of sign? Some warning
from God? She knew she couldn't get back to sleep, so she
retreated to her closet and began talking with God about
the dream, her fears that Tony was involved with someone

else—everything poured out. She read from Scripture, looked over the verses that Clara had given her, and felt her heart settle. She didn't have to rescue Tony. That wasn't her job. Her job was to be faithful to what God had called her to do.

That thought sent her in a good direction and she began thanking God for the things He had already done. Soon, she was on to Danielle, thanking Him for how her daughter was being drawn closer to His heart.

The next thing she knew she heard a bell. Was it some angel sounding a gong in her head? Did God allow people to hear bells from heaven when they were that deep in prayer? She opened her eyes and saw light coming from her bedroom window. Her head was propped against the corner of the closet and her neck felt stiff and painful.

Elizabeth sat bolt upright and looked at her watch. She'd spent the whole night in the closet! She raced to the door and opened it, finding a deliveryman dressed in a brown uniform and holding a package.

"Oh, hello," Elizabeth said, breathing in his face.

The man turned away with a strange expression. "Whoa! Um, hello. I just need you to sign for this package."

Elizabeth stood beside him and realized what he'd delivered. "Thank you so much." She signed the tablet and said, "This is a present for my daughter and I can't wait to give it to her."

The man took back the tablet and forced a smile. "Well, I hope it takes your breath away." He handed her the package and quickly ran to his truck, calling back, "Have a nice day, ma'am."

Elizabeth closed the door and studied herself in the front hall mirror, seeing the smeared makeup and wild hair. "Oh," she said, exasperated with the way she looked. She cupped a hand to her mouth and exhaled and could hardly stand the morning breath. Stinky had been right. Just one of the hazards of sleeping in her prayer closet.

Rather than hate the miles he put on his Tahoe, Tony enjoyed the driving. He had time to think, time to process what was happening in his life. He listened to sports radio in the morning to catch up on the latest. He loved turning his music up loud when he got tired and his eyes felt droopy. The coffee at various shops along the road helped too. He even listened to self-help audio that encouraged him to reach for the heights and be who he wanted to be. He could take a seminar driving from one location to the next simply by listening to speakers talk about how to seal a deal, how to be positive and cultivate contacts and look people in the eye. There were even spiritual motivators who talked a little about God wanting the best for every person. These all made him feel better inside. There were so many ways a person could improve himself—all at the touch of a button.

What he couldn't improve was his marriage. That was a given. There was nothing that could repair the brokenness.

And he knew what would happen when he got home. Elizabeth would ask questions and make him feel like he needed to leave again. There was nothing worse than coming home to a place you wanted to leave.

For some reason, he hadn't been able to call Veronica back. He didn't know why, just something inside that told him to wait. Maybe the way she had moved toward him and invited him to her apartment made him think this wasn't the first time she had done something like that with a guy who had shown an interest. Tony wasn't looking for someone who was "easy." He was looking for . . . well, he wasn't sure. Someone who wouldn't argue so much. Someone who would smile at him for a change. A woman who would help him become the person he wanted to be, the father he wanted to be, without all the drama and nagging.

He pulled up to the house and saw Danielle's jump rope hanging on the porch. At first it would hurt her to see her dad with another woman, but kids were resilient. Tony had turned out okay after his parents split up. Danielle would too, with enough time and explaining.

Tony hit the garage door opener, and as he waited, he thought about a man who had helped him early in his sales career. Gary was a friend at Brightwell who taught him how to deal with some difficult situations. Tony had been about to lose an account, and to compensate, he'd immediately lined up a dozen other possible ones.

"I know how bad you're feeling," Gary had said. "You're

frustrated, upset, and worried. And you're overcompensating. You're trying to prove to everybody you can do this."

"I'm trying to keep my job," Tony said.

"Let me give you some advice," Gary said. "A client kept is gold."

"You think I don't know that?"

"I'm sure you do, but knowing it and achieving it are different things. Spend your energy trying to keep an account rather than trying to generate ten more."

"There's no hope. They've made their decision."

"Are you sure?" Gary leaned closer. "Show some humility. Show them you're willing to do whatever it takes."

"You mean beg? Crawl in there on my hands and knees?"

"Tony, you can walk away from a client when you know you've done nothing wrong. Tell yourself they don't appreciate you. Another client will treat you better. But the truth is, the client you have now, with all their faults and hang-ups, is the one you need to work on. Bring them back."

Tony pulled into the garage and turned off the car, remembering that Gary had called the company—it had been his own account long before. He'd put in a good word for Tony and asked for another chance, and the company had somehow agreed. Tony took Gary's advice and showed them he was willing to work hard to keep their business. That was simply being a good salesman.

He wasn't sure why that memory surfaced as he returned, but as he pushed the garage door button on the wall, he took a deep breath and prepared for another fight.

When he walked in, Elizabeth and Danielle were fixing sandwiches and talking about some new journal Elizabeth had ordered for Danielle. Tony put down his satchel and draped his jacket on the counter.

"Hey, Daddy," Danielle said.

"Hey, Danielle," Tony said.

"I didn't think you were coming home until tonight," Elizabeth said.

"Yeah. I finished up everything pretty early." He looked at the food she was preparing and his stomach growled. He hadn't been able to eat much in the past two days, but his appetite was suddenly back. "You got enough for me?"

"Sure. Jennifer's mom is picking Danielle up in a few minutes, but you and I can eat."

No argument. No yelling or shouting or shaming. Just an invitation.

"All right. I'll take my stuff to our room," Tony said.

He tossed his suitcase on the bed and threw his jacket on the ottoman. Elizabeth had made the bed, like she always did. Everything was neat and tidy—but there was something different. He couldn't put his finger on it, but something in the room had changed.

Elizabeth's cell phone dinged on the dresser. From the living room came the ring of the doorbell and Danielle ran to get it. Who was picking her up? One of her friends from jump rope—started with a *J*.

He took off his tie and dropped it on the bed. Then his curiosity got the best of him and he walked to the dresser.

From the living room came the sounds of Elizabeth and the mom of Danielle's friend. What was her name? He picked up Elizabeth's phone and stared at the message on the screen. It was from someone named Missy . . . the name sounded vaguely familiar to him. Someone from college, maybe? The first message in the thread was from two nights earlier.

Liz, this is Missy. I'm in Raleigh. Just saw Tony in a restaurant with a woman I didn't recognize. Somebody you know?

His heart sank and he felt his stomach clench.

Elizabeth had responded: Are you serious?

Missy: I wouldn't lie to you.

Elizabeth: I'm sure it's just a client.

Missy: Looked pretty friendly.

Elizabeth: I can only hope it's nothing.

Missy: I'll keep you posted.

Elizabeth: Thanks, girlfriend!

Tony scrolled down and saw the message that had just arrived.

Liz, did you find out about the woman Tony was with in Raleigh?

It felt like a punch to his gut and he wondered if he'd repeat the episode in the restaurant bathroom. He swallowed hard and took a deep breath. Elizabeth knew about Veronica. Though she probably didn't know her name, she knew he'd had dinner with some female. But she hadn't called, hadn't texted, hadn't asked about it. What was up with that? Did she really think it was just a business meeting or was she waiting to pounce on him? He'd heard horror stories about wives who did terrible things to husbands. Maybe she was waiting to confirm things so she could put a plan in place for revenge.

Maybe she already had a plan.

The front door closed and he casually walked into the kitchen. Pretended he knew nothing about what she knew. Elizabeth was finishing fixing his meal.

"So what's been going on here?"

"Well, I sold another house yesterday. And I already told you about getting held up, so . . ."

Here it came. She was going to hold that over him—he was sure about it. "Yeah, look, about that. It's not that I didn't care. I was just busy, so when I knew you were all right . . ."

"I understand," she said, putting the plates on the table. "I'm sorry for getting so worked up about it."

Tony couldn't believe what he was hearing. She had apologized to him when he was the one who had been insensitive. And the part about being "busy" . . . that was because of Veronica.

"You're sorry?" Tony said.

"Yeah, I knew you were at work. Probably in a meeting. I should have just waited till later to bring it up." She turned to pour some tea for them.

This was not right. Something was definitely off. Tony took her plate and switched it with his own.

"My mind was just racing, and I took it out on you.

But you know what? I think it was really good for Danielle. I think it helped her realize how important it is to be aware of who's around you."

She came to the table and put the tea glasses down. He tried to smile at her, but his own mind was racing. Had some alien taken over his wife's body? Was she pretending everything was okay until he was comfortable? She had conveniently gotten Danielle out of the house.

"Hot sauce?" Elizabeth said.

He checked the counter and saw all the knives were still in place. "Yeah, that's fine."

"You want mild or Wrath of God?" she said.

"I don't want Wrath of God. Let me have the other one."

Elizabeth returned and sat, spreading a napkin in her lap. It was clear now what she was doing. She was baiting him. Acting all nice and pleasant and getting him food and pretending everything was fine. Even apologizing. He was on to her game and ready for the stab.

Finally he shook his head. "What do you want, Liz?"

She pretended to not understand. She had gotten good at it. He almost believed her response.

"You mean, right now?" she said.

"Yeah."

She thought a moment. "Well, I would kill for a hot fudge sundae. Just fudge everywhere." She waved a hand in a circular motion. "And two scoops of ice cream, cookies and cream. Just mounds of whipped cream on top. And one cherry."

He stared at her, not believing what he was hearing. She was going on about a sundae when he knew she was planning something horrific for him.

"And my feet are killing me," she continued. "Man, I would love a foot rub." She stared at the table as if imagining what that would be like.

Tony shook his head. "Liz, I'm not rubbing your feet."

"Okay," she said matter-of-factly. "Well, you want to pray?"

Pray? he thought. They hadn't prayed before a meal since . . . he couldn't remember when. But he would roll with the charade. He bowed his head and awkwardly said, "God, we thank You for this food and for taking care of our family. Amen."

He looked up, waiting for Elizabeth to bare her teeth or brandish some weapon or scream at him about Veronica. Instead she picked up her sandwich and dug in.

"I'm starving," she said.

Tony watched her a second before picking up his own sandwich and gingerly trying a bite. He guessed it was safe, unless she had assumed he would switch plates. No, that was crazy.

"What's the journal thing you and Danielle were talking about?"

Elizabeth smiled. "It's so cute. I've started a prayer journal with the help of one of my clients—Miss Clara. Tony, you have to meet her. Anyway, Danielle saw it and started asking questions and one thing led to another and we had this spiritual conversation about God and whether He answers prayer. I ordered a journal for her so she could write in her requests and favorite verses. She was as excited about it as some expensive birthday present."

"Is that so?"

She wiped her mouth with a napkin, the look on her face like sunshine coming over the mountains. "I'm beginning to see who she's going to be, who she's becoming. You know? I always thought of her as our little girl, that she's going to stay that way forever, and I know out there in the future she's going to grow up and have a family of her own. But that has felt so far away. Having that conversation with her made me realize it's not. It's coming soon."

"I've heard they grow up fast."

"It's going to be like a rocket lifting off. And I'm so grateful we have her. And for the way you provide for us. I know I haven't said that in a long time."

Tony stared at Elizabeth. There had to be a hidden microphone—she was going to trap him into saying something and use the audio in court during the divorce hearing. Or maybe there was a sniper outside on the back deck who was waiting for the signal to pull the trigger.

"Tony, you okay?" Elizabeth said.

He picked up his sandwich again. "Yeah, I'm fine." Tony watched her eat, trying to figure out what had happened to his wife.

Miss Clara

✦ ✦ ✦

Clara didn't want to say anything to Elizabeth that would discourage her. It was clear she was flying high with victory about her daughter and her own spiritual progress. But when the two of them were sitting at that table with hands clasped and Elizabeth began to pray for her husband, Clara had gotten the distinct impression that God was about to do something, and she could never predict what hard thing He was going to do.

Clara didn't live on feelings because they ebbed and flowed. She had decided to keep the train of her life on the parallel tracks of faith in God and loving others. The enemy tried to push her off the tracks every day and it was her job to trust God, to believe He was good and was working, and then to act on that belief by loving others.

If she'd said it once, she'd said it a thousand times. "People let their feelings push them away from God or away from believing that their life makes a difference. They think that because they don't see God working the way they think He should work, He's not there. Or they think He doesn't care and they get discouraged."

When Elizabeth left that day, Clara had climbed the steps that led to her war room. She felt every year with every step and couldn't wait to have a war room on the same floor as her kitchen. But as she climbed, the impression she'd gotten about Elizabeth and Tony grew into a rock-ribbed belief that God was working for their ultimate good. She hit her knees and flew down those twin tracks with her prayers, asking God to change hearts.

CHAPTER 11

✦ ✦ ✦

Tony had settled in for a leisurely morning without any sales calls or driving. He would go into work in the afternoon and do some paperwork, and he had a weekly department meeting to attend, which he hated, but it was going to be an easy morning. He would make an omelet with cheese and veggies for a late breakfast and watch a recap of last night's games.

Danielle sat at the table writing furiously with her pencil as he chopped onions and peppers.

"What are you doing?" he said.

"Writing in my journal," she said without looking up. She was focused on the page, like some ancient scribe who wanted to get every stroke perfect.

"Mom told me about that. Can I see it?"

She closed the journal and shook her head. "No, this is private. I write stuff in here that only me and God see."

Tony smiled and cracked four eggs in a bowl. "Well, can I at least see the front of it?"

She frowned, then handed it over. "But don't look inside."

He washed and dried his hands and took it. It was leather-bound and weighty. It felt like a Bible and had an interesting design on the front. "This is really great, Danielle. So what kind of things are you writing in here?"

She took the journal back. "Just verses and prayer requests and stuff like that."

He leaned down with his elbows on the table, right next to her. "And what's your number one prayer request right now?"

She looked at him and opened her mouth like she was going to say something, then closed it quickly. "I can't tell you."

"Of course you can. I won't laugh or anything. Is that why you won't tell me?"

"No, it's just that it's between me and God."

Connecting with his daughter was going to be more difficult than he thought. Tony retreated to the stove and turned on a burner. He was formulating his next question when his phone rang with a number from the office. He answered and found his district manager, Rick, on the line.

"Hey, Rick, what can I do for you?"

"I was wondering if you could come to the office. Something's come up we need to discuss."

"Well, I was taking the morning off after the trip. I'll be in for the meeting this afternoon. Can we meet right before then?"

"I don't think this can wait, Tony. I need you to get here as soon as you can, okay?"

He didn't like the sound of Rick's voice, but it was clear the only reaction was simple obedience. "Yeah, Rick, sure thing. I've got Danielle—I'll figure it out and see you in a few."

"I appreciate it," Rick said.

Tony put his phone away and turned off the burner. Breakfast would have to wait. He called Elizabeth but her voice mail answered. He clicked off the phone angrily.

Then he got an idea. "Do you think I could drop you off at your friend's house? Jeanette or Jeanie . . . ?"

"Jennifer," Danielle said.

"Yeah, Jennifer. Could you call her?"

He retreated to his bedroom and showered and dressed. When he came out, Danielle had her jump rope and was ready. "Her mom said it would be fine. Where are you going?"

"Rick called me to a meeting—my boss. And when the boss says, 'Jump,' you learn to ask, 'How high?' Where did your mom go this morning? To work?"

"Yeah, then to Miss Clara's house."

They drove to the end of the street and Tony realized he had no idea where the girl lived.

"Turn here," Danielle said. "Her house is down that way."

He pulled into the driveway and walked up with his daughter. Jennifer opened the door and the two were off into the house. The girl's mother came to the door and introduced herself.

"I'm really sorry about this," Tony said.

"Oh, don't be."

"My boss called and I need to get to work. I'll have Elizabeth pick her up on her way home, if that's okay."

"It's no problem at all," the woman said. "Danielle can stay all day if she wants. Or I can drop her off at the house when Elizabeth gets home from work."

"That would be great," Tony said. "Thank you."

Tony called Elizabeth on his way to the office but the call went straight to her voice mail again. He left a quick message, telling her that Jennifer's mom would drop Danielle off at home later, then hung up, steaming that he couldn't speak with her.

When he got to the office, Sharon, Rick's secretary, saw him and quickly picked up the phone. She wasn't her usual bubbly self but Tony felt there was probably something going on in her life. Maybe a marriage problem. Or maybe he was projecting his problems onto her.

Rick opened the door and ushered Tony in. Also in the room was Tom Bennett, the vice president Tony didn't care for. Plus Clinton Withers, head of the human resources department. Strange. Clinton only attended meetings where there were hirings and firings.

Rick shook hands with Tony and motioned for him to sit. Suddenly he felt like he'd walked into an ambush.

"Tony, there's no easy way to say this," Rick said, his eyes on his laptop. "I had a conversation with Greg yesterday."

"I know Greg," Tony said, his stomach curling into a tight ball. "He's an inventory rep." He tried to look innocent like he was unsure of what Rick was talking about. Tom and Clinton just stared at him.

"Greg says your numbers are off. And it's not a onetime thing. He saw the same thing last week after your trip to Asheville. He says there's a pattern."

Tom leaned forward. "He's padding, Rick." He said it with a sneer like he enjoyed the accusation. "It's clear what's going on."

"Wait," Tony said, not sure how to defend himself.

Rick turned the screen around and spoke with some regret. "Numbers don't lie, Tony. Greg double-checked. This is the fifth time he's noticed. And it makes me wonder if this hasn't been going on for a while."

"I'm sure there's just a mix-up," Tony said, trying to sound confident. His palms were sweating and he had a hard time swallowing. He needed something to drink. He needed a trapdoor. "Let me go get my samples and count again. . . ."

"That won't be necessary, Tony," Clinton said. "In cases like this where there's a clear breach, termination is the only option. It's spelled out in your contract."

"Termination?" Tony said.

"You're gone, Tony," Tom said. There was a little glee in his voice.

"You mean that's it?" Tony said. And the switch flipped inside. The competitor, the person who had to be right, to win the argument. "I'm your best sales guy. I spoke with Coleman the other day. I've got a bonus coming because of the Holcomb contract. You'd let me go just because some numbers don't match up?"

"He's never earned his bonuses," Tom said. "It's all been a smoke screen."

Rick looked at him sadly. "Tony, you know how much I like you. You know I took a chance with you. Believed in you. Spoke up for you with Coleman and the others."

"I told you it was a mistake," Tom said.

"And I don't understand what's going on in your personal life," Rick continued. "I don't know what may have caused you to do this. But there's a zero-tolerance policy for this type of thing."

"You knew that when you signed the contract," Clinton said.

Tony nodded and dropped his eyes to the floor. They had him dead to rights. The only thing left to do was admit guilt and ask for mercy. But if he admitted he was guilty of padding the numbers, he'd have to tell them the real truth and there would be more problems. Legal problems.

Tony looked up. "What happens to my salary? The bonus?"

"You'll be paid up until today," Clinton said. "There will be no bonus check because of the termination. No severance. I will need your key card and your phone before you leave the building—you can give those to Jerry."

A security guard discreetly entered the room. Tony had seen Jerry at the front of the building but never knew his name. He never thought he needed to know it because the guy just opened the door and said, "Good morning." Now Jerry would be the last person in the building he'd see.

The air went out of the room. Tony had never believed they would notice the missing sample boxes. He didn't think it mattered—a few pills? Sure, the number of boxes had mounted, but still, with all the money the company was raking in . . .

"My house," he said. "My family. Insurance. How do we pay the bills?"

"You should have thought of that before you fudged your numbers," Tom said, jumping on Tony's words.

"I'm sorry, Tony," Rick said. "I really am."

Tony signed the papers and Jerry escorted him to his desk. There was a box on top of it to store his personal items. He had a picture of Elizabeth and Danielle with the words *Best Dad Ever* around the frame. *Yeah, right. Best dad ever gets tossed out on his ear.* It wasn't fair. It wasn't right.

But it was. That was the shame of it. He deserved what he was getting.

"Another thing," Rick said, meeting him in the hall outside his office. "I forgot to talk to you about the car."

The car. Tony had forgotten about his Tahoe. It had become his second home.

"We'll come to get it tomorrow," Rick said. "Unless you'd rather we drive you home now. Whatever you think would be easier for—"

"Let me drive it home," Tony said. He couldn't imagine being driven home by his boss, like a teenager who had failed a driver's test. Like some drunk being driven home from a party. The truth was, he wanted to be alone and away from all of this. All of the accusations and stares.

He felt like a dead man walking through the hallway. People turned away as he walked past cubicles and open office doors. Their faces were full of pity and shame and maybe a little bit of relief. It was something he'd only seen once before at the company, and he'd promised himself he'd never become *that guy*. Now here he was, walking the plank that led to an ocean of unemployment.

Rick walked side by side with him to the elevator. The man tried to find something to say but couldn't. Jerry pushed the Down button and they waited until the elevator dinged.

Tony turned. "My accounts. You'll have to explain what happened."

Rick shook his head. "We can't talk about HR stuff. We'll just tell them you moved on to another opportunity. Don't worry about your accounts, Tony. We'll take care of them. You just take care of yourself, okay?"

Tony nodded and rode to the first floor, and the guard walked him to his car. How would he tell Elizabeth? How could he explain? And how would she respond? She would explode. He was sure of that. She would think about herself and Danielle and the house payment and his "indiscretion." She would categorize it as "sin." She would take it personally, say that he had brought shame on the family, and there would be tears and a turned back and rejection. It would be the nail in the coffin of their marriage.

The family. What would he say when he walked into the house at Thanksgiving with her relatives there? What would he say to Michael or to anyone else from church? And who was going to hire a guy who'd been fired for stealing from his employer? So many questions. Yes, Tom was right—he should have thought of all this before he ever took a box of pills.

Danielle wouldn't understand why Dad was hanging around the house so much. And Elizabeth . . . the distance between them would only grow.

He looked in the rearview and watched the building recede in the distance. Instead of taking the familiar route home, he drove aimlessly around town. No more going on the road. No more setting up meetings. No more bonuses. All he had was a hefty life insurance policy that would provide for Elizabeth and Danielle and another that paid off the house. He was worth more dead than alive.

When Elizabeth left Clara's house, she checked her phone and saw that Tony had left a message. Something about dropping Danielle off at Jennifer's. He had told her he'd watch Danielle and here he was leaving her. Probably going to work. That's where his heart was. She wished he would put as much energy into his home as he did his job.

She pulled away from Clara's and another thought struck her. If Tony was at work, he had done the responsible thing and taken Danielle to someone's house. And she was grateful for how hard he worked—the way he provided for their family. There were plenty of men who didn't seem to care about working for a living and becoming successful. Instead of thinking negatively, she turned that around, made a different script.

"Lord, Tony has a long way to go, but You've given him a desire to work hard and I thank You for that. Thank You that he does care about us. I'm going to choose to look at what he's doing rather than all the things he's not doing. Thank You for helping me see that today. I pray You'd bless him today and help him do his job well."

This was the kind of thing that was beginning to happen. Rather than her heart being turned away from her husband, it was drawing closer to him.

She called Jennifer's mom to tell her she was heading home, and Sandy offered to drop Danielle off there. It was raining hard when Elizabeth made it home and pulled into the garage. She asked Danielle where Tony had gone and she said something about a call from his boss.

There were dishes in the sink and some things still left on the stove. The garage door clacked. "Oh, I hear him," she said.

Danielle stared at the book she was reading. "He wanted to see my journal."

"Did you show it to him?"

She shook her head.

"Why not?"

"Because there's stuff in there about him. Things I've been praying about and asking God."

"What are you asking, sweetie?"

"You know. That you two would stop fighting. That he would be able to spend more time with us. That he would . . ."

"That he would what?" Elizabeth noticed that Danielle was wearing her *Love* shirt, the pink one with purple sleeves and the word spelled in glittery letters.

"That he'd become friends with God again. It seems like they used to be friends, but now they're kinda not."

When Elizabeth could speak, she said, "I think that's a really great prayer."

She sat next to Danielle and opened a magazine. If Tony hadn't eaten before he left for work, he was probably hungry. She could make him an omelet in a few minutes. When he didn't come inside right away when the garage door went down, she wondered if there might be something wrong with his car. Or maybe he was on his phone with the mystery woman from Raleigh.

She closed her eyes. *No, Lord, I am not letting my mind run that direction. I am going to trust You and hold on to You rather than think the worst.*

Tony walked inside and immediately went toward the bedroom.

"Hey," she said warmly.

He didn't respond. Not even a nod or a grunt. He just walked right past them into the bedroom.

How do I look at this positively? she thought. *Lord, does he need me? Should I go in there or just leave him alone?*

She thought of something Clara had said to her. "You start treating him the way he wants to be treated, not the way you feel loved. Tony is a man and sometimes you have to switch things around. You start loving him that way and you'll show him your heart is turned toward him."

When Elizabeth went through something difficult, she needed to be alone, to shut the door and take a bath or a nap or read. Just get away from it all. But at least in the early days of their marriage, Tony had needed to process the ups and downs of life together. He vented. And she didn't do well with the venting—it scared her. Maybe she could change things up a little.

Deciding to take the chance, she walked through the open bedroom door. "Tony?"

He had his back to her, unpacking his satchel on the bed. She could tell from his demeanor that something was wrong, but she couldn't see his face. Was there fire in his eyes? Had she done something?

Before she could ask, he spoke. "First off, I don't want any grief from you, okay?"

Now he turned and looked at her, his muscles tight, his face full of anger or hurt. "Because I'm really not in the mood to talk about this right now."

His level of anger shocked her. What could have happened? She collected herself and, in a tone as conciliatory and caring as she could muster, said, "Tony, what's going on?"

He pulled his tie off like it was a noose around his neck. "I just lost my job." He slammed the tie on the bed and went back to his satchel.

Elizabeth took a breath and tried to stay calm. She couldn't imagine what the meeting had been like—was it a layoff at the company? Was he fired for something else? It didn't matter. What mattered was, her husband was hurting. He was probably asking a million questions about the future.

"Okay. So we'll just do what we gotta do," she said, trying to sound measured and in control. Reassuring.

"What? No sarcastic comment?" he said. He had that look on his face, that bewildered, what-did-you-say? scowl.

"Tony, I think we'll be fine." She said it with all the confidence she could dredge up. At that moment she wasn't sure they would be fine. But she had to give him something.

Tony turned, his face twisted in anger. "Liz, you heard me, right? I just got fired." He threw his head forward to put an exclamation point on the sentence. "So that means no income, no company car, no health coverage. We can't even afford this house anymore."

There it was, the stark truth. Her mind whirled and she rubbed her neck, trying to think quickly. "I understand. Listen, I'll just pick up some new properties while you look for a different job, okay?"

Tony stared at her, a blank look that seemed to hold them both in disbelief. "So that's it? You're just gonna roll with it?"

"What else am I supposed to do?"

Tony studied her eyes a moment, then turned his back and kept going with the satchel. "Sometimes I don't get you, Liz."

Elizabeth stayed quiet. What could he need from her? What happened to the inside of a man who'd had everything he based his life on pulled out from underneath him? Yes, she was scared. Terrified, even. But if God was for them, if God was watching out for both of them, what could this job loss do? Wasn't He bigger than this problem?

Yes, He was. She couldn't say that right then, of course. It wasn't the right time or place. But it was true. And part of her wondered if, just maybe, this whole situation, whatever it was, could actually be used for good in their lives.

"I'll go start dinner," she said.

The chopped peppers and onions. The omelet. She would make that for him. She would just do the next thing, take the next step. What else could she do?

God, please help me love my husband right now and be strong for him. Help me trust in You and not what I can see. Help me not lean on my own understanding. Help me not panic but fully trust.

Miss Clara

✦ ✦ ✦

The phone call came late that evening as Clara was getting ready for bed. She was sitting at the table in the living room, going through the book of Philippians, when Elizabeth called to share the news of Tony's job loss. Clara listened and closed her eyes and prayed a silent *thank You* to God. She had been through this type of thing too many times not to give thanks.

"I'm proud of you for responding that way to your husband," Clara said. "It shows God is working in your heart—and Tony noticed the difference, didn't he?"

"He sure did," Elizabeth said, her voice cracking.

"I'm going to say something that will seem a little strange at first."

"Okay," Elizabeth said hesitantly.

"Sometimes the best gifts God gives us are not the easy times when everything goes our way. The best gifts are the hard times when your life is reduced to a couple of good questions: What is this all about? Why are we here? Sometimes it's a diagnosis. Sometimes it's a slamming door when someone you love walks out. Might be a bill you can't pay. And at first you think the answer will be healing or that loved one returning or a pile of money that drops right out of heaven. Now I'm not against healing. I'm for it. And I'm for reconciliation. If God opens up the storehouses of heaven and rains down hundred-dollar bills, I'll get out a basket and gather them like manna."

Elizabeth laughed, though Clara figured tears were running down her cheeks at the same time.

"But here's the thing I've discovered after walking with the Lord a long time, Elizabeth. God is not interested in making me comfortable or happy. His goal is to make me holy, like His Son. And I've never met a follower of Jesus who hasn't encountered some suffering and pain. God doesn't tell us to pick up a memory foam cross. It's rugged and it's heavy. You can run and try to find some easier way, but eventually He leads you through the thorns and briars and that valley of the shadow. But I promise you, if you trust Him, He will lead you to green pastures and peaceful waters. Not just when you get to heaven, but right now. Peace and contentment in the middle of the storm. In the middle of the disappointment and fear and anger."

WAR ROOM

STILL PHOTOS FROM THE MOVIE

all photos by David Whitlow

War Room seeks to create a nation of prayer warriors. In this scene, a pastor in a church is highlighted in a montage of American life.

Miss Clara's wall in her home features a host of mementos signifying answered prayers.

Tony Jordan (T. C. Stallings) faces temptation from a number of sources, including his job as a pharmaceutical sales representative.

Beth Moore, in her first acting role, appears in *War Room* as Mandy, a real estate agent and a friend to Priscilla Shirer's character, Elizabeth. Moore is a *New York Times* bestselling author and acclaimed Bible teacher and speaker.

Elizabeth Jordan (Priscilla Shirer) makes amends with her daughter, Danielle (Alena Pitts).

Michael (Michael Jr.) challenges Tony
to rethink his attitude toward his wife.

Miss Clara (Karen Abercrombie) prays with Elizabeth.

Miss Clara offers a prayer of praise after receiving good news from Elizabeth.

Danielle longs
for more attention
from her father.

Tony's boss Rick (Scotty
Curlee) delivers bad
news to Elizabeth.

Elizabeth studies her Bible in her prayer closet and prays for her daughter, her husband, and her marriage.

Coleman Young (Alex Kendrick) visits the Jordans' home to discuss Tony's unethical behavior.

Danielle and her father practice for the jump rope competition.

WAR ROOM

BEHIND-THE-SCENES PHOTOS FROM THE MOVIE

Members of the cast and crew of *War Room* pray over the film.

Priscilla and Beth preparing for a scene

Michael Jr. and T. C. have fun between takes.

Writer and director Alex Kendrick on the set of the film *War Room* with Make-A-Wish program participant Rachel Aarhus. Rachel was an extra in the film as part of her wish.

Alex Kendrick discusses a basketball scene with producer Stephen Kendrick.

Dr. Tony Evans, respected pastor, author, and speaker, and Alex Kendrick on the set of *War Room*

Alex feels at home in the pulpit as he prepares to direct a church scene.

Alex Kendrick, Dr. Tony Evans, Beth Moore, Priscilla Shirer, and Stephen Kendrick pray over Angela and Roland Mitchell, the owners of the home used as a *War Room* set, and ask God to bless their home in Jesus' name.

Clara let the words sink in. She could hear Elizabeth's gentle sobbing on the other end of the line.

"You take heart now. Be encouraged. The bad times are really the good times in disguise. And I'm going to get down on my knees tonight and ask God to break through. God is walking with you, Elizabeth. Don't you forget that."

"I won't, Miss Clara."

CHAPTER 12

✦ ✦ ✦

Tony was in the dark when he heard Elizabeth's voice, distant but clear. She was in trouble. He stood, struggling to see where he was—a warehouse? There were boxes and containers around the dimly lit room and some kind of hazy fog. He ran toward her voice but seemed to go the wrong direction. He switched to his right, then back again. The closer he came, the more fear he could sense in her voice.

He spotted a corridor and then, across the way, he saw her. White shirt, gray jeans, and standing over her a hulk of a man in a black hoodie. He sprinted toward them as the man took a swing and knocked her to the ground.

Nobody did that to his wife! Nobody hurt her like that!

With every ounce of strength he had built up over the past years, the weight training, the workouts, the basketball games and jogging, Tony sprinted toward the two. He would just take the guy down. He would sail into him and tackle him like a defenseless quarterback who didn't have the sense to know there was a linebacker ready to flatten him.

"Tony!" Elizabeth shouted. "Please, help me! Please!"

His heart beat faster and his legs felt like lead. What was she doing here, in this place? What was *he* doing here? She struggled to get free from the man, but he was too big, too strong. Was it the robber in the alley? Had he found her and brought her here?

"Tony! Please! No, no! Tony!"

The man loomed over Elizabeth, his back to Tony as he rushed forward, gaining momentum, the bile fueling him as it rose inside. The attacker raised a hand to hit his wife and Tony couldn't believe it. Why would anyone attack Elizabeth? Why would anyone want to hurt her?

Tony flew at the man and, instead of tackling him, turned him around with every ounce of strength he could muster. Then he pulled back in horror. The man standing over Elizabeth, the man who had thrown her down, the man who was ready to attack her again . . . was himself. He was looking into his own menacing face. Tony couldn't believe it—couldn't process the vision before him. How could this be?

Before he could react, Tony felt his air constricted as a hand gripped his throat and squeezed. It not only blocked the air, but his grip was so tight, the blood flow lessened and he was in danger of passing out. Struggling to get free, Tony desperately tried to pull the hand away. When that didn't work, he tried to throw some punches, but they were weak and ineffective against the force that was now focusing on him.

Somehow, with a turn of the head, Tony spun and threw a ferocious punch that landed squarely on the man's face. The two fell to the floor and struggled, the attacker gaining the upper hand and getting on top of Tony. The man punched again and again and Tony was helpless—he tried to protect himself, tried to block the man's fists, but each time a punch landed, he heard a sickening crunch. There had to be blood everywhere.

In the dim light, the attacker—the other Tony—drew his right hand back and prepared to throw the killing blow. Silhouetted against the scant light in the room, the man let go and Tony closed his eyes tightly, waiting for the pain, waiting for the impact.

The impact came on Tony's shoulder. He awoke startled, on the floor next to the bed. His whole body shook from the dream. He looked down and noticed his legs were tightly wrapped in the covers, a sign he'd been thrashing and turning in his sleep.

What in the world was that? he thought. *It was so real.*

His heart rate felt like he'd just run a hundred-yard dash. He told himself to calm down, it had only been a dream, but the feelings wouldn't subside. He had been the one standing over his wife, hurting her. He had thought she was calling him for help, but she was just trying to get him to stop. He closed his eyes. He couldn't shake the image of the other Tony throwing Elizabeth to the ground and attacking her.

He struggled to get out of the covers and stood, letting his heart rate settle. It was light outside. How long had he slept? He glanced at the clock, which read 7:14. He tried to remember the night before—he'd fallen into bed, physically and emotionally drained.

Elizabeth wasn't in the bedroom now. He wished he could talk with her, see her—just make sure she was okay. Maybe the dream was some kind of warning? Maybe she was being stalked by the guy who had jumped her in the alley? But the guy in the dream had been himself.

He noticed something taped to the mirror over Elizabeth's dresser. A note in Elizabeth's handwriting. She'd always had the neatest writing. He remembered the hand-written notes she used to send him and the feeling it gave him to see his own name written in her hand.

Went to work early. Can you take Danielle to practice at 10:00? Liz.

Tony looked at his face in the mirror. He flexed his jaw—it almost felt like a punch had landed. But that was crazy. It was only a dream.

He went to his closet to find his gym bag but it wasn't

there. He tried to think where he'd put it last and wandered into the living room. He hadn't left it in the car, he was sure of that.

Danielle sat at the kitchen table crunching her favorite cereal, Coney Bombs, and reading the box. It was one of those generic brands that mimicked the national brand but was half the price. They were going to be eating a lot of that from now on. Her journal was open and on the couch across the room. What was it about that journal that had captured her? It was probably a phase she was going through, like the expensive doll phase and the expensive toy horse stage with the expensive toy corral and the barn that cost more than a real barn. It hit Tony again that he didn't have a job, and who would hire somebody who had cheated his employer? There would be no more expensive dolls or horses in that house.

"Danielle, have you seen my gym bag?"

She looked up. No *Good morning* or *Hey, Dad* or anything like that. She just said, "No, sir."

Her words troubled him, but he shook off the feeling and wandered back to his bedroom, trying to recall his steps. Maybe Elizabeth had put the bag in her own closet. She was always tidying up, moving things around so the house would look less cluttered.

He opened her closet door and froze, staring in bewilderment. Instead of all her dresses and blouses and jeans and scarves and sweaters and the collection of shoes that rivaled some queen in a far-off land, it was empty. At first he thought she'd moved out. It was the first step in her leaving him—that's where his mind went.

Then he saw the pillow on the closet floor and the Bible. The only things on the walls were taped notes. He thought they were to-do lists, things she might need to get done at work or around the house. Then he examined them a little closer and saw that they were names—and there were Bible verses written on the notes with phrases underlined and words circled and highlighted.

He'd seen movies where a main character discovered the secret life of a spouse. Or a husband or wife had gone off the deep end mentally and written crazy stuff on papers they kept in a shed in the woods. Was Elizabeth losing her mind?

As he studied the content of the messages, he began to think differently. It almost looked like some spiritual game plan by a coach who wanted to win against a rival team. Or a strategy of how to win a battle in a war he didn't even know was raging.

One of the notes had Danielle's name at the top of the page.

I pray that you would give her a spirit of wisdom and revelation in the knowledge of Christ. I pray that the perception of her mind might be enlightened so she would know what is the hope of His calling, what are the glorious riches of His inheritance among the saints, and what is the immeasurable greatness of

His power to those who believe, according to the working of His vast strength.

—EPH. 1:17FF

There were other verses and prayers for their home, their finances, people in the community, friends, and extended family. There was a page marked *Cynthia and Darren*, and underneath a prayer for their marriage, their finances, a job, and wisdom for the future.

Tony knew Elizabeth was a spiritual person. She took God seriously, but he'd never seen her this serious. And the change in Danielle's spiritual life had obviously been her following Elizabeth's lead.

He leaned down to the note taped closest to the pillow, right at eye level if you were kneeling. He read the words in his wife's handwriting.

Lord, I pray for Tony, that You would turn his heart back to You. Help me to love him, and give him a fresh love for me. I surrender my rights to You as Lord and ask You to bless him as he honors You and to expose him if he walks in deceit. Build him up as the man You intend him to be. Help me to support and respect him. I ask for Your help to love him. In Christ I pray.

Tony stood there, stunned. It was like looking inside someone else's soul. He felt almost ashamed, like he was looking at something that was supposed to be hidden. If Elizabeth could open his closet, see inside his soul, what would she find? What notes had he been stashing? He hadn't told her about why he'd been fired. He hadn't told her about Veronica or any of the old flames he'd thought about contacting on social media. A comparison of the closets of their hearts showed a stark difference.

Tony studied another sheet on the wall. It was like a shopping list of people and prayer requests, and some of them had been checked, as if already answered. Cynthia had received help from a church. Elizabeth and Danielle had grown closer in their relationship. Her desire for God had grown stronger. But there were several other requests that were left unchecked.

Tony to come back to the Lord was at the top. Under that was *That our marriage be restored.* Those two items stopped him for a second. Elizabeth hadn't nagged him about much of anything the past few days. She'd become quieter. When he revealed the news about his job loss, she had been supportive instead of lashing out or accusing. Was that partly because she'd been praying so much?

Miss Clara's house to sell. That was one of the most practical requests on the list and the one that seemed most likely to be checked next. All that had to happen was for Elizabeth to find a buyer in order for that check to go on the paper. The others . . . well, he wasn't sure how any of those about him and their marriage could be checked.

Tony heard movement behind him and turned to see Danielle at the bedroom door holding his gym bag.

"Daddy? I found your bag next to the washing machine."

"You can set it right there," he said.

She put the bag on the floor and started to leave.

"Danielle, when did Mama do this to her closet?"

She thought a moment. "Umm, a few weeks ago?"

Tony turned back to the words that seemed to float around this space. The day before he had thought seriously about ways he could end his life and give his family financial stability. They'd been fleeting thoughts, of course. Tony was a fighter, and he wasn't going to give up. Not yet, anyway. But he wondered if there was something he hadn't considered. Was there a different way out of his problems and the hole he had dug? Was there a possibility that God could forgive him and give him a second chance?

"Daddy, are you going to take me to the community center?" Danielle said, breaking his train of thought.

He showered, dressed, and made breakfast. Danielle was ready to go and sat on the couch writing in her journal while he ate. As they drove to the community center, he thought again about his dream and shuddered. The feelings it brought were too close to the bone and the soul.

The community center was a beehive of activity with kids and parents. Several girls practiced their double Dutch routines, where two people swung two ropes and jumpers navigated the middle. Tony had jumped rope in training and he was pretty good at going fast, but this was another level of coordination, timing, and teamwork.

"What time does your practice end?"

"At noon," Danielle said.

"I'll be back to get you then," he said.

Jennifer ran to Danielle and the two walked over to their team. Tony scanned the center and saw Michael in his blue paramedic uniform. He was filling something out at the front desk.

There were so many things swirling around in Tony's brain and his default was just to keep it to himself, protect himself, hold it in. But Michael was the kind of guy you could talk to and not feel . . . well, judged.

"Michael?" Tony said.

"What's up, man?" Michael said. "What are you doing here?"

"Dropping Danielle off before I head to the weight room. What's up with you?"

"I'm renewing my membership. Then I'm getting my coffee and hitting my shift, bro."

Tony thought a moment, fighting the battle to step over some unseen line in his mind—the line between vulnerability and self-protection. Finally he said, "Well, look, you got a few minutes?"

"For you? No, I got stuff to do."

Tony stared at him. Then came a big smile on Michael's face. "I'm just playing. What's up?"

They got their coffee and grabbed a table away from

everyone else. Tony didn't know whether to discuss his job situation or what had happened with Elizabeth. He decided on the latter and explained what he'd seen in Elizabeth's closet.

"It kind of freaked me out," Tony said.

"So the whole closet was empty?" Michael said.

"Yeah, except for the papers on the wall."

"And what did she do with her clothes?"

"Michael, I don't know. Some other closet. Why does that matter?"

Michael sat forward. "Dude, I don't think you understand how important this is. When was the last time you heard of a woman giving up some closet space?"

Tony frowned and shrugged.

"All I know is, you can fight against your wife, and probably hold your own, but if God is fighting for her, you can hit the gym all you want to, but it's not looking too good for you."

Tony stared into the distance, wondering if he should talk about the loss of his job, the marriage struggles, all the stuff that weighed him down like a thousand-pound barbell.

"Man, I wish my wife would pray for me like that," Michael said. "Plus, I could use the closet space."

Tony wanted to laugh, but his heart wasn't in it.

Michael stood. "I gotta catch my shift. I'll check with you later."

Tony sat for a few moments thinking. All of his life had

been tied up with what he did. His identity was his job and what a good salesman he was. With that gone, how would he define himself? And if he had stayed with Brightwell for the rest of his life, would he have anything more than he had right now? He'd have a pension and some kind of retirement plan and insurance, for sure. But would he have anything of lasting value? Would he have a wife who loved him in spite of how he'd acted? Would he have a daughter who wanted to be with him?

He glanced at his watch and walked toward the gym, where Danielle and her teammates practiced. He stopped at the front desk and caught the receptionist's attention.

"Excuse me. Can you tell Danielle I'll be back to get her after practice?"

The girl smiled and took a scrap piece of paper from a pile. "Sure, I'll tell her. My pleasure."

He thanked her and drove home, the radio off. It was still and quiet when he walked in the door. Empty. It was almost as if God were showing him what life would be like if he continued living his own way. He would wind up alone, separated from the people he loved and, more importantly, from the people who really loved him.

What a fool he had been. He had told himself that he worked hard because he wanted to provide for his family. The truth was, he wanted what he wanted. He had made the decision to throw himself into his sales, and the more success he had, the more he threw himself at it. The whole thing had wrapped him up and clouded his vision.

When had he ever asked Elizabeth what she wanted? When had he ever asked if he could do something for her? What would make her life easier or better? He'd always been consumed with whatever was on his mind, whether it was work or his next trip or the big game. It was never Danielle or Elizabeth and what they were interested in or what would help them.

When had he ever prayed for his family? That thought hit him between the eyes. He had always thought of himself as a good, God-fearing person. He'd given his life to Christ years ago and read his Bible and knew that the only really satisfying life was found in living for God and following Jesus. But the inexorable draw of day-to-day living, the ebb and flow of a career, caused a slow drift away from the truth. He could see that now.

The loss of the job, the accusation of padding the numbers, and the truth of what had really happened brought him to the brick wall of himself. And the dream he had the previous night also confronted him. He would never strike his wife. He would never harm her or take out his frustration physically, but he could see that he had hurt her, that he had done the next best thing to a gut punch with every selfish choice he made.

He went to Elizabeth's closet and sat in a small chair staring at the prayers on the wall. The verses. The requests. The people in her life. Tony didn't even recognize some of the names and for that he was ashamed. How could his wife be fervently praying for people when he didn't even know who they were?

They aren't important.

Those words came to him softly, in his heart. These people weren't important—but the people who *were* important, he remembered. He wrote down their names. He memorized them, used mnemonic devices to make sure he knew they were important. So why didn't he do that with the woman at the community center who knew his daughter and Elizabeth?

His eyes rested on the sheet that Elizabeth had written about him, the things she was praying over his life. She prayed he would love her and Danielle, that he would be honorable in his work, that he would hate his own sin. She hadn't even known how his life had become unraveled, hadn't known of his sin, and this was what she was praying.

Hate his own sin.

He stared at the words. What did it mean to hate your own sin? It sounded so spiritual, so Christian. But that was really the crux of it, wasn't it? In order for him to change, he had to see the ways he was hurting his family, the ways he was hurting his employer—and those he came in contact with, like Veronica. He closed his eyes and thought of how close he'd come to throwing it all away. If he'd ordered something else on the menu, he might not have become sick. He might have gone with Veronica that night.

Or maybe it wasn't the food that had sickened him.

Maybe it was something else, something deeper than his stomach.

He stood and moved to sit on the bed, facing a picture of Elizabeth from their wedding. She looked so happy, standing straight and tall, the white dress highlighting her dazzling smile. If he could have bottled the joy that poured out of her in that picture, he'd be a rich man. She'd been so full of hope, ready to be loved. The light on her face had grown dimmer in the past decade.

At the wedding, the pastor had talked about what it meant to love someone like Jesus loved. And he charged Tony to do that. Tony didn't remember much of the message, the challenge, but he knew he hadn't lived up to that ideal. Not even close.

A sadness that cut to his very core fell over him. But it was more than sadness, more than regret. It was a deep conviction. It was a verdict on his life. As he stared at the picture, he flashed to the dream where he'd been attacking his wife. Like some music stab in a movie that makes you jump, a jolt went through him and made him flinch. The wave hit him again and he was rolling beneath it, struggling for breath.

He stumbled from their room, wandering through the house he had worked so hard to buy. All the stuff, the furniture, the nicest television, the granite countertops, the expensive bookcases. What did any of this mean?

A verse flashed through his mind, something he had memorized when he was a child in one of those children's programs at church. It was tucked away back there in some hidden room in his mind, stored until this moment.

"What is a man benefited if he gains the whole world, yet loses or forfeits himself?" This wasn't just about losing his wife and daughter. It wasn't just about serving them and memorizing another list of names written in his notebook. It was deeper.

Elizabeth hadn't been praying for Tony to become the husband she wanted because she was unhappy. She had been praying for him because she knew *he* was unhappy. What was that old quote? *"Our hearts are restless until they find their rest in God"*? Something like that.

He moved into Danielle's room, looking at the pictures she displayed. She loved to color and draw. On a table near her desk was a card she had colored: *I ♥ DOUBLE DUTCH*. He picked up a picture of her smiling, looking up into the camera, sitting in a big leather chair. The innocence of childhood. The hopes and dreams that lay ahead. He stared at the picture of his little girl as a newborn. What kind of legacy was he leaving for her? Would he even be in her life a year from now? Ten years? He didn't want her to wind up feeling abandoned like he had felt.

He had criticized her for quitting basketball. He had missed her heart. All the chances he had to spend time with her, to play a game or watch a movie or go for a walk—he'd been too busy for the most important thing.

It all came together for him in that moment. His eyes watering, his heart breaking at the choices he had made,

Tony thought, *I don't want to miss any of this. I don't want to miss life, real life.*

He had contemplated ending his life. He truly had thought that his family would be better off without him because they would get his life insurance. But looking at how much his wife and daughter loved him in spite of the way he had treated them pushed him toward a different ledge. Their life wasn't about money and nice things and a beautiful house. It was about relationships. It was about showing and receiving love. He had missed that truth. He had worked so hard to provide something good, but he had trusted in the things he could do, the things he could possess, and they had risen up to possess him. He had missed the whole point of his marriage and his life.

The emotion became overwhelming, and he tried to shake it away but couldn't. He wondered if there might be somebody praying right at that very moment—maybe Elizabeth or Danielle, maybe Miss Clara. They were praying, *God, do something in Tony's heart,* because he could feel it, all the way to his toes. And instead of running his car into a phone pole or finding a gun to end his life, he decided he would surrender in a different way.

He knelt slowly on the floor of Danielle's room and bowed his head. It was the familiar posture of some holy person relating to God, but Tony knew he wasn't holy. It took a moment to form the words, but then they came through his tears.

"Jesus, I'm not a good man. I'm selfish. I'm prideful.

And I'm hurting this family. But this is not who I wanted to be. I don't like the man I've become. And I don't know how to fix it. I don't know what to do."

The words were heavy. It took every ounce of strength in him to get them out, to push them forward from his lips. Finally he couldn't push anymore. He said the only words he could raise from the well.

"Forgive me, please." He leaned over, his head on the floor now. "Forgive me, Jesus."

It was a prayer of surrender. A prayer of a helpless heart. And he wasn't doing this for Elizabeth or Danielle. He wasn't doing this so he could get his job back, because he knew that wasn't going to happen. His surrender wasn't because he thought he could make God do what he wanted. That idea was gone. He prayed because he knew it was his last resort and that it was the first thing he should have done, long ago.

With his head on the carpet of Danielle's room, Tony wept. He wept for all he'd done to distance himself from the people who loved him. He wept for the wasted years. Each tear was a plea for help and a desire for surrender. And when he stood, it felt like that thousand-pound barbell pushing down on his soul had been lifted. God had been spotting him all along. And for the first time in what seemed like forever, the weight had been replaced with something that felt like hope.

CHAPTER 13

✦ ✦ ✦

Elizabeth had been encouraged by her visit with Clara. Every conversation brought out some new facet of a lesson learned and gave her hope that things could change. She just had to stay the course. Keep moving forward, holding God's hand, and trusting Him.

She was in her car, ready to drive away, when she felt the need to pray again for Tony. There was no lightning, no fish symbol in the clouds above her, no voice that whispered some mysterious message. It was just a feeling that she needed to stop and pray.

"Lord, I don't know if Tony is in trouble or if he's upset about his job or if he's just working out at the gym. But I pray that You would draw him closer. Help him see there's no sin so great that You aren't ready to forgive. I pray You would give him hope. I pray You would allow him to see how much You love him and want him to come back to You. And give me the ability to love him well, through whatever we face."

She sat there pouring out her heart to God. It was funny—not long ago she would have seen prayer as wasted time. Now she looked at it as the most important thing she did.

After a few minutes she felt a peace about going ahead with her day, but she kept praying as she turned on a song about the goodness of God.

She stopped at the office and met with Mandy. She didn't tell her everything about the situation, but enough that the woman came over and gave her a hug.

"I'm so sorry about Tony's job," Mandy said. "Let me see if I can find you a few more properties in the interim."

Tony walked into the community center and stopped at the front desk. It wasn't the younger girl this time, but a woman he recognized as a friend of Elizabeth's. What was her name?

"I'm back for Danielle," he said.

The woman smiled. "They're not quite finished yet, Tony. But you can watch them from right over there. The team's getting pretty good."

Tony smiled. "I'm sorry, I can't remember your name."

"It's Tina," she said.

"Thank you, Tina."

He pulled out a scrap of paper and wrote her name on it as he walked into the noisy gym. There were teams scattered around the hardwood working on their routines. He spotted Danielle and for the first time saw them practicing. Her coach was calling out instructions, and Danielle and Jennifer were in perfect sync. He'd been upset that she had quit basketball, but seeing her jumping rope with that smile brought him joy. Her footwork was impressive, and when Danielle cartwheeled into the ropes, he couldn't believe it. Even when they missed and the ropes stopped, Danielle smiled from ear to ear and her coach clapped and praised them and then gave a few pointers.

Tony hugged her tightly when she was finished and they walked toward the car, passing the front desk.

Tina, he said to himself. *Tina.*

In the car, they pulled out of the parking lot and he instinctively wanted to fill the silence with the radio. But he didn't turn it on. He could tell there was something more important. Tony looked in the rearview mirror at his daughter. "Hey, you know what?"

Danielle's face was expressionless.

"I thought your jump rope routine was going to be something simple. But it wasn't. It was pretty difficult. You were really good, Danielle. I was impressed."

The more words he said, the more she reacted. First

in her eyes. Then her mouth. Then her whole face lit up. Just a few words was all it took to open her heart up like a flower.

"Thanks," she said quickly, as if obeying some inner script, and a smile spread across her face. She looked at him, then back down, still smiling.

"When did you learn to do a cartwheel like that?" he said.

She told him about Coach Trish, how she helped them perfect the things they'd done in the gym to make their routine more complicated, a higher risk, just like a gymnastics routine. He got lost in the conversation, in her explanation of how she and Jennifer had practiced for hours together and how much fun they'd had. He was so absorbed that he didn't see the car in front of his house or Elizabeth standing in the driveway until he pulled in. Rick was talking with Elizabeth and he had his clipboard out and Tony remembered what had happened at the office the day before.

"Daddy, why are they here?"

"They've come to get this car, Danielle."

"Why do they need your car?"

"It's kind of a long story."

"Is that all they're taking?" she said, a tremble in her voice.

"Now you don't have to worry about that, sweetie," Tony said. "We're going to be all right, okay? Look at me.

You listen to me. Everything is going to be all right. Do you believe me?"

There was a question in her voice and in her eyes. But she said dutifully, "Yes, sir."

She got out and walked slowly toward her mother. Tony followed. The whole scene was humiliating, but he was ready.

"Rick," Tony said.

"Tony," Rick said, his face showing real regret. "I'm sorry about this."

He looked the man in the eyes and for the first time saw the hurt there. It was killing him to do this to Tony and his family. He didn't want to fire Tony, but he'd been forced to act. Tony saw how his actions had not only affected his family but those he worked with.

"It's not your fault," Tony said with conviction.

Rick held out a pad with a printed sheet on top. "I need you to sign that we came for the car. And clean out any items that belong to you."

Tony nodded and signed. "I already did."

Rick took the paperwork and paused. "You're a talented guy, Tony. I'm sorry to see this happen." He took the keys from Tony. "You take care."

Elizabeth politely nodded as Rick got in Tony's car and drove away, followed by the other man from Brightwell Tony didn't know. Danielle stayed close to them as they watched the cars drive away.

"Why are they taking Daddy's car?" she said.

"We'll talk about it later, baby, okay?" Elizabeth said.
"Why don't you go inside and knock out some chores
before lunch, all right?"

"Okay."

Danielle walked inside, leaving Tony and Elizabeth
alone on the driveway. He wanted to tell her everything
that had happened. He wanted to look her in the eye and
apologize. Instead, he smiled sadly and held out a hand.

She took it and squeezed. "You okay?"

He nodded before he walked into the house.

Elizabeth found Danielle in her bedroom making her bed.
"How did practice go?"

"Fine," Danielle said.

Elizabeth sat on Danielle's chair and Danielle seemed to
instinctively know to stop and listen.

"Honey, I can't explain everything right now, but I want
you to know we're going to be fine, okay?"

The look in her eyes was one of fear. "That's what
Daddy said."

"He did?"

She nodded. "He said everything is going to be all right
and to believe him. But I don't know what is next after they
take his car."

Elizabeth hugged her and kissed her forehead. Part
of loving a child was not telling her everything. Danielle
didn't need to live under the weight of a job loss. Elizabeth

had assumed this was a layoff or downsizing, but Rick's words and Tony's admission that it wasn't Rick's fault confirmed something else had happened.

"You just keep writing down what you're feeling in your journal, okay? And you and I will keep talking about this."

Danielle nodded. Elizabeth left the room and went downstairs to find Tony sitting in the corner chair in their bedroom, leaning over with his elbows on his knees. She wanted to encourage him and let him know she was all-in, fully on his team.

"I picked up a few more houses to sell this morning. I've asked Mandy to give me everything she can for the next couple months."

"That's good, Liz," Tony said, looking up at her. Then he paused. "Can we talk?"

"Sure," she said. She sat across from him on the edge of the bed and it felt like something was happening in the room. All the prayer, all the pleading with God . . . Was Tony about to tell her he was leaving? Was he choosing some other woman from Raleigh or Atlanta? Elizabeth quieted her heart and took a deep breath. She just needed to listen. Not react too strongly.

Please, God, she prayed. *Help me to hear him and let him just say what he needs to say. Help me not be afraid.*

"I just don't understand why you're treating me this way," Tony said.

Because I love you, she wanted to say. *Because I care.* But she didn't say it. She didn't say anything, hoping to draw him out, let him speak.

"When I told you what happened with my job, I expected you to hit the ceiling, Liz," Tony continued. "So in my mind, I was ready to defend myself. Except this time I can't."

Elizabeth listened to his words, but more than that, she listened to his heart—the intangible things between the sentences. When she saw the emotion welling up in his eyes, it was all she could do to hold it together.

Tony looked out the window, then around at the room. Then he hung his head. "I hate saying this, but I deserved to get fired. I was deceiving them. And I was deceiving you. I almost cheated on you, Liz. I thought about it. I almost did it. But you know all this. And you're still here."

Her eyes stung. It was like watching her personal Jericho, the walls falling down right there in their bedroom.

"I see your closet," he said. "I see the way you're praying for me. Why would you do that when you see the type of man I've become?"

Her lip quivered as she watched the tears stream down his face. He was broken. He was at the end of himself. And it was a beautiful sight.

"Because I'm not done with us," she said, the strength of her voice surprising her. It was like she was speaking to Tony and anyone else who might be listening. "I will fight for our marriage. But I've learned that my contentment can't come from you. Tony, I love you. But I am His before I'm yours. And because I love Jesus, I'm staying right here."

The dam broke and Tony fell to his knees, weeping. He bent over, his body racked with sobs. "I'm sorry, Liz. I asked God to forgive me. But I need you to forgive me. I don't want you to quit on me."

His emotion became hers and the two of them wept. "I forgive you," she said. "I forgive you."

Tony put his head on her knees. "I'm sorry. I'm so sorry."

Elizabeth closed her eyes. She couldn't believe what had just happened. She put a hand to her chest and shook her head in amazement. "Thank You, Lord," she whispered.

Tony kissed her hand and they held each other there, crying, rejoicing, wrapped in love—and not just their own. Elizabeth glanced at the door when she saw movement outside. It was Danielle, listening. It looked like perhaps she was crying too. Before Elizabeth could invite her in, she was gone, back to her room, probably. Back to put a check mark beside her own answer to prayer in her closet.

Miss Clara

* * *

Clara saw the caller ID and picked up quickly. Any news from Elizabeth was like communication from the front lines of an extended battle. As soon as she heard Elizabeth's voice, she knew it was good news. Her tone was somewhere between gratitude and amazement.

"Tony just told me he's gotten right with the Lord," Elizabeth said. "He asked me to forgive him."

"This happened just now?"

"A little bit ago," Elizabeth said. "And he said he wants to start over."

"He did? Oh, sweet Lord!" Clara was about to jump out of her skin—not surprised at what God had done, but at how quickly Tony's heart had turned. "I told you, Elizabeth. I told you God would fight for you."

"He has, Miss Clara. He has fought for me and for our marriage and for my little girl."

Clara held it together until she hung up the phone, and then she did her happy dance—if you could call it that. It was something that happened on the inside, even when her outside didn't have the strength to follow. Then she threw back her head and let Satan know he'd lost a battle.

"Ha-haaaa! Devil, you just got your butt kicked!" she screamed. "My God is faithful! He's powerful! He's merciful! He's in charge! You can't fire Him, and He'll never retire! Glory! Praise the Lord!"

Clara imagined angels doing the same thing somewhere in heaven. Then she headed upstairs to her war room to put another check on the wall of answered prayer. She did it as an act of worship and thanksgiving. She did it to make the devil mad that he had lost another fight he thought he was going to win.

The whole thing made her want to pray bigger prayers. She believed anew that God was in the big-prayer-answering business.

CHAPTER 14

✦ ✦ ✦

Tony knew it wasn't going to be easy, moving forward and putting his life back together, but he felt like he had hit bottom and there was nowhere to go from here but up. He'd gone through the valley and now there was just the slow climb out to where he could get a vision for his life again. Things would get better, a day at a time.

The next morning he saw Danielle sitting at the bottom of the front stairs putting on her sneakers. She had noticed the change in him. Her face looked less pained since he'd become real with God and confessed to Elizabeth. Funny how a ten-year-old could have her life changed by a father's prayer.

He knew he needed to talk with her, to move toward his daughter, but he wasn't sure how. He didn't want to make the mistake of revealing too much—that wouldn't be fair to her. But he also couldn't second-guess himself the rest of his life. He wasn't going to get all of this right. Something inside told him to simply chance it—get in the game and see what happened. He greeted her and sat beside her.

"Hey, Daddy," Danielle said.

"Listen, I need to tell you something."

Danielle looked at him. Such innocence. She had her whole life in front of her and he had another chance to be involved, to help her. The best thing he could give her was his heart, what was going on inside. These were things he usually couldn't say because he didn't know he felt them half the time. But God had done something, had shown him a path to life, so he kept talking.

"I don't think I've been a very good dad to you. And I haven't been very loving to your mother either. I can do better, Danielle. You both deserve better from me."

A good start. He hadn't gone into detail, but if she wanted him to, he would. He just laid things out there clearly and in a way she could understand.

"But you know what? I've asked God to help me. And I wanted to ask you if you would forgive me and give me another chance. Think you can do that?"

In a way, this was the same thing he had done with God. At first he imagined God at the portals of heaven, His arms crossed, scowling at him. Tapping His foot, waiting for Tony to get to the point. He knew this wasn't how God really was, that God wouldn't react the way he would. If he could have pictured God with the face his daughter showed him, he might have returned sooner.

For a few seconds, she stared at him. Then the smile came and Danielle nodded, and just that look melted his heart. It said, *"I accept you and love you and always will."*

Just like that. Forgiveness with a smile and no questions. Love looked a lot like that, he thought. If he could love like that, if he could respond like his daughter, the rest of his life would go a lot better.

"I do love you, Danielle," he said.

"I love you too, Daddy."

He kissed her on top of the head and walked away, as light as a feather. She followed him outside with her jump rope and did some warm-ups, explaining their routine and what Trish had been teaching them. When she sat on a step beside him, he decided to pick up the subject again.

"Danielle, is there anything I could do better? Something that would tell you how much I love you?"

She made a face and got wrinkles in her forehead. It was clear this wasn't a question she'd considered. "You mean like buying me a present?"

"I guess it could be that. But I was thinking more—is there anything we could do together that you'd like?"

She shrugged and said, "I don't know."

It was another moment of unbridled childhood. She couldn't think of anything and that was okay. He had offered a lamp with only one wish attached and she didn't seem to want to rub it at the moment.

Tony smiled. "All right. You think about it. If something comes to mind, you let me know."

Elizabeth came outside and sat beside him, and they watched Danielle jump rope. With all of his anger at his wife, all their bickering, he had forgotten how beautiful she was. No, he hadn't forgotten—he'd just pushed the truth aside and allowed the clouds of life to cover it.

"Your little girl seems happy with her daddy again," Elizabeth said.

"It honestly doesn't take much. I just asked her to forgive me for being such a cruddy father and she said yes like it was the easiest thing she'd ever done."

"Kids will give you a second chance. It's the grown-ups who have a harder time."

He looked at her. "Is that so?"

She smiled. "What?"

"One of my big fears in asking you to forgive me was that you'd hold all the stuff I've done over me. And you'd come back in a day or a week or a year and bring it all up again. You haven't done that."

"Well, it hasn't been a week or a year, either," she said.

"No," he said, "I can tell you mean it. I can tell this is not about me getting everything right and living up to some list of rules and regulations."

"I'm glad you said that," she said, digging into the pocket of her jeans. "I just came up with a list this morning."

They laughed and he realized it had been so long since they had genuinely laughed together. He couldn't remember the last time. It had probably been the last time they had . . .

Danielle stopped jumping and caught them talking together. She ran to them, out of breath, and jumped in front of them. "Kiss her, Daddy! Kiss her!"

"Now don't rush things," he said, laughing and waving a hand at her. "Your mama and me are working on not fighting. That's the first step."

"Kiss her!" Danielle said, swinging her rope and jumping. She got into a rhythm and sang, "Kiss her, kiss her, kiss her . . ."

Tony shook his head.

Danielle stopped and her face turned glum. "You asked me to tell you one thing you could do, didn't you? Well, this is it."

Before Tony could object again, Elizabeth said, "Go ahead and give the girl what she wants."

He raised his eyebrows and leaned back, looking at Elizabeth's face. She turned her head to offer a cheek and he leaned in and gave her a peck.

"On-the-lips," Danielle said, talking in time with her jumps. "On-the-lips!"

Tony looked in his wife's eyes, studying them. He didn't want to take things too fast. He wanted to give Elizabeth time to see his genuine heart.

"Kids these days," he said playfully. "They ask so much."

"You're the one who asked her the question," Elizabeth

said, matching his gaze. She moistened her lips with her tongue.

He leaned closer. "It is cheaper than a new jump rope."

He kissed her on the lips. It wasn't the longest or most romantic kiss of their marriage, but the feelings it stirred inside Tony surprised him.

"Yay! Yay! Yay!" Danielle said, continuing her jumping. "Do-it-again! Do-it-again!"

Jennifer and her mother drove up. Tony put an arm around Elizabeth and they walked to the car, greeting Jennifer's mom.

"It's Sandy, right?" Tony said.

The woman smiled.

✦ ✦ ✦

Elizabeth knew real estate was kind of like marriage. You could have the best house in the world but if you didn't have an interested buyer, you'd sit alone at the open house. But you could never tell what a new day would bring. The right person in the right situation who came along could make all the difference. One phone call from someone driving around who saw a nice neighborhood and a sign was all it took. A friend of a friend knew somebody who was looking and suggested they call. It was all part of an unseen network of people and needs and wants.

The kiss from Tony was one of those things the new day had brought. The feeling lingered all day. The touch of his lips, the closeness she felt. Kissing was as much about the heart as about the lips, and her heart had done a backflip when he leaned in and connected with her. Still, she felt some reservation. She had been grateful that Tony had turned to God, but she'd also been hurt by what he'd revealed.

Elizabeth had wondered about Tony's decreased interest in intimacy in the past year. When they had first been married, she worried that she and Tony would have different levels of longing. She heard married women talking about husbands who wanted sex every day, and that had sounded good at the time. But the wives had complained, at least most of them. A few had said their husbands didn't want sex at all, and that troubled her. Would she and Tony be compatible in this area?

That question was quickly put to rest when they discovered both had a fairly equal level of desire. But after Danielle was born, things changed. Her body changed. Her energy level fell and she was emotionally tied in with her daughter. She supposed it was hormones and all the changes her body had gone through.

Soon she and Tony got in a groove as a couple and moved forward. They were at least going in the same direction. They would find each other occasionally—nothing planned—and enjoyed each other, but their intimacy was hit-or-miss at best. In the last year Tony had backed away from her and had thrown himself into the gym, working out and staying fit seeming to fill some inner need. She read articles online and found a book at the library on the subject, but the content troubled her. It said a husband who backed away from his wife sexually could be a flashing light on the marriage dashboard. Maybe he was getting toned for someone else?

That night, after Tony had gotten Danielle to bed, he came to Elizabeth as she sat on the chair in her bedroom. She had picked up the marriage book she'd been reading but lowered it when he walked into the room.

He knelt in front of her. "I need to tell you something."

She closed the book. The look on his face telegraphed a message she wasn't going to like.

"Sounds ominous," she said. She meant, *It sounds painful.*

"Not really," he said. He took a moment, then looked her in the eyes. "I think we need to see somebody."

"What do you mean?"

"Like a counselor. A pastor. Somebody who can help us take the next step."

Elizabeth searched his eyes. She'd been in enough Bible studies with other women who had marriage problems to know that getting a man to go to any kind of counselor was like getting a wild horse into a minivan. Through the window. And the seat belt buckled. That he was suggesting it felt like a huge gift.

"Okay," she said.

"I just think there are some things a third party could help us work through, you know? Somebody who's been through this kind of thing before."

She nodded. "Yeah, of course. I'm in. You choose."

"I was thinking of calling the church," he said. "They have a family pastor, don't they?"

"Yeah, Pastor Wilson."

"Good. I'll call in the morning."

She put the book on the edge of the chair and balanced it. There was something behind this. It felt like the tip of the iceberg was showing above the choppy waters they'd been through. "Is this because there's something else you need to tell me?"

Tony said he hadn't been unfaithful. But he'd been on the road a long time. Elizabeth had prayed earlier that day that God would help both of them uncover their hidden thoughts and feelings so they could get them out in the open and deal with them. Kind of like finding the edge pieces of a puzzle. If you got those on the table and connected, you could find the middle easier.

"I know you heard about Raleigh," he said. "The lady I had dinner with. When I came back from the trip, I saw the message from Missy."

"You looked at my phone?"

"It was out when I was getting changed that night and the phone dinged. I saw what she said and the whole conversation. I wasn't trying to spy. I didn't go through all your messages, trust me."

"That's what this is about, Tony. Trust. And I'm working on forgiveness and trying to build that trust, but when I hear you saw that and never said anything about it . . ."

He sat back on his heels. "Look, don't read too much into it. I'm telling you now, okay?"

"Don't tell me what to read into something. I've been fighting for you, for our marriage, and this hits deep. It's one of the things I know we have to work out."

He set his jaw. "This is what I'm talking about. This is what I'm afraid will happen. I come to you, I try to talk, and you throw up a wall."

"You built the wall yourself, Tony."

Her heart was racing now and she could tell this could go really badly. She took a breath, tried to find a way to go that they hadn't been before. Tried to see the good in him rather than just look at the bad.

"Look, I know you're trying," she said. "I think you have a good heart and you're turning toward us."

"You think?" he said, a little hurt, like a kid who thought he had done well at making a bed that turned out lumpy.

Before she could respond, he put up his hands in defense. "You're right. You're always right."

"I'm not trying to be right here."

"But you are. And I see that. This is why I'm suggesting we go to the pastor or whoever. I want to work this out. I'll do whatever it takes to prove you can trust me. We just need a referee. Somebody who can help us hear each other and not fight the same battles over and over."

She nodded and her heart calmed. She liked those words. They were strong and comforting. And they matched the same way she felt.

"So who was the woman in Raleigh?" she said. Her mouth felt dry from the emotion that throttled her. Part of her didn't want to know. Part of her wanted to just move on and forget the past and tell herself it had no bearing on the present or future. But the other part, the bigger part, wanted to know everything. Had to know everything. She braced herself for the truth.

"She works for Holcomb," he said. "She was handling the contract we had signed."

Was that all? Elizabeth thought, but she didn't say it. She didn't say anything. She just looked at him, waiting for the truth.

"We were going through the contract together and she had a meeting scheduled, so I suggested we go to dinner."

"Is that something you'd done before?"

"Every contract is different—"

"No, I mean, with women you worked with. Have you gone to dinner with other women?"

He thought for a moment, and that unnerved her. He looked like a little boy who had stuck his hand in the cookie jar just as his mother walked into the room.

"I don't recall going alone. I mean, there were times when a group would get together at a conference. This was the first time I'd actually . . ."

"You'd actually what?"

Tony took a breath and threw his shoulders back. "It was the first time I'd actually felt like I wanted to pursue someone else. I don't do one-night stands, Liz. I'm not that dumb. But I think I'd finally given up on you and me. And this woman was attractive and I thought I would test the waters."

Elizabeth hadn't been prepared for the pain those words would bring. He was talking about the night she'd prayed so hard. The night she'd really believed that God was working.

"Go on," she said. "What happened that night?"

"We were at a restaurant having our meal. I thought it would kind of break the ice between us. But there was no ice to break, really. She was ready. After dinner she suggested we go back to her place and open a bottle of wine."

Elizabeth's jaw dropped. "And what did you say?"

"I said I was fine with that. I mean, it surprised me because she didn't seem like the type who would just jump at somebody."

"I guess you were wrong," Elizabeth whispered. Her heart was heavy now and the forgiveness she had offered seemed more conditional with each word that slipped from his mouth. This was going to be a lot harder than she thought. "What's her name?"

"Veronica."

Elizabeth rolled her eyes. *Veronica? You were going to fall for a Veronica?*

"What does she look like?" she said.

"She's a little younger than us. Pretty."

"You mean younger than me, right?"

"Elizabeth, don't get defensive."

"Don't tell me how to get. I can react to this, okay?"

"I agree—you can react, but I want you to know nothing happened."

"What do you mean nothing happened? You were at a restaurant alone together. You talked and laughed and maybe played footsie under the table. Then you went back to her apartment for wine."

"I didn't go back with her. I got sick. Right after the meal—it was the craziest thing. I can't explain it. We finished the meal, she was ready to go, and I got this feeling in my stomach. I barely made it to the bathroom before I tossed my cookies."

That made her feel better. The image of Tony in the bathroom heaving his expensive dinner made her wonder if it was food poisoning or something God had done. Did food poisoning work that fast? Jesus had turned water into wine and calmed a storm, so He could certainly turn a stomach. That almost brought a smile to her face.

"I stayed in the bathroom for a while—and when I came out, I told Veronica I couldn't go with her."

"But you wanted to."

"Liz, don't hold this against me."

"I'm trying to understand what you're telling me. I'm sorry if this gets a little messy, okay?" She was raising her voice. She put up her hands and waved them down, like she was bringing a plane in for a landing. "What did she say?"

"She wanted me to come to her place anyway. She said she could take care of me."

The bile rose and Elizabeth wanted to scratch the woman's eyes out. Another woman trying to take care of her husband. But she couldn't have said that if Tony hadn't initiated the dinner.

"She knew you were married?"

"I didn't bring it up, but I didn't take my ring off. And I mentioned we were having problems."

"That was convenient. Alone on the road, your marriage in trouble, a lonely man, and a woman named Veronica." She said the name like it was a curse word.

"Liz, I feel terrible. I haven't wanted to tell you. I want it to just go away."

"But you know Missy saw you. And she told me."

He nodded. "Right. But I would like to think I would tell you this at some point whether you had found out or not."

"I'd like to think that too," she said. "But we can't know that, can we? We'll never know if you would have told me because we don't live in a world of alternate choices. You can't step in a time machine and come home."

"No. All I can do is tell you the truth and pray that you'll forgive me and give me a chance to let you trust me."

He could have yelled at her and told her she was being obtuse or overbearing or unforgiving. That had happened before. Seeing him here on his knees showed there really was progress, but there was no getting around the hurt she felt. She kept picturing him with *Veronica* at the restaurant. Veronica who wanted to nurse him back to health. Veronica who had a bottle of wine chilled and waiting.

"How could you go out with somebody else while we're still married?" she said.

He shook his head. "I don't know how I could go for anyone but you. I guess I thought we were over. I thought our marriage was hopeless because every time we were with each other, we fought."

"You promise nothing happened?" she said.

"Baby, nothing happened but me losing everything I ate that night and then some. I was miserable. I can't even look at fettuccine on a menu and not feel queasy."

You poor thing, she thought. "Has she called you? Did you get in touch with her the next day?"

"I was going to text her and apologize, then I deleted it." He pulled out his phone. "Wait. It's still in my drafts." He held the phone out to her and she read the message. "I never sent it. And I never called her back."

"Why not?"

"I think it's because I knew it was wrong. I knew it wasn't good for me or her to go down that road."

"What if she calls? She's going to call, you know. *Veronicas* always call again once they've been stood up."

"I won't answer. That's not an option anymore. And I don't need to be in any more meetings with her because I don't work with Holcomb."

The last words seemed to bring a curtain down on his face. Then he looked up with some new thought. "Listen, if you want access to my phone, if you want to check to see if I'm telling the truth, you can look at it anytime you

want. E-mails. Facebook. Whatever. I'm an open book
from here on out."

She nodded and looked at the book balanced precari-
ously on the chair's arm. This was a good way to build
trust. How long it would take, she didn't know. She wished
she could turn the pages to that chapter, after all this was
done and over, but life wasn't like that. You couldn't skip
ahead. You had to live it.

"I'm pretty tired," she said. "I think I need to go to bed."

He put out a hand and helped her up. "Thank you for
listening. For hearing me out. I appreciate it."

She nodded and tried to smile.

"I'll let you know what the pastor says. I'll call tomorrow—or maybe send an e-mail tonight, okay?"

"Okay."

Later, Elizabeth lay in bed trying to push down the image
of Tony in the restaurant. She pictured Veronica as some
voluptuous vixen with a low-cut dress and come-hither
eyes, batting at him. Probably thin and leggy. How could
she compete with that? But he had said he wasn't interested
in Veronica. Elizabeth didn't have to compete. He was
interested in her again. He was doing the hard work of
rebuilding and wanted to meet her in the middle, but here
in the middle was the struggle. Like two parties negotiating
the sale of a house and finding problems with the roof or
an air conditioner that leaked, she was having a hard time
negotiating with her own heart.

It all came down to trust. In the end she had the choice to trust or not trust Tony. It was a decision totally in her power. And ultimately that trust was a reflection of what she believed about God. This was something Clara had told her early on.

"This problem with Tony is more about you than it is about him," Clara had said.

"I don't know what you mean."

"I mean that God is taking you somewhere you may not want to go."

"Why wouldn't I want to go?"

"Because it's hard. And messy. You will find out things about yourself that you don't want to discover. You will find out things about your own heart that you don't want to change. You see, everybody wants to make the problems in their life the fault of somebody else. We need a scapegoat. It's easier that way because you get rid of the goat, you get rid of the problems. Or you turn the goat into a handsome prince and your life is different. Nobody wants to look at the goat in the mirror."

"So you're saying my problem is not Tony? It's me?"

"I'm saying God is using Tony to help you dig deeper. If you let God take you to this place and you are fully there with Him and willing to change whatever He wants you to change, there's going to be new life."

"I'm confused," Elizabeth said.

"I don't doubt it," Clara said. "You can influence Tony. You can pray for him and ask God to work in his heart.

You can love him with the kind of love only God can give you. But you can't make decisions for him. You can't change him. You can only allow God to change you. You can change the way you think about him and yourself and God. You can believe the truth about the power of God and join Him in what He wants to do.

"Really, what I'm talking about here is the difference between you working hard to change things and revival. I hear people talking a lot about revival and what they want God to do to change society and the culture and how much sin there is in Hollywood and everywhere else. I pray for revival. But I've lived long enough to know that it doesn't start with anybody but me. Right here." Clara pointed a bony finger toward her own heart.

"If you find yourself getting anxious, nervous, questioning whether Tony can change, you're not really questioning him, you're questioning whether God has the power to do what He said He could do."

Elizabeth rose from the bed quietly, Clara's voice ringing in her memory. Tony's breathing was heavy. He could always fall asleep so fast and she envied that. She went to her closet, closed the door, turned on the little light, and stared at her handwriting on the walls.

"Oh, God, I want to trust You," she prayed. "I want to believe in You and Your power and not try to make all this happen myself. Would You give me the faith to really believe? Would You give me a love for Tony I don't have?"

And then it hit her. The doubt she had about Tony,

the questions about Veronica were important. She had
to deal with those. But what scared her the most was the
doubt she had about *herself.* She wasn't sure she could
accept Tony and forgive him. She wasn't sure she could
fully love him—because that meant she was exposed, her
heart unprotected. She wanted to hold back some little
part of herself, but love meant becoming fully open, fully
vulnerable to someone else.

There was a quote she had seen, something that Clara
had written down . . . No, it was in one of her Bible study
books. She was sure of it now, and she knew which shelf
the book was on. Tony was asleep and she didn't want to
wake him, but she didn't want to wait to read the quote.

She turned out the light and crept into the bedroom,
letting her eyes adjust to the dim light. She got down on
all fours and crawled to the bookshelf, pulled four of the
studies out, and retreated to the closet. Finally she found
the quote she was searching for, from C. S. Lewis's book
The Four Loves.

To love at all is to be vulnerable. Love anything,
and your heart will certainly be wrung and possibly
be broken. If you want to make sure of keeping it
intact, you must give your heart to no one, not even
to an animal. Wrap it carefully round with hobbies
and little luxuries; avoid all entanglements; lock it up
safe in the casket or coffin of your selfishness. But in
that casket—safe, dark, motionless, airless—it will

change. It will not be broken; it will become
unbreakable, impenetrable, irredeemable.

That sent Elizabeth to 1 Corinthians 13. She went
through the chapter picking out the words that stood out
to her and asking God to make her patient and kind. She
didn't want to keep a record of wrongs, but it was so hard.
Patience was sitting vulnerably in God's waiting room.
Kindness was how you lived out to others the way God
loved you. She read through the whole passage praying
individual verses, and the words came alive. She intuitively
knew that this kind of love was not something she could do
on her own. It came only with strength God provided, so
she prayed God would empower her with that kind of love
and understanding for Tony.

She was in her closet until it was almost light, talking
with God and praying. Crying. It was one thing to pray
and have God answer that prayer by making her husband
sick to his stomach. That was miraculous. It was one thing
to pray God would break her husband's pride and bring
him back to his family. That, too, was a miracle. But it was
a huge leap to believe God had the power to restore and
rekindle her own heart. It was an even bigger leap over the
canyon of her despair to believe God could take away her
pain about being rejected.

CHAPTER 15

✦ ✦ ✦

Elizabeth couldn't figure out how Miss Clara's son had convinced her to move before there was even an offer on the house. But she jumped at the chance to help, once the decision was made, and enlisted Danielle and Tony for the project. It was the first time Clara had met Tony and she smiled and gave him a big hug when he arrived, patting him on the shoulder.

"That man has enough muscles to move this whole house," she said to Elizabeth when he went inside. "I wish my son could be here to help, but he's out of town."

"I'm looking forward to meeting Clyde. I've heard so much about him."

"How are you and Tony doing?"

Elizabeth smiled. "We're moving toward each other. But there are still a lot of boxes to unpack."

"And that pastor at the church, he's helping you?"

"It was the best idea Tony ever had. We've only seen him once, but he's good. He's gotten to the core of some of our issues."

"And it was Tony's idea—that's the important thing," the woman said. "You don't know how rare that is."

Elizabeth followed Clara around the house, writing labels for each of the boxes. Her items were divided into three sections. The first was the smallest, furniture and boxes that would go in the new apartment at her son's house. The other slightly larger section was for storage. And the final, bigger lot that filled the living room was made up of things Clara wanted to give away. Elizabeth had suggested having a garage sale, but Clara wouldn't hear of it.

"God has not blessed me with all these things in order to sell them for pennies on the dollar. I've prayed for my things to get into the right hands and I believe He's going to make that happen."

The giveaway stuff was handed out to neighbors and people from church. Some items had sticky notes with names on them, set aside for specific people in Clara's life. Wall art, a coffee table, and bookshelves to a young couple just starting out. Many of her books were donated to the church library. By the time the moving truck arrived,

Elizabeth couldn't believe how organized and pared down things had become.

She loved seeing Tony and Danielle involved in the project. They took it on with equal gusto, though Tony did have everyone stop for a few minutes to show Danielle's moves with the jump rope.

"That girl has real talent," Clara said.

Elizabeth walked over to her as she wrote a few more box labels. "I'm going to miss coming over here to see you."

"Well, you can come see me at my son's house. He's just four blocks away."

Tony had opened a window to get some furniture through and Clara watched him.

"And Tony's going to be all right. You just keep praying for him."

"Every day," Elizabeth said.

"Now, when is my house going to sell? I don't want just anybody to buy it. It's got to be the right people."

"I'm praying for the right people, Miss Clara. Every day."

Tony walked out of the moving truck and headed back into the house. He pulled out his cell phone like he'd gotten a call or a text. He stared at it a moment, then punched the screen. Elizabeth wondered which call he'd rejected.

They drove to Clara's new home and helped unload things into the apartment prepared for her. Tony and Michael, his paramedic friend, moved the couch three times until they got it just right.

"Now don't go putting anything in the closet in my room," Clara said.

Clara's daughter-in-law took her aside. "Mama, Clyde made you a nice sitting area over by the window where you can look out at the neighborhood and pray."

"I love that," Clara said. "And I'll watch the sun come up and read my Bible there, but I need my closet for the heavy praying I do every day."

Her daughter-in-law smiled. "I told Clyde it's enough that we finally got you here."

A teenage girl walked out of the house, her head down as if she didn't want to meet any of the company helping her grandmother.

Clara saw her and called her over. "Hallie, I want you to meet a friend of mine. She's helping me sell my house."

Elizabeth greeted the girl and shook her hand. She looked a little too thin and her face was pale.

"Nice to meet you," Hallie said, not looking up.

"It's going to be nice having your grandmother even closer than before, isn't it?" Elizabeth said.

"I guess so."

With that, the girl left, and Clara put a hand on Elizabeth's shoulder and lowered her voice. "If you wouldn't mind, I'd like you to add Hallie's name to your prayer list. The Lord has some work to do in that young lady's life. And I want to be here when He does it."

Elizabeth promised she would pray for her and entered a note on her cell phone. She made a mental note to ask

Tony who had called his phone, then decided she would let it go. That was part of building trust, she thought.

✦ ✦ ✦

Tony's mind was always whirring with ideas about a small business he could start or companies where he might work. Networking was the key to any job search, and he had asked some of the men from church about employment possibilities. No one knew of anything currently, but they all said they would keep Tony in mind.

Michael suggested he become a professional brooder. "You know, that statue of the guy who sits and thinks all the time? You look a lot like him."

"I haven't found anybody who would pay me to do that," Tony said.

Tony knew Michael cared and he wanted to open up about what had happened, but it was painful. If he could keep it inside and get a new job, everything would be all right. He could put the past where it belonged and move ahead.

With the workout he got moving Clara's things, he figured he could start an exercise club in a truck. People would pay him to tone their abs by moving furniture. The families who were moving would pay him for the service and everybody would win. He'd call it "Ab-Haul" or something like that. The thought made him smile, but he had to come up with more than a good idea.

There was someplace he would fit, where he could use

his sales abilities, his people skills, and his love for athletics and training. When he got to the gym, when he played ball or ran, he felt alive. If he could wed his passion on the court and in the weight room with life, he could make a difference. He'd always seen his best skill as managing people—getting people on the same team and moving in the right direction.

Too bad you didn't try that with your own family.

That was the voice in his head, the accusing, deriding voice that chopped him down at every turn. As he was moving Clara's things, he'd received a call from Veronica. It stopped him in his tracks, but he quickly rejected the call. He'd made that decision—if she called, he wouldn't answer. Then he took the next step and deleted her contact information. He wanted to show Elizabeth what he had done, then decided against it. He didn't want to be the puppy that needed a pat on the head every time he didn't pee on the rug. This was part of the new Tony, the strong, decisive man God was rebuilding, but he had to admit the accusing voice sometimes got to him.

Jennifer and Danielle were jumping rope in the driveway and he watched them, wanting to enter into the fray. But the accusing voice said, *You were never there for her when she started jumping rope. Why would you want to start now? You've ignored her. She's not going to forgive you and let you back in. Stop trying.*

Tony sat on the step, amazed at how well the girls

jumped. Danielle looked over. "Dad, why don't you try? We'll get both ropes going."

His first reaction was to reject the idea. Jumping rope was for girls. But for some reason he stood and said, "Sure."

When he reached for the rope to turn it for one of them, Danielle said, "No, I mean, you go in the middle. See if you can do it."

"See if I can do it?" Tony said. "There's no *seeing* about it. When I jump in there, your arms will fall off before I miss."

"Let's see you, Mr. Jordan," Jennifer said with a smile.

"Yeah!" Danielle yelled, and they started turning the ropes.

He tried jumping in three times before he actually made it without stopping the ropes, and that time he only jumped twice. Danielle laughed and said her arms weren't falling off yet. Tony was determined. In his life, whatever he decided to do, he did it. And he was successful at what he put his mind to. Pretty soon, he was running in place, the ropes swirling around him, whistling in the wind. He made a turn and the girls giggled. As he got into rhythm, Danielle's eyes widened and her mouth got stuck in a grin she couldn't stop. She shook her head at Jennifer as if this were the proudest moment of her life.

Tony was fully there in the middle of those two ropes. Instead of feeling on the outside of his daughter's life, he was smack inside it, and with each jump he thanked God for the chance to change, the chance to be part of his family, the chance to love and be loved and make mistakes.

"Daddy, why don't you jump with us?" Danielle said when he missed again. He realized she meant for him to be on the team, in competition.

"Yeah, that would be awesome!" Jennifer said.

"No, no, no. They don't let parents do that."

"Yeah, they do," Jennifer said. "But no parents do 'cause they can't keep up."

"Dad, it's an open league. You can jump in the freestyle competition. They'll let you!"

Tony stared at her, a sweat breaking out. "Tell you what. Let me think about it."

Jennifer and Danielle both jumped for joy and he tried to calm them. "Now if I'm going to do it, I want to do it right. So let's try it again. Get it going!"

The pattern began again, the ropes cutting through the wind and whipping around Tony, his feet moving quickly, his muscles engaged, and the sweat rolling.

You'll make a fool of yourself, the voice said. *Don't even think about joining that team.*

Tony smiled and jumped and kept on jumping until Danielle complained that her arms felt like they were going to fall off.

✦ ✦ ✦

Elizabeth awakened to find Tony gone from their bed. She put on her robe and walked through the living room, searching for any trace of him, calling out in the empty house. Danielle was still asleep up in her room.

He wasn't in the kitchen and the front door was still locked, so he hadn't gone for a run. She finally checked the garage and found him there. It was weird not seeing his Tahoe in the garage. He sat in a lawn chair in front of a folding table, staring at a storage box on top like it held some hidden treasure—or maybe a nuclear device that would destroy the planet, she couldn't tell which.

"Tony, what are you doing?" she said.

"I'm struggling."

She came down the steps and closed the door behind her. "With what?"

Tony lifted the cover of the box, revealing drug samples with the Brightwell logo on them. He kept staring straight ahead, unable to look up at her.

"What is this?" she said.

"It was my bonus plan."

She studied one of the bottles, the questions forming. "Where did you get these?"

"I've been keeping some for myself each time I take samples to a client."

"I thought they had to sign for what you gave them."

"There's ways around that."

"Tony, you've got to take these back." She said it with conviction and with the knowledge that she was right.

"Liz, I could be prosecuted for this."

The weight of his words fell on her.

Tony stood and walked around the garage like a caged

lion. "Look, I've already lost my job. So now I'm supposed to go and tell Danielle her daddy might be going to jail?"

Ask him a question, she thought. *Draw him out. Find out what's going on underneath the bravado.*

"Then why are you struggling?" she said, letting the question hang there between them.

He stared at the box, then at the garage floor, anywhere but at her face. She'd rarely seen this look. Tony was always the take-charge, move-ahead, swing-for-the-fences kind of guy. Now he seemed caught in a rundown between bases, and the one running after him was God.

"Because I know God is telling me to take them back," Tony said, slumping down into the lawn chair again.

"Sounds like you know what you want to do, then."

"Not what I want to do. What I need to do. What I have to do."

Elizabeth pulled out a chair and sat beside him, studying the boxes of medication. "What kind of a drug is it?"

"Predizim. It's a stimulant. It's not oxycodone or anything like that. It'll keep you awake. Kind of like several of those energy drinks in one little pill."

"Did you sell them?"

He looked down. "About a year ago I got this idea after a box got stuck at the bottom of my sample case. Right after I signed the Bradley deal."

"You were so excited about that."

"Yeah, until they gave me a lowball bonus. The company is making billions and they reward the guys out there selling with peanuts. That's what went through my mind—I'm not saying it was right."

"I understand," she said.

"So I saw this as a way to make a few extra bucks on the side. To make up for the bonuses."

"How did you do it?"

Tony explained how he'd rearranged the cartons that held eight boxes and kept two for himself. "I put them in their supply closets and had the doctor sign for it. Doctors never took the time to check the numbers. That's what I thought."

"But who did you sell the extra bottles to?"

Tony's face fell. "I found a pharmacist who bought them under the table. He gave me a couple of other names in a couple other cities. But the biggest market for this is a college campus. Kids cramming for a test, writing papers in the middle of the night, they thrive on this."

"You sold these to college kids?"

"It's not like I stood on the street corner and peddled them. I'd find one or two people on campus and supply them. I'm not proud of this. It makes me sick now."

"I know," she said. "And I'm glad you're telling me. I think it's a good step."

"I couldn't say this to the pastor. Or anybody."

"No wonder you're out here. The weight of this must be . . ."

He nodded. "And the weight of telling it feels just as bad. I thought when I gave my life to God, things would get easier. I thought I'd hit bottom. But if they prosecute me, I could go to prison."

Tony was right—there was a lot to lose by going back, but something inside Elizabeth rose up. Doing the right thing was always the best route to take, even if it hurt. She wanted to say something, tell him what he had to do, and then she thought of Clara and the mistakes she said she'd made in trying to change her husband.

Elizabeth stood and looked at him with concern and love, putting a hand on his arm. "Tony, you don't have to do this alone. I'm here. I can get Clara praying. And when that woman prays, things happen."

"I've been praying about it all night," Tony said.

She took his hand. "Lord Jesus, You know the struggle that Tony has. You know the indecision, the shame, the pain of his choices. I pray You would remind him right now of whose child he is. And that when You look at him, You see the perfection of Your Son, Jesus. Thank You that You have conquered sin. Thank You that the evil one is not in control. Give Tony the courage to do what You're asking him to do, in Your timing."

Before Elizabeth could say, "Amen," Tony's voice echoed through the garage.

"Jesus, help me," he prayed. "Please, Lord. Help me do the right thing."

Miss Clara

✦ ✦ ✦

A short time after Tony's turnaround, Elizabeth called with an urgent request. "I can't go into detail, Clara, but Tony confessed something. And we both believe he needs to do something really difficult."

"That's good. That means God is working in his heart and changing him from the inside out. This is not just about getting his family back. He really wants to obey God. This is wonderful!"

"It doesn't feel so wonderful because . . . there could be repercussions."

"You hang in there and give the repercussions to the Lord," Clara said.

After she got off the phone, Clara recalled something she'd told Elizabeth in one of their earliest meetings. "Once the power of God is unleashed in a life, things don't stay the same. And that's what prayer does, it unleashes the power of God. You see, prayer is not about getting things right. You don't get your prayers answered because you kneel in just the right spot or say just the right words."

"But you have your war room," Elizabeth had said.

Clara nodded. "That's where I feel closest to God. But I can pray by the birdbath just as well."

Elizabeth's next question that day had been a meaty one: *Why pray at all?*

"If God knows everything and if He's working out His will in the world, what's the point?"

"Mm-hmm," Clara said. "The answer to that question is simple, but not easy. We pray because God tells us to. He commands us to. So we obey. And John says whenever we ask anything according to God's will, He hears us. So why would God ask us to do something that makes no difference? That's really your question."

"Right. But you do believe it makes a difference."

"I do or I wouldn't waste my time or the cartilage in my knees."

Elizabeth laughed.

"Prayer brings us closer to the heart of God. It opens your heart to those around you and makes you long for what He longs for. And it's clear from the first page to the last that God does respond to the requests of His people. I don't pretend to understand it, but it's true."

With those words in her mind, Clara danced to her war room, telling Satan he was losing big-time because God was on the move. She prayed for courage for Tony and peace for Elizabeth's heart. She prayed that the victories would begin to come in a hurry.

CHAPTER 16

✦ ✦ ✦

Tony rode the elevator to the forty-seventh floor of the Bright-well building in Charlotte. The security guard at the front desk had called upstairs and someone in the office had given him clearance. It was weird not having an access key, but that was the price of his indiscretion.

His stomach was in a knot when the door opened. Almost as big a knot as after his dinner with Veronica, but this time he didn't feel sick. This was a good tension, if there was such a thing. Humiliation mixed with determination.

He walked into the offices and several people glanced at him, then turned away. He stopped at Julia's desk outside Coleman Young's office. She did a double take when she saw him and reached for the phone.

"It's okay," Tony said. "I'm not here to cause trouble. I'd just like to speak with Coleman. Five minutes is all I need and then I'll be going."

Something about his demeanor, or maybe it was something he said with his eyes, convinced Julia he was sincere and didn't pose a threat. She looked down the hall and held up a finger for him to wait.

Julia walked toward the conference room. Tony strained to hear the conversation but only heard Coleman say, "Do you know what he wants?"

Tony sat in the waiting area, cradling the box of samples on his lap like a child waiting to see the principal. He held the incriminating evidence—or did the evidence hold him?

Just dump the box down the trash chute and be done with this, the voice in his head said. *You don't have to do this.*

Julia's high heels clicked on the tile floor. "Tony, Coleman's waiting for you in the conference room."

He thanked her, then took the long walk down the hallway. It felt like walking to an execution, even more so when he saw Coleman and Tom in the conference room. Coleman's face was stern. Tom looked at him like he was week-old roadkill.

Tony set the box down. Coleman was on one side of the table and Tom on the other, a wide gulf between them.

"Coleman, Tom," Tony said, his voice shaky. "Look, I appreciate you guys meeting with me. I just need to bring something back that belongs to the company. And apologize for taking it."

"What's in the box?" Tom said, breaking the awkward silence.

Tony lifted the top, revealing the stolen Predizim. Tom walked over and picked up a bottle. When he spoke, it was with the same accusing voice Tony had heard in his head.

"So you weren't just padding your numbers. You were stealing samples. And then selling them, is that right?"

Tony nodded.

"Let me get this straight," Tom continued. "We give you a high salary with awards and benefits and trips. And you decide to thank us by taking even more for yourself? Do you realize we could have you prosecuted for this?"

"Tom," Coleman said, interrupting. His voice calmed the room somewhat and Tom turned away.

Coleman stared at the box as if trying to make sense of what he was seeing. He moved closer to Tony and sat on the edge of the table. "Why would you bring this in now?"

Tony swallowed hard. "Because I've needed to confess what I've done. And ask for your forgiveness."

"Forgiveness, oh, that's rich," Tom said, laughing. "How long have you been doing this? How much money did you make?"

"About nineteen thousand."

"Nineteen thousand," Tom said, obviously not believing him. "Is that all? Really?"

"Tom," Coleman said, calling off the dogs again. He looked at Tony with a measure of pity and disbelief. "Tony, it doesn't make sense to do this after you've already been terminated."

"I realize that. But, Coleman, I needed a wake-up call. I had the job, I had the income, but I was losing everything else. I've gotten right with my family, and I've gotten right with God. But I need to get right with you. So I'm ready to accept whatever decision you make."

"Including arrest?" Coleman said slowly.

"Whatever the consequence."

"Well, that makes it easier for us," Tom said quickly. "Coleman, it's time to call the authorities."

"Not yet," Coleman said. He studied Tony's face and paused. "Tony, are you willing to sign a statement?"

He nodded. "I am."

"Then I want two days to think about it."

"Two days?" Tom said, incredulous.

"Yes," Coleman said, his eyes still trained on Tony. "You'll hear from me by then."

Tony glanced at Tom. Steam wasn't boiling from his bow tie, but it probably wouldn't be long.

"Thank you," Tony said and slowly walked out of the Brightwell office. He wondered if the next time he saw Coleman or Tom would be in a courtroom.

✦ ✦ ✦

Elizabeth prayed for Tony as she turned the jump rope for Danielle and Jennifer. So much of their marriage the past few years had been separate. He had gone his way, she had gone hers. She had convinced herself that he couldn't change, that he was stuck in all the patterns of life. She, of course, hadn't seen the ways she had been stuck. You never see your own face until you look into something reflecting it, but it sure is easy to see the flaws in everyone else.

Elizabeth had wondered through the years if she'd married the wrong man. Why hadn't she seen Tony's ways of handling problems when she was younger? Why had she pushed down the warning signs and told herself she could change him?

The truth was, God had done in a few weeks what she had tried to do for sixteen years. And God had done the same thing in her.

"When's Daddy getting back?" Danielle said when they took a breather.

"Should be any minute," Elizabeth said.

"Good. I want him to do the ropes so we both can jump."

There wasn't any hesitation in her. Danielle had seen the new Tony and accepted him and believed he would jump into her life. She didn't hold back trusting him. Elizabeth wanted that same kind of trust—not to act on what had happened in the past and the old wounds that still hurt, but to believe the best and treat him as though he had always treated her kindly.

"Danielle, when he gets back, we're likely going to need to talk. He had an important meeting today."

"But he's going to jump on our team," she said.

"He is?" Elizabeth said.

"He told us he can teach us a couple of moves we can use in the competition, too," Jennifer said.

Elizabeth smiled at that. Tony was a good coach, a good motivator, a good salesman. He'd sold his daughter and her friend on the idea that they could win a competition that, by all accounts, was going to be quite competitive.

"Is he getting a new job?" Danielle said.

"He needs to find a new one, but this meeting isn't about a job."

Jennifer picked up the rope and Danielle got in the middle. Elizabeth and Jennifer swung as Danielle went through her part of the routine. They had endless energy and endless grace to give, it seemed. Maybe it was that childlike way of looking at life that Elizabeth needed. If she could forgive her husband and move on like Danielle had, her relationship with Tony would be a lot better.

She had prayed for him and watched God work on his heart, but there were still areas—words he said, ways he looked at her—that brought up the old wounds. In those moments she had to consciously tell herself the truth and act not on what she saw and the feelings stirred, but what she knew was happening inside of him, the change that was taking place. After all, she reacted in some old ways too. None of this was easy or quick. God hadn't waved a magic wand over their marriage and made them all lovey-dovey. In fact, they hadn't been intimate in weeks, maybe months, and part of that was the news Tony had shared about

Veronica. Though he hadn't actually had an affair, Elizabeth felt little trust with him. But she could feel a thawing in their frozen relationship and the temperature rising between them. The pastor at their church had encouraged them to take things slow and go on dates together and let their relationship rekindle. That made a lot of sense to them both.

Tony pulled up in her car and the garage opened. As he parked, Elizabeth stopped swinging the rope. "Hey, girls, why don't you go inside and grab something cold to drink, okay? We can start back in a little bit."

He got out and slowly walked toward them, hugging Danielle and giving Jennifer a fist bump. Elizabeth studied his face, trying to discern what might have happened. Tony was always so hard to read. At least he hadn't been taken away in handcuffs.

"Well?" she said.

He shook his head. "I don't know. I mean, Tom just wanted to throw me in jail. But Coleman says he wants two days to think about it."

"Really?" She said it with equal measures of incredulity and cynicism. She knew Coleman was all about the bottom line. You make a sale and he rewards you. You falter and you pay the price. Tom hadn't liked Tony from the beginning—at least that's how Tony had seen it. But Coleman had always seemed neutral. Pleasant to her and Danielle, but all business. "Did he seem angry?"

"I couldn't tell." Tony shook his head and looked at the

trees surrounding their house. Green and leafy and full of life. "Liz, this was the most awkward thing I've ever done."

"Yeah, but you did it. Listen, you did the right thing." She moved toward him. "Now we just have to pray and wait."

Pray and wait. That's what she had done in the past few weeks. And in the waiting came the strengthening of the muscles of faith. It was a whole-faith workout to wait and allow God to do what He wanted to do. As Clara said, it was time to just get out of His way.

"Why don't you change and come practice with your daughter?"

"Liz, why should I practice for a competition when I might be in jail?"

"You don't know that. Whatever happens, we trust God, right?"

She was saying it to herself as much as she was saying it to him. It sounded a little cliché, a little trite, but she didn't care how it sounded. She cared about Tony.

Tony thought about it a moment, the wheels spinning inside. "Right," he said with determination. He turned to go inside, then shook his head. With a bit of a laugh he said, "This is crazy. You know that, right?"

Elizabeth smiled as they walked inside. While Tony changed, she dialed Clara and let her know what had happened with Tony's meeting. The woman was hungry for information about the progress the two were making and how Tony was changing, but it never felt to Elizabeth like her prayers hung on results. Clara was on her knees for them no matter what good or bad thing happened.

"I want you to hear me," Clara said as Tony and the girls went outside to practice. "God is working here. He's done a big thing in your husband's heart. And it doesn't matter what that company decides. I don't care if they hire him back as vice president or they bring a SWAT team to your front yard. The circumstance doesn't matter. It's your reaction to it that matters."

"Well, I'm hoping the SWAT team is not an option."

Clara laughed. "It reminds me of Joseph. You know the story of the boy getting sold into slavery by his own brothers. That's betrayal. And then he's falsely accused and tossed into prison. And all the while God is working in his life. Old Joseph, he's just being himself. He's just interpreting dreams like God allowed him to. And when the story is all told, you see how God's hand was over all of it, good and bad. He uses it all, Elizabeth."

She looked out the window at Danielle and Jennifer turning the ropes and Tony jumping in, hopping on one foot, then the other. The smile on Danielle's face was priceless. There was a glow about her as she watched her dad.

As Elizabeth watched, it became clear that the motion of the ropes, all the jumping and struggling to stay in rhythm and not stop the movement, was just like their lives. The marriage rope swung and she and Tony were trying hard to keep both feet above it as it crossed below them. The finance rope also swung over them, and the spiritual rope—there were just so many ways to trip and get tangled. She wanted God to hold them both up, suspend them in midair so they never touched the ground—but He wouldn't. There was something about the jumping that made them stronger—and something about the missing that made keeping their feet moving in time more sweet. Clara was right. God used it all. He used the hard times to draw her closer. He used the struggle to bring them together.

That evening they sat in Elizabeth's closet, her war room, and prayed for the situation with Coleman and Tom. She asked God to work things out so that Tony wouldn't have to be prosecuted. She prayed for a new job for Tony and provision for their family. "Help us trust You no matter what," she prayed.

Tony hesitated before he began. Praying together wasn't something he was comfortable with—and in the beginning he'd just let Elizabeth pray and he held her hand and squeezed it at times. She gave him this, not requiring that he be at the same place she was. But soon he was praying aloud with her, and his voice and his heart came shining through. Elizabeth couldn't believe the sense of unity she felt when she heard him speaking with God.

"God, I want a new job and I don't want to go to jail," Tony prayed. "But I know there are consequences to my actions. I know what I did hurt people. I've hurt my family. I hurt my employer. And I thank You for forgiving me and grabbing hold of my heart and not letting me go any further toward things that would have destroyed me.

"Right now I pray for Tom. He hates me. I could see it in his face. And I can understand why. So, Lord, give me some opportunity to be kind to him. Some chance to show Your love to him. I don't have any idea how You could do that, but I believe You can make it happen. And I pray for Coleman, Lord. He has a lot of pressure on him to succeed. A lot of pressure from the shareholders and all those people who are working under him. I pray You would bless him. I pray You'd bless the company and use it to help people. Give the research team wisdom as they're working on new medicine. Most of all I pray You would draw Coleman and Tom to Yourself. Would You use even this situation with them to help them see their need of You? Their need to be forgiven?"

They were in the closet for nearly an hour. When they finished praying, Tony held a hand out and helped Elizabeth up, and she drew close to him. She looked in his eyes and he put his hands on her shoulders. For a moment she thought he would kiss her.

Instead, Tony bit his lip and looked at a verse on the wall. "As we were praying, I got the impression that the Lord wants us to talk to Danielle. I don't think it's fair to lay a big burden on her, but I don't think it's fair to keep her in the dark, either."

"I trust you," Elizabeth said. And the words were out of her mouth before she realized she meant them.

✦ ✦ ✦

Tony saw the fear in Danielle's face when, after the dinner dishes had been put away, he asked her to sit at the table with them. "We have something to talk about."

"Don't be scared, honey," Elizabeth said, rubbing the girl's back.

"You're not getting a divorce, are you? Because that's what's happening to Cindy's parents. They sat her and her brother down at the kitchen table just like this."

Tony leaned forward and caught his daughter's eyes. "Your mother and I love each other. We're working on our marriage so we can be the people God wants us to be. So we can be good parents."

"You're not moving out?" Danielle said. "That's what Cindy's parents did first. Her dad moved out—"

"I'm not going anywhere."

As soon as Tony said the words, he looked at Elizabeth and could see the pain in her face as well. He couldn't say that he wasn't going anywhere. That decision was up to Coleman. Well, really, it was up to God.

"Danielle, the reason I got let go from work—the reason they took my car—was that I did something wrong."

"What did you do?"

"I kept some medicine that didn't belong to me. At the time I thought it was fine—I thought nobody would ever notice. And I sold some of it."

"You stole from them."

"That's right."

"Why, Daddy?"

"To make some extra money. I thought I deserved more than they were giving me. They caught me. And it was wrong. I took back the things I had stolen and showed them."

Danielle's face showed the pain he felt inside, but it was a double hit seeing it through her eyes. He had let her down and that look tore at his heart.

"God will forgive you, Daddy."

He reached out and patted her hand. "He already has. That is a good lesson. When we make mistakes, we can ask Him to forgive. And He'll do it. But mistakes also have consequences."

"What do you mean?"

"When I went back and apologized, they let me know that there could be consequences. They're deciding if they want to punish me for what I've done."

"If God can forgive you, why can't they?"

Tony glanced at Elizabeth and she gave him a look like *You're on your own with this one.*

"I hope they will forgive me, but even if they do, I might have to be punished."

"What does that mean? Punished how?"

"They could do a lot of things. Like make me pay them back for what I didn't return. I'm going to do that whether they ask for it or not."

"What else could they do? Take your cell phone away?"

Danielle looked at her mother, then turned back to Tony. When she saw the expression on his face, she said, "Could they make you go to jail?"

"I don't know, baby. I don't think that's going to happen, but I'm going to do everything I can to stay right here, to be your daddy, to jump in that competition with you and the team, and God is going to get us through this together."

"Are you sure?"

"God can do anything," Tony said. "And He loves you so much. He loves all three of us and wants the best for us. So you keep praying and we'll keep praying, and let's see what He does, okay?"

Danielle nodded and looked at the table.

Tony reached for her hand again, and Elizabeth put her hand on Danielle's head as if blessing her.

"Father, you are our Daddy, and I thank You that You love us so much," Tony prayed. "Help us not be afraid of what's ahead. Help us to trust in You no matter what happens . . ."

"And help those people forgive my daddy," Danielle whispered.

"Yes, help them forgive me, Father. And whether they do or not, I thank You for forgiving me. In Jesus' name, amen."

Miss Clara

✦ ✦ ✦

Clara had coffee ready when Elizabeth arrived. She'd originally suggested they meet once a week, but their conversations had become much more frequent. Elizabeth told her all about Brightwell, what Tony had done, how he had felt convicted and confessed, and how they were now waiting for the hammer to fall.

"There's not going to be a hammer falling that God won't allow," Clara said. "You know that, don't you?"

Elizabeth nodded. "Doesn't make it any easier."

"I suppose it doesn't," Clara said. She thought a moment. "You know I was thinking about old Bartimaeus today."

"Who?"

"Bartimaeus, the beggar. He was blind but he'd heard of the miracles Jesus had performed, so when the Lord passed, old Bart yelled out and wouldn't keep quiet, even though they told him to hush. How can you be quiet when the One who made you is walking by? How can you shut up when the Lord is near?

"So Jesus, in His kindness, told them to get old Bart and let him through. I imagine that man walking stiff-legged, his eyes cloudy, his face unshaven, clothes tattered. And I can see the compassion and love on the Lord's face. Jesus asked him a question. Instead of Bartimaeus launching into what he needed, Jesus said, 'What do you want Me to do for you?'

"You see, Elizabeth, prayer is God drawing us close and asking what's on our hearts. Now most people, if you tell them that, will go to their list. 'Lord, give me this and that and the other thing.' But Bartimaeus did something different. He asked the Lord for one thing—he asked to see.

"Right there is a truth you can hang on to. The first thing God wants to do is help you see. See yourself. See your sin. See your helplessness without Him. And then—oh, this gets my blood pumpin'—then He opens your eyes and brings everything into focus.

"I envy Bartimaeus. The first thing he ever saw in his life was God. Can you imagine that? God looking you in the face. But God doesn't leave you there. He helps you act on what you've seen. This is the hard work. This is where God meets your greatest need: vision. He enables you to see how utterly helpless you are in your own strength."

"That's not a popular message these days," Elizabeth said.

"That's a fact. Most people think 'God helps those who help themselves' is in the Bible. Listen, God helps those who have come to the end of themselves. And that's where Tony is. I know it feels terrible, but it's a very good thing."

"Well, I appreciate you praying for us."

"What's the man's name who is making this decision?"

"Coleman Young."

Clara closed her eyes tightly. "Lord Jesus, You know this Coleman Young. Father, open his heart to Tony. Don't let him rest. Don't let this decision go out of his mind. Help him see the truth about Tony wanting to set things right. Even now, Lord, would You help him show grace? And glorify Yourself through this somehow."

Clara felt a stirring inside, a peace that washed over her. "And, Lord, I'm going to ask You for something in Tony and Elizabeth's life—and their daughter's, too—that is going to sound impossible in these circumstances. But I know You can do it. Would You not just keep Tony out of jail, but would you bring him home? Would You help him avoid prosecution and help him pay back the money he owes and, Lord, would You give him something to do that keeps him close to his family and fulfills the desires of his heart? Give him something to do with his life that will be perfectly suited for everyone involved."

After Elizabeth left, Clara went to her war room and stayed for hours. She was still praying for Tony and for Coleman Young when she drifted off to sleep.

CHAPTER 17

✦ ✦ ✦

After her meeting with Clara, Elizabeth spent the day at Twelve Stone Realty trying to focus on her work, but finding it hard. She couldn't shake the fear of Tony in a courtroom, Tony being led away, Tony in shackles and a prison jumpsuit. These weren't reality, she knew—that wasn't the way it would happen, even if Tony were convicted and sent away. But the end result would be the same. Tony would be gone from them, and they would likely lose the house, and she and Danielle would have to pick up the pieces and move on, at least for a time. She beat back the voice in her head, but it was like a rushing stream with a current so strong that it was hard not getting carried away by it.

His choices have put you in this spot. What makes you think he won't do this again down the road? Coleman isn't going to forgive Tony. You and Danielle might as well move back with your mother.

That voice was strong in her head, telling Elizabeth she and Tony would never make it and she should just look for someone new. Clara had said the way to drown the voices was to wash yourself with truth, so Elizabeth turned to the Scriptures she had memorized. She wished she could put an eviction notice on her thought life to get the bad voices out, but it didn't work that way.

She kept praying, kept asking God to soften Coleman's heart to the situation, to help him understand the change in Tony. But just because a person changed didn't mean he could walk away freely. She knew that. Still, he was a good man. He was trying to be a good husband and father and a productive member of society. She just wanted Coleman to see the real Tony, not the one who had made such mistakes.

On her lunch break she dialed Clara and spoke with her for some encouragement. Just hearing her calm voice again sent a wave of peace over Elizabeth. As they spoke, a thought went through her mind—since Clara no longer lived in her house, maybe Elizabeth and Danielle could rent her home while it was in process. She didn't mention the idea, but it seemed like an idea that might have come from God.

This was where Elizabeth's mind went all day, trying to figure out the future, trying to calm herself with ways to make things work out. Life was one plea bargain after another with God if He would just make things happen the way she wanted. She had a constant running battle with herself about what Coleman would decide and whether Tom would influence him or people on the legal team. It was like predicting the outcome of some sporting event, but this wasn't a contest for a trophy or bragging rights, this was the life of their family.

In the afternoon, Mandy pulled Elizabeth into her office with a dispute from another Realtor, a man who had a reputation in town as being hard to work with. He had billboards and ran ads on TV and radio and was known, at least by the general public, as the man who would sell your house the fastest and get you the most money, all while smiling and being your best friend. Every Realtor who had worked with the man knew a different story. Lies and hard-ball tactics and signings that left people in tears. Veteran Realtors, people who had seen every trick in the book for decades, wilted when they heard a property had listed with his agency.

"Don't let this guy eat your lunch," Mandy had said. "He growls and throws his weight around and wants every-thing to go his way. But you have something powerful, and the buyers do too. Your clients have what he wants the most—the money to buy that house. Don't forget that."

Elizabeth nodded and went through the disputes about the sale with Mandy giving good advice. Then Elizabeth sat back. "That's not the only thing eating my lunch."

Mandy's face showed a compassion that moved Elizabeth. She was a consummate businesswoman who rarely let her guard down, but every now and then she surprised Elizabeth. She showed her humanity in small ways and this was one of those times.

"I don't know everything that's going on with you and Tony. You've been guarded about it lately, after talking so much about the money squabbles you had about your sister. I understand that. I respect it. But I can see there's been a change in you."

"Really?"

"Yeah, Lisa and I were talking the other day. You've always done your job well. You're professional, courteous, thorough with all your contracts. But lately it seems like you're living at a different level."

Elizabeth smiled. She'd been praying about an opportunity to talk with Mandy and Lisa about what had happened to her spiritually. Was the situation with Tony that entrée to their hearts?

"One of my clients has really challenged me to get closer to God and start praying for Tony," Elizabeth said. "Rather than make it all about Tony changing and being the man I want him to be, she's encouraged me to allow God to change me."

Mandy scrunched her face in thought and tried to guess the client. After two guesses, Elizabeth revealed it was Clara Williams.

"That sweet old woman has you praying?"

Elizabeth nodded. She told Mandy about the closet—the war room—and how she had finally given up and decided to let God take over. "I had made all of my problems Tony's fault. I thought if I could just get him to live how I wanted, we could get along. But God wanted to do something bigger than change Tony or my situation. He wanted to show me my own heart. And that was a painful process."

"But Tony was mean to you, about your sister, about the money," Mandy said. "Are you going to become one of those women who just grit their teeth and take the abuse?"

Elizabeth smiled. "No, that's the irony of this whole thing. At first, I thought exactly like what you're saying. I thought Clara meant I had to let Tony make all the decisions. He has ten votes and I have one. That kind of thing. But we're supposed to work together. He's supposed to love me like Jesus loved the church. And he wasn't doing that."

"Not even close."

"The counselor we've been seeing has given us permission to call each other out on any kind of ugliness. That's part of what love is. I don't want to nag or be overbearing, and he doesn't want me feeling like he's a steamroller. But the truth is, Tony and I both needed to change. I just saw it first."

Mandy gave her a curious look. "Well, I'm glad for you, Elizabeth. I really am. But I don't understand. If you give a man that kind of power, he is going to run over you." Her phone rang and she glanced down. "I need to take this."

Elizabeth nodded and went back to her desk and the contract she was preparing. The brief talk with Mandy showed her that even in the middle of the questions and doubt and pain, God could use her to maybe plant a seed in someone's heart. That was the craziest thing about all this. She thought she had to get everything neat and tidy in her life in order to be used by God. But here she was at her weakest, her most vulnerable, with all the questions unanswered and in the middle of her struggles. That was the moment when God could break through and show Himself powerful. Even with all the voices swirling in her brain about the future, God could show up. That was reason to give thanks.

Clara liked to use the old hymns at times in her prayers and Elizabeth had found a hymnal at a used-book store. "It Is Well with My Soul" was one of Clara's favorites, and she had told Elizabeth the story of the hymn writer, all the problems and loss the man had been through. The words of the hymn washed over Elizabeth there in the office as she pulled out her journal and looked at her own handwriting. Bits and phrases stuck in her mind, and she identified with the "sorrows like sea-billows."

When she had first come to the verse that began, "Though Satan should buffet," she had read the word *buffet* wrong. She thought it was like a smorgasbord at a cafeteria-style restaurant. But the *buffet* the writer was talking about was the smacks and whacks of the enemy she was feeling—all the ways the devil was having a field day with her marriage, her family, her heart.

Though Satan should buffet, tho' trials should come,
Let this blest assurance control,
That Christ has regarded my helpless estate,
And hath shed His own blood for my soul.

She could see why Clara clung to the words. No matter what happened to her and Tony, no matter how choppy the waters became because of the evil one's influence, she had a choice. She could choose to be tossed about and blown off course, or she could be controlled by the love of God. She could choose to look at how far God had gone to show her love—the death of His only Son. She could choose to see the rescue plan God put in place for her soul, how much He cared, how much He wanted to bless her. She could either look at the circumstances she was in, which were pretty dire, or she could see the big picture, that God was ultimately in control and would walk with her no matter what happened.

This truth, that God was with her, was like an anchor that sank deep into the surf of Elizabeth's life and kept her in one place. It didn't matter how much she bobbed on the surface of all the troubles—her soul was anchored by God's grace.

Tony took Danielle to the community center in the afternoon and warmed up with the team. Raising a sweat made him feel better. Getting his muscles loose and his body going helped him focus on something else. But the cloud that hung over him was too dark to push completely away. It was like the bully at school when he was in third grade. Just the thought of walking onto the playground made him seize up with fear. He'd had to push himself, will himself onto the playground instead of cowering. Coleman's decision was that specter now, along with the influence Tom surely had. Every time he thought of that man with the bow tie, Tony's stomach clenched and all he could see was the box of stolen pills he'd put on the table. All the guilt and shame out there for everybody to see.

He shook the thought off again, stretched out a little more, and joined the group. Trish, Danielle's coach, had done a great job with the team, instructing them on different moves that would score points with the judges and getting their rhythm down. In a competition like this, with all the spectators and distractions, repetition was the key—getting the muscles to remember the feeling of the ropes' rhythm and their body movement. She had tried to get the girls to the point that they didn't even have to think about their routine, they just did it. And to his surprise, Trish didn't seem threatened by Tony's involvement. She could have thrown her weight around and balked at having him join them after she'd worked for so long, but instead, she encouraged him to take on the role of assistant coach.

"I can see you know what you're doing with the girls," Trish had said. "You ever coached before?"

"Not much," he said. "But I had a lot of good coaches when I was younger."

The girls were ready to begin the practice and Trish had given them some final instructions. She looked at Tony and held out a hand as if she were saying, *"Go for it."*

Tony looked at Danielle and the others and something welled inside. Maybe it was the emotion of knowing he might not be able to even compete with them because of his uncertain future, something that was out of his control. But in that moment, a truth came over him that took his breath away.

The way he saw his daughter and her friends must be the way God saw him.

Tony didn't see the team's faults and the way they fell short on small areas of the routine. He saw what they were capable of doing with a little encouragement. And if this was the way God saw him, as someone He could empower, who was Tony to disagree with God?

He leaned down, his hands on his knees. "Here's the thing I see when I look at you guys. You have unlimited potential. You can do anything you set your mind to. The only thing that can hold you back is not being able to see that and go out and do it.

"When you make a mistake, when you don't do the routine like you want, you can choose to beat yourself up and say nasty things about your performance. You can focus on the mistakes and try to get every jump right and get your form right and follow every direction. But you'll never get there by trying *not* to make a mistake. You can't perform at your highest level focusing on the things you *don't* want to do. Does that make sense?"

Jennifer raised a hand and Tony nodded to her. "It's like when I play the piano. Every time I try not to make a mistake, I make one."

"Exactly. Great example. With music, you hear the tune and see it on the page and you play it. You just let your hands work through it. And with our routine, you do the same thing. You jump with abandon into the middle of those two ropes swinging around you. You leap in there knowing that when you land on the floor, you're going to hit square and bounce right back up like there are springs on the bottoms of your feet."

Danielle and Jennifer and the rest of the team smiled ear to ear. They were drinking in his words and catching this new mind-set.

"It happens that way with turning the ropes, too," Joy, one of the other team members, said.

"Absolutely," Tony said. "And never think that your job is less important. Every member of the team shares an equal part in the outcome."

There were smiles all around and Tony choked up, remembering a coach he'd had who said the same thing about a football team he'd been on in high school. The equipment manager had been a disabled kid who loved football but had no skills. He'd pick up the dirty clothes and do whatever grunt work the coach asked, and the coach pointed him out to emphasize that everyone who contributed played a part in the team's success.

"Here's the other thing," Tony said. "Sometimes you concentrate so hard, you get focused on your footwork or timing or winning and not letting the team down, and you forget we're having fun. Guys, what we're doing here is really fun, okay? So smile. The judges will notice. They don't keep score on how many teeth they can see, but it will influence them, I guarantee you. A person who is happy about what they're doing attracts attention because we all want to live that way. If they see you fully into this and smiling, everything changes. Don't just perform a routine, let the routine perform from the inside out. And let's show the crowd something they've never seen before."

When he finished, every member of the team put a hand in and shouted their team name, "Comets!" They had been captured by every word. Even Trish smiled at the encouragement and challenge.

Tony glanced at the clock on the wall to see how much time they had left in practice. What had been a high point for his day came crashing down. How much time would he have with his daughter before the decision was made about the rest of his life? The cloud was back.

That evening, Elizabeth watched Tony rinse dishes at the sink while she placed them in the dishwasher. They had tucked Danielle in before they tackled the dishes and Elizabeth was sure, with all the activity of the day, that she was now asleep.

In the past, the unwritten rule had been that Tony took care of the lawn, the trash, the upkeep of the cars—everything outside—and Elizabeth took care of the inside. But lately he'd taken a more active role in everything from dishes to vacuuming. He'd even suggested that since she was the one with the job, he should be the one to make dinner.

"What about the laundry?" she said playfully. "As long as you're taking over the domestic duties . . ."

"You know how I feel about the laundry," he said. It was the first time he'd smiled all night.

When he went back to scrubbing, she studied him. "You're nervous."

"I'm trying not to think about it."

The truth was, they were both nervous. She was just trying not to show it. "What time are you supposed to be there?" she said.

He looked out the back window as if he were calculating his freedom by the view. "Nine o'clock."

Tony had told her he thought he would never set foot inside Brightwell's building again. It looked like he had one more trip up the elevator.

The doorbell rang. Elizabeth looked at the clock and then back at Tony. Strange. It was late and they weren't expecting anyone.

She followed as Tony opened the door to find Coleman Young standing on their front porch. He wore a sport coat and had a serious look on his face.

"Coleman?"

"Hello, Tony." He looked at her. "Hi, Elizabeth."

"Hi, Coleman, how are you?"

"I'm fine, thank you." There was something in his voice that didn't sound quite right. He looked straight at Tony. "I know this is unexpected, but I wondered if you might give me a few minutes to talk?"

"Yeah, sure," Tony said. "Come on in."

Elizabeth sat by Tony and they both faced Coleman, the last person on earth either one of them thought would be sitting in their living room. She pulled her hair back and took a deep breath, praying silently as she did. *Lord Jesus, help me to accept whatever it is Coleman has to say.*

Tony wondered if they should offer Coleman something to drink. Maybe tea or decaf. A glass of water with some kind of powder in it to make the man see Tony's situation.

Coleman spoke before he could offer anything. "Tony, I've been thinking about your visit. In fact, it's probably all I've thought about the past two days." He clasped his hands in front of him and spoke with an even, measured voice. "What you did was wrong. And I was disappointed. But we've fired salesmen before and life goes on. Then you showed back up. And I've never seen anybody do what you did. I've never seen a man take total responsibility for his wrongdoing, no matter the consequence."

As he continued, Coleman's voice seemed to get softer, his eyes showing concern and also a desire to understand. "I kept asking myself why. Why would you do that?"

The question hung there between the three of them. Tony wanted to shout, to jump in and explain again, but his heart was beating so fast he could barely control his own breathing. He felt Elizabeth right beside him, hanging on every word Coleman spoke.

"The only answer I could come up with is that you are sincere in your desire to make it right. And that you do regret what you have done. So I have chosen to believe you. I can't give you your job back. But I've decided not to prosecute."

Tony could hardly breathe, hardly think about what Coleman had just said. His soul felt numb while at the same time joyous and grateful. Tears formed in his eyes and he tried to control them, fight them, but there was no fighting now, only joy—unspeakable, inexpressible joy leaking through every part of him.

He looked down, trying to form some kind of response. He glanced at Elizabeth, who looked like she was in a state of wide-eyed shock.

"I do think it would be appropriate to return the nineteen thousand to the company."

Tony nodded, finding his voice for the first time. "We've already decided to do that."

A smile crept across the man's face. "Well, if you're willing to sign an agreement to that effect, I think we should all move on."

The tension in the room had lifted, and Tony felt Elizabeth take his arm.

"So if you don't mind me seeing myself out, I'll give you your evening back."

Tony and Elizabeth shook the man's hand and whispered their thanks, unable to say much else. Coleman walked down the hall and out the front door.

When it closed, Elizabeth turned toward Tony, unable to hold back the emotion.

"Tony, that was grace," she said, her face already streaked with tears. "That was God's grace toward us."

Tony looked at her, their tears flowing in a symphony now. He raised his eyes toward the ceiling and past that to some other realm he knew was there. "Thank You, Jesus."

A few moments later he heard movement in Danielle's room. While Elizabeth went to call Clara, Tony crept upstairs and found Danielle at the door, listening.

"Did somebody come over?" she said.

"Yes, sweetie. Let's get back to bed."

She yawned and crawled under the covers, and Tony tucked her in again. Then a look of concern came over her.

"Was it the police? Are they going to take you away?"

He smiled and the emotion was still there. "It was a man from the company, Mr. Young. He wanted us to know he accepted my apology."

"He did?"

"Yes, he did. He said there isn't going to be any police officer and there's not going to be any jail."

"Oh, Daddy." Danielle sat up and hugged him, and it felt like God Himself had given Tony an embrace.

✦ ✦ ✦

Elizabeth found Tony sitting in bed after she hung up with Clara. She asked Tony about Danielle and he explained their conversation, tears coming to his eyes.

She covered her mouth, again too overcome to believe what had happened to them. "That Clara must have awakened the whole neighborhood. I've never heard a woman her age talk so much about kicking Satan's butt."

Tony laughed. "She's not just talking about it, she's doing it."

Elizabeth sat on the bed and stared at her closet. "This is going to take some time getting used to."

"What's that?"

"Forgiveness. Grace. I mean, it's one thing to hear it from Coleman. It's another thing to believe it and act on it."

"It's the same with Coleman as it is you and me," Tony said.

"What do you mean?"

"I keep waiting for you to jump on me for something I forgot to do. Hearing the old voices, the old patterns. Forgiveness is a two-way street, you know?"

She nodded. "We have a long way to go, Tony. But we're headed in the right direction, don't you think?"

He nodded and the way he looked at her brought up feelings she'd lived without for a long time. He held out a hand and she took it and climbed under the covers. He reached for the light and the room went dark.

Tony leaned close and whispered, "You want to pray?"

Elizabeth laughed. "Yes, we can start with prayer."

Tony slid his arms around her and pulled her close, then prayed softly, praising and thanking God for His mercy, His forgiveness, and His intervention in their lives. He also thanked God for a wife who was willing to fight for him. Elizabeth tightened her embrace, agreeing with every word. When he finished, Tony kissed her. Slowly and tenderly. And she kissed him back.

For the first time in forever, the connection that had been absent returned. They enjoyed a closeness that had been missing far too long. Sweet and loving. Passionate and fulfilling. God had brought them together again. And it was beautiful.

Miss Clara

✦ ✦ ✦

Clara believed that praising God was not a part-time proposition. It was full-time with benefits. Praise was part of the muscle memory of her spiritual life. She praised God for the good things that came her way and thanked Him for the things she didn't understand because she knew from experience that He was working in both cases. God was always working and always deserved praise.

Some, of course, saw this as wishful thinking and letting God off the hook, but Clara had read about people who had suffered great injustice and still gave glory to God. The people who loved Jesus and had followed Him stood at a hill outside of Jerusalem. As lightning flashed and blood poured from the sinless Son of God, they couldn't believe what they were seeing. At that spot on the planet, on that day in history, God put to rest the question of whether or not He was worthy of praise for the good and the bad because He took the worst thing to ever happen and turned it into the best thing. He snatched victory from the enemy and provided salvation for anyone who would call on the name of the Lord.

Giving thanks in every circumstance, for Clara, meant saying to God that she was willing to look at things from His perspective. Giving praise was freeing herself from having to understand everything. She could surrender it all.

When she got the call from Elizabeth about Coleman Young's decision regarding Tony, she felt like she could have flown to the moon. There would be no prison, no stain on Tony's record, and he would be able to continue living with his family and growing in grace and paying back his debt.

Clara threw her hands up and thanked God with a whoop that should have awakened any sleeping angel for a billion miles. She didn't know if angels slept, but she did know that angels rejoiced when a sinner repented. She marched to her war room and put a check beside that request, gave another whoop, and praised God again.

Praising God did something to her heart nothing else could. She had read Psalm 22, which said God was "enthroned on the praises of Israel." She believed that God drank her praises in and enjoyed her whoops of joy.

But the benefits weren't just for Him—they extended to her. When she praised God, she agreed with Him that He alone was worthy and she was not. He alone was in control and she was not. He alone deserved the credit, and He alone was holy. So praise was a humbling act. And the more she humbled herself, the more peace washed over her. She didn't worry and fret when she told God the truth about Himself. When she reminded God of who He was, she was reminding herself about the truth. And when she did that, she was no longer wrapped up and tied in knots with what the enemy wanted.

"Let us exalt His name together." Those words were a recipe for joy. She wanted that joy to spill from her life on everyone she contacted.

"Lord, I thank You that this kind of praise will never end. Praising You is something we'll be doing forever! That's what I want to do. I want to praise You with every breath and every prayer and every heartbeat until I see You face-to-face. I want to praise You for the way You're changing me from the inside out and the way You're changing Elizabeth and Tony. And with all the bad stuff going on in the world, the wars and killing and injustice, I'm going to praise You.

"A body can't lose when they praise You, Lord. Hallelujah!"

CHAPTER 18

+ + +

Tony sat with Michael at a corner table in the community
center café. The place was abuzz with activity. Moms held
lattes and talked, waiting for kids to be released from
morning programs.

The look on Michael's face was priceless. His shaved head
had wrinkles on its wrinkles from the way he was frowning.

"Man, I didn't know you were going through all that at
work and at home. Why didn't you tell me?"

Tony shrugged. "Pride, I guess. I wanted to keep all of
that hidden."

"Bro, we're supposed to be there for each other, you
know? That's what friends are for."

"I see that now. And that's why I wanted to tell you."

Michael took a sip of coffee and smiled. "That's awesome, though, about your marriage—your faith in God. I gotta be honest. I could tell something was up from how angry you were playing ball. You were like the Tasmanian Devil out there, swirling around. You remember that night?"

Tony nodded. "Yeah, there was a lot going on that night."

"I started praying for you then. Off and on, you know."

"Off and on?"

"I'd drive past your house, or see Danielle and Elizabeth here, and I'd think about you. Ask God to do something with your sorry little heart."

Tony laughed. "Well, He answered. I'm serious now. No more going to church just because it looks good or my wife wants me to. God has shown up. He's revealed what's most important."

Tony told Michael more about why he'd been let go at work. He was afraid Michael might judge him and scold him for taking the samples, but he listened to the story without comment. When Tony was finished, Michael said, "That's a tough lesson."

"It was even tougher going back and confessing, but I knew I had to do it."

"Good for you. If it had been me with that Tom guy, though, I'd have wanted to smack him upside the head."

Tony laughed. "Believe me, I wanted to. I still want to. And if I ever get the chance, I don't know what I'll do."

"Revenge is a powerful motivator," Michael said. "But

I'd hate to see you do something you'd regret. You know, Jesus said you're supposed to pray for your enemies. Maybe you ought to try that. It's hard to hate somebody you're praying for."

Tony smiled. "I have prayed for him, believe it or not."

"You mean, like, 'Lord, break his teeth'?"

Tony laughed. "No, I'm just praying that someday I'll have a chance to reach out to him somehow."

"That's good, bro. Because Tom was just calling you out for what you did. You admitted it was wrong, right?"

"Yeah, sure."

"Okay. So when you look at it from his perspective— I'm assuming he's not a believer—he just wants to make you pay for the wrong stuff you've done."

Tony nodded. "So I'm supposed to just take his meanness?"

"No, I'm saying to look at it from a third perspective. Sometimes the hardest way to think about people who hurt you is how God sees them. And every time you want to smack them upside the head, remember God wants them to turn to Him just like you've done."

"Can't I see him that way *and* smack him upside the head?" Tony said.

"Let me put it this way. Let's say you do something mean to me. I hold it against you so much that when the call comes that you're having a heart attack, I say no, I don't want to help this guy. You think that's a good idea?"

"No."

"Why not?"

"You'd lose your job."

"True, but there's a bigger reason. I gave my word to help whoever's lying on the ground, no questions asked."

"I get you. So I need to forgive him even if he doesn't ask for it or think he needs it."

Michael nodded. "You'll get a chance."

"I'm never going back there. There's no chance."

"Then write him a letter. Hire a plane to write it in the sky." He thought a moment and sat forward. "We have a men's Bible study over at the station on Tuesday mornings. Eat breakfast together. Pray. Talk about our struggles. Talk about what forgiveness looks like. We have it in the community room because some of the other guys object. They call us the God squad. Stuff like that. We'd love to have you join us if you could spare the time."

"Man, time is all I have right now," Tony said.

"Yeah, any job prospects? Must be a ton on your shoulders with that house payment."

Tony nodded. "And we're down to one car. Liz picked up a few more houses and she needs the ride. Tell you the truth, I'd love to find something close, you know, that didn't involve traveling all the time."

"So I'm looking at the death of a salesman? I thought you loved the travel."

"I did. I loved the money even more. I loved making the sale and the bonuses. But when your priorities change, all that comes into focus, you know?"

Michael nodded. He started to respond, then held up, noticing someone behind Tony. "Hey, Ernie!"

Ernie Timms, the director of the community center, passed with his usual bewildered look. He was carrying a large box and heading toward his office.

"Michael," Ernie said with a blank stare. He nodded at Tony.

"Where you going with the box?" Michael said.

"Cleaning out my office. You heard about the change, didn't you?"

"What change?" Michael said.

"They're letting me go. Board made the decision yesterday. I'm clearing out."

Michael stood, concern etched on his face, and put a hand on Ernie's shoulder. "I had no idea. I'm sorry, man."

"Just one of those things, I guess," Ernie said as if he was trying to take it in stride and be a man.

"I know how you feel," Tony said. "I was let go from my job at Brightwell."

"Sorry to hear that," Ernie said.

"Sit down. I'll buy you a cup of coffee," Michael said.

Ernie looked at the box, then at the hallway leading to his office.

"Come on. It'll help to talk, don't you think?" Tony said.

"Yeah. Probably."

Michael went for a cup of coffee and Ernie sat.

"Was it all of a sudden?" Tony said.

"I knew it was coming. I'm not really cut out for this.

Too many administrative plates to keep spinning. The main job of the director here is getting everybody on the same team, you know? I was never good at organizing. I'm not really a people person. That's what they told me when they let me go. But they gave me a good severance package, so I can't complain. It gives me some time to look."

Tony listened. A few weeks ago he wouldn't have cared about somebody else's problem. He would have been glad Ernie had been fired because it would mean less confusion at the gym over court time. He'd only judged things on how much they affected his own life. Now he saw a guy who was hurting, a real flesh-and-blood person with a family and hopes and dreams that were coming to an end, and his heart was moved by the man's struggle.

Michael returned with the coffee and the two of them listened to Ernie's tale. When the man had told them everything, he sat with the coffee in his hands, staring into the distance.

"You know, the job loss that Tony's been through has been a game changer for him," Michael said.

Ernie looked at Tony. "Really?"

"I can honestly say I'm at peace right now," Tony said.

"You found a job that quick?" Ernie said.

"No, I haven't found another job. I don't have any idea what I'm supposed to do next."

"Then how can you be at peace?" Ernie said.

Tony hesitated. He didn't know where the man was spiritually, and the last thing he wanted to do was bash the guy over the head with religion. But it seemed so natural just to tell him what God had done in his life.

Michael raised an eyebrow at Tony, giving him the look of a teammate who had just passed the ball to him under the basket.

"I guess you could say God got ahold of me when I hit bottom," Tony said. "I was running after achievement and success and money. But God woke me up to what's important. And when I ran toward that, He gave me peace. Real contentment. Even though I'm not really sure what's ahead."

"That's great," Ernie said. "For you. I mean, I'm happy for you."

"What about you?" Tony said. "Do you have a relationship with God?"

Ernie frowned. "I go to church. Every now and then. My wife goes."

"Does she pray for you?" Michael said. "Because Tony's wife prayed up a storm and his whole life came unraveled."

"Your wife prayed and you lost your job and you're happy about that?" Ernie said.

"I'm not happy about losing my job," Tony said. "And my wife didn't pray for bad stuff to happen. She prayed for our marriage. She prayed I'd come alive to God. But I was going down a wrong path, you know? I was trusting in myself and my own abilities. And that's over. I'm not leaning on my own understanding anymore."

Ernie took a sip of coffee and stared at the table.

"This is a lot to take in, isn't it?" Michael said.

Ernie nodded.

"You mind if we pray for you?" Michael said. "Don't look at me that way. We're not going to throw snakes around and roll on the floor."

Ernie stood. "I appreciate it, but I need to get going."

Michael nodded. "Okay. We'll catch you some other time. But know that we're going to pray for you and your family."

"I appreciate it," Ernie said, leaving with the box and his coffee.

"Sad," Tony said. "That he wouldn't listen."

"He listened," Michael said. "He's just not ready to hear. And that's okay. Breaking through people's hearts is not your job. That's God's business. You be faithful to share what God's done. That was awesome the way you picked up and told him what had happened to you."

"Yeah, but he walked away. That was a failure."

"I seem to recall somebody else doing the same thing with me," Michael said. "And he's sitting right there looking at me."

Tony smiled. "Guess I got a new name for my prayer list."

Elizabeth fidgeted with her phone, trying to calm her nerves by scrolling through her Facebook feed. Tony was driving them to the double Dutch competition. She looked at her notifications and saw the photo she'd taken of Tony holding Danielle, both of them wearing their Comets T-shirts. She had ten comments from people, all of them encouraging the team to do well.

"Will Miss Clara be there today?" Danielle said.

"She said she wouldn't miss it," Elizabeth said.

"Did you bring my snack?"

Snacks were her daughter's middle name. Though they had talked about not being superstitious, Danielle was convinced that when she ate peanut butter and gummy worms on celery sticks, she jumped better. "Yeah, baby, I've got it right here."

"Danielle, are you nervous?" Tony said, looking in the mirror at her.

"Very," Danielle said.

"Are you nervous?" Elizabeth said to Tony.

A wide grin spread across Tony's face. "Oh yeah. But I'll be fine just as long as I don't fall on my face."

"Are you really still going to do that flip?" Elizabeth said. Tony had been telling her some of the moves they were practicing, and she wasn't entirely confident Tony could wed his gymnastic ability with the jump rope competition.

"Am I gonna do the flip? Yeah, we're gonna do the flip." Tony spoke in a high voice and it made Danielle giggle. To Elizabeth it was proof that God had been at work. Before the change in their relationship, she and Tony hadn't been able to ride in the car for ten minutes without arguing. Now the mood in the car was playful.

"And that's not all, huh, Danielle?" Tony said.

Elizabeth turned and saw her daughter with a grin as wide as Tony's.

"You ain't seen nothing yet, Liz," Tony added.

"Okay, now I'm nervous," she said.

They drove toward the venue, a gymnasium on the north side of Charlotte. Tony had wanted to get there early for the team to get a feel of the room and the atmosphere. The building wasn't far from the Brightwell offices, and as they looked at the stately building in the distance, Elizabeth put a hand on Tony's shoulder.

"You miss going there?" she said. "The polished floors and nice office?"

"I miss the paycheck. And the challenge every day. But I wouldn't trade what I've learned. There's no going back now."

"I think God has something good in store for you," Elizabeth said. "And Danielle is praying some specific things for your next job."

"Is that right?" Tony said, looking in the mirror again.

"Yep. I'm praying that God will give you a job that's close to the house, that won't make you travel, and that will give us enough money so we don't have to move. Oh, and one that will let you stay on our double Dutch team."

Tony laughed. "That's being specific."

"Well, Miss Clara said God likes to answer the specific ones," Danielle said.

"She said that, huh?" he said.

They pulled up to a stop sign in a residential area and

Elizabeth spotted a car parked weirdly in a nearby lot. The door was open and the trunk popped, and a man in suspenders and dress pants talked on a cell phone. When he turned a little, she saw his bow tie. He gestured wildly as he yelled into his phone.

"Isn't that Tom?" she said.

"Yes, it is," Tony said, lingering at the stop sign. "Looks like a flat."

Elizabeth watched the man, imagining the conversation he was having with whoever was on the other end of the phone. It served him right, being inconvenienced like this. A little part of her was glad he was going through something hard.

Tony pulled past him, then turned left into the parking lot and behind Tom.

"Daddy, are we going to be late?"

"No, sweetie. This is not going to take long."

"What are you doing?" Elizabeth said.

"Something I've been needing to do for a while." He parked and set the brake, giving her a look that tried to say everything. She couldn't quite understand. "I'll be right back," he said.

Elizabeth wanted to caution Tony—to remind him not to do anything rash. If he tried to hurt Tom in some way, Coleman might reconsider his decision not to press charges. But she didn't say anything. They were past words about this because Tony had made up his mind. She could tell by the way he slammed the door and walked purposefully toward the disabled car, toward the man whose name he couldn't say without flinching a little.

Lord Jesus, will You help Tony right now? Will You give him Your heart and mind, O Lord?

"What's he going to do, Mom?" Danielle said. She had unbuckled and was sitting forward now.

She wanted to shield her daughter in case Tony did something rash. There wasn't anyone around. No one could see.

"I'm not sure, Danielle."

Clara had said all of life was a test about whether or not you really believed God. Every day you had a thousand choices to show God you were serious about following Him, serious about obeying Him, and one of the greatest tests was whether you would seek revenge against someone who did you wrong. Tony had been one to let his anger get the best of him at times. Elizabeth reached for the window, thinking about rolling it down to say something.

Tom wiped the sweat from his brow on his shirt, then looked up to see Tony striding toward him. Tom took a step back, a look of fear on his face. He stepped away from the car as Tony leaned into the trunk to grab something. He came up with the tire iron.

Tony had always believed in working out and keeping himself in the best shape possible. The T-shirt accentuated his biceps. He looked massive compared to Tom, and as he stepped forward, Tom took another step back.

Anyone passing the scene or looking out their window

might have seen a black man with a deadly weapon moving toward a white man. If they had known the backstory, they might have dialed 911, and Elizabeth wondered if Tom would reach for his phone to call for help any second or if he'd just turn and run away as fast as he could.

Tony got close enough to speak to Tom, but Elizabeth didn't hear any words. The two just looked at each other. Then Tony squatted by the car and began to loosen the lug nuts.

Elizabeth smiled and Danielle strained to see. "What's he doing, Mom?"

"He's changing Tom's flat tire."

"Who is Tom?"

"He's a man who was mean to your dad after he confessed what he'd done. He works at the same company. And instead of being mean back, your father is showing him grace."

Danielle studied her father loosening the lug nuts and then putting the jack underneath and raising the car. He placed the spare on and tightened the lug nuts, then lowered the car and tightened them again.

When he had the tire on, he put the flat in the back along with the tools, brushed off his hands, and walked toward Tom again. The man's face seemed to have softened—or maybe he was asking the questions that she and Danielle had asked. Why had Tony done that? He could have just driven past and never thought a thing about it.

Tony reached out a dirty hand and Tom hesitated. Then

he took Tony's hand and shook it. No thank-you. No questions. He just shook it and Tony returned to the car.

"Why did you do that?" Danielle said.

"Because that's how I want to be treated, Danielle."

Elizabeth smiled and thanked God for changes of the heart. As they drove past Tom, he was staring at his back tire as if he'd never seen one before in his life. As if he'd just witnessed some kind of miracle. Elizabeth knew he had.

Miss Clara

✦ ✦ ✦

Clara asked Clyde to drive her to the double Dutch competition and he said he had a meeting in Charlotte that morning and it would be no problem. He shook his head at his mother's request. "Are you spectating or participating?" He smiled at her and gave her a look that warmed her heart.

On the way they talked about the latest news, what was going on with Clyde's work, and eventually the conversation turned to her granddaughter, Hallie.

"The other day she wandered into the backyard after school," Clara said. "I was doing the most powerful thing I can do."

"You were praying."

"You better believe it. I hear people say, 'Well, all we can do now is pray.' That's the best thing you can do. So I was praying as I sat at the window and here comes Hallie walking out there in the yard. She didn't look at me. Kept her back to me. But I'd been praying for a slap week that she'd come to my door, that she'd just pass by without me asking her again, and there she was."

Clyde stopped at a light and turned toward her. "Did you go out there to talk?"

She waved a finger at him. "No sirree. I didn't peck on the window. I didn't holler through the door. I just waited. And I prayed."

"What happened?"

Someone honked behind them as the light turned green.

"She walked around a little bit like she was waiting for me to do something. And when I didn't, she came to the window and looked in, like she was concerned about me. I waved and pointed to the door. And she finally walked inside."

"You would have made a good fisherman."

Clara laughed. "Maybe it's age and experience that makes me so patient. Just sitting there and waiting made it her idea to come in."

"Did you have a good talk?"

"I'd say we had us a good start to the conversation. You can tear down a wall with a bulldozer, but it's usually better to go brick by brick."

"I'm glad you're living with us, Mama. I really am."

Clara pointed to the gymnasium even though Clyde's GPS was telling him where to turn. He parked at the front and opened the door for her. "You call me when it's over and I'll come get you, okay?"

She found Elizabeth inside and the first thing they talked about was what Tony had done for the man who had treated him so unkindly at work. Clara just about burst out a hallelujah right in that gymnasium. A few minutes later she found Tony, who was stretching and getting ready, and asked if she could have a minute.

"Sure, Miss Clara," Tony said. "What's up?"

"Elizabeth told me about the flat tire you changed. Now where did you get the strength to do that? And I'm not talking about the physical strength."

Tony smiled. "Well, if you want to know the truth, I've been praying for Tom. A friend of mine encouraged me to do that, and then I came across the passage in Matthew about loving your enemies and praying for them. It was all over but the tire changing at that point."

Clara chuckled and shook her head. "That's a good passage. But it's a hard one."

Tony's eyes twinkled like stars. "You know, when I saw Tom in that parking lot, I knew it wasn't just chance that we were passing him. He was yelling at somebody on the phone—probably late for a meeting, all frustrated and hot and sweaty."

"Can't that man change his own tire?"

"Tom's not the tire-changing type, if you know what I mean."

"So when you saw him, you knew it was the Lord telling you to do something?"

Tony nodded. "It's one thing to pray for your enemy. To ask God to move into his life and bless him. That's a good start. But it's another thing altogether when you're given the opportunity to become the answer to your own prayer. I couldn't have orchestrated that. And I didn't tell Tom why I was doing it. I didn't give him the gospel. I didn't preach a sermon. I just changed his tire, shook his hand, and moved on."

"You may not have preached, but you showed him the gospel in action. You showed him what it means to live from a forgiven heart."

Tony smiled. "I guess I did, didn't I?"

"God did it through you. And I love what He's doing. My guess is, down the road, you're going to have a chance to talk to that man about the reason for the hope you have. I'm going to pray that happens."

"That'll be two of us, Miss Clara. Thank you for what you've meant to our family."

She pursed her lips. "You don't know what your family has meant to me, young man. Now go out there and do some flips for Jesus."

Tony moved back to his team and got ready for the competition. Clara praised God again for the way He was working.

As the gymnasium started to fill, she found Elizabeth. "A lot of people want to do great things for God. A lot of people want to change the world. I just shake my head when I hear that. God is the only one who can change the world because He's the only one who can change hearts and minds. Tony didn't run out and try to do something good for Tom to show him love and forgiveness. He prayed and asked God to do something in Tom's life. And when he had the chance, he took it. But that only came after drawing close to the heart of his heavenly Father. Sometimes a miracle looks like a tire change."

"That's what happened with me," Elizabeth said. "I didn't do anything to turn Tony around. I just got close to God and asked Him to work."

Clara looked out at the teams and found Danielle and Tony. "That little girl of yours will probably do the same thing for you."

"What's that?" Elizabeth said.

"She will, at some point down the road, cause you to get on your knees. All children do that to their parents. And when that happens, you remember what I said. Don't think the problem with Danielle is something to solve. This is God's way of drawing you to Himself and helping you rely on Him instead of your own wisdom."

"I'll try to remember that," Elizabeth said, smiling. Then her face turned serious. "I am concerned about your house. I've had a few nibbles about it, but—"

Clara shook her head. "God is going to bring the right family along. In His timing. Don't you worry."

That seemed to calm Elizabeth. Then she cocked her head. "Miss Clara, does God care about sporting events? When we pray for one team to win and somebody else prays for another, how does He handle those?"

"You're asking me about the nature of God. And that's a deep subject. There are some people who don't pray because they say they don't want to worry God with little things. Lost car keys. A parking spot. Some game you want to win. I believe God cares about it all. If He numbers the hairs on your head and sees every sparrow that falls, He cares about the little things. Because the little things influence the big things.

"When people say they're not going to pray about such and such, they're really telling God to stay out of that area, that they can handle things. And that's dangerous. I'm not saying we need to fast and pray for ten weeks about which toothpaste we buy, but at the same time, God is over cancer and cavities alike.

"Now I don't believe that God is more interested in who wins than He is in who grows. God wants us to be drawn to Him in the wins and losses. He uses our abilities and inabilities to praise Him. So one player may make a fantastic catch and praise God in the interview afterward. But another player may be humbled by getting beat on that play. Is he any less capable of praising God?

His praise in difficult circumstances is in some ways better because he's trusting God."

"So it's not wrong to pray that Danielle's team wins?"

"No, I was praying the same thing driving over here. But I was also praying that God would keep working in Tony's heart and in your family to bring you together. That's a double Dutch win, if you ask me."

CHAPTER 19

✦ ✦ ✦

When Tony walked into the gym with his family and the other members of his team, the venue had taken his breath away. He knew the organizers would stage things well, but he hadn't expected this. Bleachers were set up on all four sides, leaving room in the middle for the competition. A sign above read, *Citywide Double Dutch Championship*.

"This place is huge," Jennifer said.

Danielle's eyes had gone wide in awe. "Wow" was all she could say.

"This is why I wanted to get here a little early," Tony said to Elizabeth before she headed to the bleachers. "Give them time to get comfortable with the surroundings."

"You still going to do the flip?" she'd said under her breath.

"Baby, don't you worry about the flip."

Tony stretched and helped the team do the same. Miss Clara came to him and talked and his eyes watered as she walked away, throwing her arms out at her sides and flailing like she was doing some dance of joy. Maybe she was. She had good reason to be joyful.

Trish called everyone together in a corner of the gym for some last-minute words. As she spoke, Tony went to the judges to see what order the teams would compete. Then he hurried back to the group.

"I'm so proud of you for everything that you've done, and I can't wait to see what you guys do out there," Trish said. Then she turned. "You want to say something to them, Tony?"

"Yeah, thanks, Coach. Listen. I just spoke with the judges. They've agreed to let us go last."

"Yes!" Danielle said, unable to contain her excitement.

"Remember what we talked about," Tony continued. "We want the last thing they see to be impressive. All right? I know you guys are nervous. Believe me, I am too. But we're going to take that nervous energy and turn it into rocket fuel. All right? You guys are with me?"

The girls all nodded and agreed.

He put his hand in the middle and they put their hands on top of his. "All right, let's blow them away. 'Comets' on three. One . . . two . . . three, Comets!"

✦ ✦ ✦

Elizabeth sat next to Clara in the packed gymnasium. She had brought her friend an official Comets T-shirt and the woman put it on over her green collared shirt. There wasn't an ounce of pride in Clara, and it was fun to see her in action in a group of strangers. She talked with people she didn't know like they were long-lost friends. She asked questions about kids who were jumping and actually found three people she was going to add to her prayer list before the competition began. This was the life of a prayer warrior—always on duty, always willing to enter the battle.

"So they have two ropes going at the same time?" Clara said.

"Two ropes going in opposite directions," Elizabeth said.

Clara watched the teams warming up and shook her head. "Whoooeee, that's some serious hand-eye coordination."

Family members of the teams fidgeted in the hall and bleachers, talking about the weather. Elizabeth overheard one mother talking about a daughter who had sprained an ankle and was competing anyway.

Elizabeth wasn't sure how Clara would respond to the competition, whether she would sit and observe or really get into it, but all her preconceived notions of how prim and proper the woman might be went out the window when the teams were announced. She stayed seated until the Comets were introduced, then stood and whooped for Danielle, Tony, and the rest.

"I like to support my team when I can," she said, noticing Elizabeth's open mouth. "Paul says to do whatever you do with all your heart, so I don't care what it is. Stringing beans, doing dishes, or rooting for my favorite double Dutch team. I try to be all over it."

Elizabeth shook her head and thanked God for bringing this force of nature into her life.

"Oh yes, oh yes, oh yes," the announcer said. "Who's ready for the Citywide Double Dutch Championship?"

The crowd roared and Clara stood and clapped.

The announcer went over the rules for those who were new to the competition and gave instructions to the participants. Then it was time to begin. "Our teams are revved up and ready to go. We're starting off with the speed round. Here we go!"

"So the speed round is where they just get in there and jump like crazy, right?" Clara said.

"Right. The team puts their fastest jumpers in the middle and they're timed and awarded points. After that is the freestyle, where they do all the creative moves."

"And Tony is going to do a flip?"

"How'd you hear about that?"

"Danielle told me to watch for it."

Three teams competed at the same time, and an official kept track of how many jumps were completed in the time allotment. Elizabeth was amazed at the fluid motion of the competitors and how the jumpers and those turning the ropes worked in tandem. It was easy to just focus on the girls and boys jumping and forget the two competitors swinging the ropes. Everybody had to be focused and dialed into the action.

"Would you look at that?" Clara said. "I can't believe how fast they're going. It's like they're just moving their hands—I can't even see the rope anymore. How can the referees or whatever you call them possibly count how many jumps they make?"

Clara was right. As the participants jumped, they seemed to get in a zone and be able to work together as one person instead of three. Elizabeth compared the speed of a couple teams to the Comets. The official had a counter to click with each jump, and as she watched, she concluded that the Comets hadn't scored as high in this round as some of the other teams. They would have to overcome that in the freestyle round.

"Time!" an official called out.

Her palms sweaty, Elizabeth looked at Clara. "I think I'm too nervous to watch."

Clara threw her head back and laughed. "You know you're a captive audience now! Come on, Comets!"

So many sports segregated male and female, but the double Dutch competition had both. There were more girls than boys but not that many more. The sound of the ropes swirling and the feet pounding the hardwood mingled with the encouragement from the crowd and teammates.

"I don't understand how the scores for this round and the next round work," Clara said.

"It's like figure skating," Elizabeth said. "The speed round is like the technical round where skaters do specific jumps. The freestyle is like the long program. The teams try to wow the judges with style points."

"So after the speed round, it's all up to the judges and their determination," Clara said.

"Exactly. Tony said he was really glad they were going last so they could leave the judges with a final impression."

"Mmm-hmm," Clara said.

When the speed competition was completed, there was a short break. Danielle came over, out of breath and sweating.

Clara gave her a big hug. "I saw you out there jumping as fast as you could! How do you like it?"

"It's fun!" Danielle said. "I'm still a little nervous about the freestyle, though."

"You and your coaches have prepared well, I can tell that. And I'm going to be praying for you."

"That seems like an unfair advantage," Elizabeth said, smiling.

Clara laughed. "It just might be. But I'm okay with it."

The announcer called the teams back to the floor and the seven judges took their positions at the scoring table.

Elizabeth hugged Tony before he rejoined the team. "Is God going to help you do that flip?"

"Just you watch," Tony said.

+ + +

Tony gathered with his teammates as they watched the first team move to the center of the court. The announcer said, "All right, the speed scores will be added to the freestyle scores. So let's start the freestyle competition. First up is the Moon Jumpers."

The crowd went wild for the team in yellow. They had some pretty impressive moves and Tony could see Danielle and the others watching with trepidation. He called them together while the Mustangs were introduced.

"I can see you guys comparing yourselves. You're watching them do that handstand thing and noticing their speed, right?"

"We're not as good as they are," Jennifer said.

"We're not as fast, either," Danielle said.

"Did you see what the one girl did?" Joy said.

"Hey, we're the Comets," Tony said. "And what do comets do? They rise up and shoot past the earth and leave everybody gasping, right? Well, that's what we're going to do. Those teams are good—and they're fast. You enjoy watching what they do, but concentrate on your routine. Leave the comparing to the judges, okay?"

Trish gave them some encouragement as well and the team seemed a little more at ease.

Tony took Trish aside. "I wonder if we should have asked to go first instead of last. This is killing me."

Trish smiled and shook her head. "You guys are going to be great!"

The Tigers were next and one of the competitors tried a backflip that was unsuccessful. Tony glanced at the judges, who wrote down something on their scorecards. If they had a perfect routine going, should he attempt the flip? A little doubt crept in. Was he doing the flip because of his own ego? The competition was about the team, not about his personal ability.

You're trying to show off, the voice in his head said. *You're just trying to bring attention to yourself. This is not about you. This is about the girls.*

Tony shook off the voice and told himself the truth. He wasn't going to let anything hold him back. He was created to be there with his family, to be the very best he could be, and he was going to be that for his daughter, his wife, and his team.

When one team did a break-dance move where both jumpers went totally flat on the gym floor, then jumped from that position, he couldn't help but shake his head in awe. He'd never even thought anyone could pull off something like that, and the way the judges looked at their scorecards, he knew the team had hit a home run. With each team, the tricks and moves seemed to become more complex. The Speed Angels had four guys doing some mind-blowing tricks, spins, and flips. They missed one critical jump, but the performance left the crowd and, presumably, the judges in awe. Tony saw one judge turn to another and say, "Wow." He began to wonder if his team had any "wow" in their routine.

The tension mounted as their turn neared. Tony pulled the girls together for one final pep talk. "All right. Let's leave everything on the court, okay? Let's go out there and show them what we can do!"

"And now for the final team in our freestyle competition, let's hear it for the Comets!" the announcer said.

The crowd cheered and the Comets took their places. Tony glanced at Elizabeth, and she gave him a tense smile. He stood back from the others, right at the edge of the floor, and closed his eyes. *Lord, I give this performance to You and I thank You for the energy, for the friends here, and for my family.*

The music began, the ropes swung, and Tony took a deep breath. He saw his cue and took off running. What happened in the next few minutes was pure magic. He somersaulted into the ropes, did a high, arching backflip, and landed squarely, jumping immediately in time with the spinning ropes.

The crowd went wild and Tony fed off the energy. He couldn't really hear individual voices, but he heard a roar in his head and kept an internal beat as his teammates prepared.

Next, Jennifer jumped in and took his place, doing some amazing moves within the ropes. Then Tony leapfrogged into the middle and was joined by Danielle. They jumped on one leg, then the other, touching feet in the air—an incredibly difficult move they had practiced on the driveway for hours. Danielle moved out and Tony was alone again, doing a backflip that brought the crowd to their feet.

✦ ✦ ✦

Elizabeth had watched the team practice, she'd seen Tony and Danielle on the driveway and in the garage when it rained, but she wasn't prepared for the scene that played out in front of her. It was as if all of their work, all the pain and sweat and nervousness, coalesced into one amazing performance.

The pinnacle for her was when Tony picked Danielle up, spun her behind his back, kept jumping, and was joined by Jennifer in the middle. In the end, the ropes fell in perfect time with the music cutoff, and they stood to wild applause.

"That was good!" Clara yelled above the din. "That was real good!"

Elizabeth couldn't hold back the emotion. This was just one more piece of evidence that God was working in Tony's life and in their family. She knew there would be some rough roads ahead. But she wanted to bottle this feeling and keep it around to pour out every now and then.

Tony grabbed Danielle and spun her around on the court like they were doing a victory dance. It wouldn't be long before Danielle would be walking down an aisle with him, moving on with her life. Elizabeth could see it flash before her eyes. She didn't want to miss anything with her family. Not one moment.

Tony put Danielle on his shoulders and she couldn't hold back the smile. "That's my dad!" she screamed. "That's my dad!"

Yes, it is, Elizabeth thought. *That is your dad.*

She looked at Clara, who was taking in all the sights and sounds. "What did you think?"

Clara gave her a big grin. "I think next year you and I should be on the team."

Tony listened to the announcer give the details of the scoring and stood with his team as the third-place winner was announced. His heart fell a little when it wasn't the Comets. There was no way they could have scored higher than the others.

"And in second place, the Comets!" the announcer said.

Danielle turned to him with eyes and mouth wide and they floated to the center of the floor together. They took their place as a team and accepted the trophy to wild applause.

"You guys were amazing out there," Trish said over the noise.

Each team member received a medallion and took turns holding the trophy, which would go in the community center back home. Parents took so many pictures, Tony thought smiling should be an Olympic sport. Elizabeth came down and they took a family photo.

"Miss Clara, you get in here," Danielle said.

"No, I don't belong with you guys," she protested.

Tony reached out. "You belong here as much as we do."

Tony had a lot of pictures of sporting events through the years. Memorable football games and photos snapped with celebrities. None of them compared to the feelings behind the photo with his family and Clara. He was going to keep that picture on his desk at work for a long time. Then he remembered he didn't have a job. He decided he would frame the picture in faith, believing God was going to provide some office for him.

On the ride home, Tony asked Elizabeth if Clara had gotten home okay. "We could have given her a ride."

"She called her son to pick her up and slipped out while we were taking pictures," Elizabeth said. "I was hoping to meet Clyde—I've heard so much about him."

"I'm sure you'll get to meet him," Tony said.

"Hey, how about some music to celebrate?" Danielle said from the backseat.

"Got just the thing," Tony said.

He turned on a song and the three of them danced to the beat, moving from side to side in perfect synchronization, smiling and laughing.

Elizabeth's phone rang and she tapped Tony on the shoulder. "Hang on. Wait, you guys. This might be a buyer." She made a silly face at him. "It's time for my professional voice."

From what Tony could hear, it was someone named Reverend Jones who wanted to look at a house on Monday morning. Just when Tony's work life had imploded, Elizabeth's job had picked up. Instead of seeing this as threatening or feeling bad about not providing, he thanked God that Elizabeth could pick up some slack in their income.

"I've got somebody looking at Miss Clara's house," Elizabeth said when she was finished with the conversation.

"That's awesome, baby. You should call Miss Clara right now and tell her."

"No, I don't want to get her hopes up yet. I just want to see how it goes."

"Can I come with you?" Danielle said from the backseat.

"You really want to?" Elizabeth said.

"I never get to go to work with you."

"Well, okay," Elizabeth said, smiling.

When the car got quiet, Tony looked in the rearview mirror. "Hey, Danielle, you all right with second place?"

Her face was as bright as an angel's. "I kind of feel like we got first place because I like being together."

Tony smiled and looked at his wife. Danielle had said it perfectly. They were together. It had taken a lot of work, a lot of tears, a lot of turning from how he'd always lived, and a lot of jumping rope, but they were together.

Tony had always measured success in the amount of money he made or how fast he could run compared with everyone else. He'd always measured success in numbers or crushing an opponent and coming out on top. For the first time in his life, he felt like being together was better than any other feeling on earth. Success wasn't about numbers because those numbers could be taken away. And the fact that he was part of the team and they were moving forward side by side was better than any amount of money, any medal or trophy, or any praise he'd ever received.

Success wasn't about anything someone could give you or that you could earn. It was about allowing God to work in and through your life. And that meant the good stuff and the bad could be used for His glory.

Tony turned up the music and the three of them danced and sang the rest of the way home. Together.

Miss Clara

✦ ✦ ✦

Clara parked at the cemetery and took the long walk to Leo's grave. She thought about the pastor who had said, "A lot of people don't pray because they don't believe it works. But unfortunately it doesn't work because we don't really pray." She knew he was right. And she was always surprised what she learned about wisdom and understanding when she spent time praying.

"Leo, the Lord is moving. In Elizabeth's life and Tony's. In Hallie's life. I wish you could have heard what she said to me the other day about how handsome you looked in your uniform. She's right—you were handsome."

She ran her hand along the smooth stone and thought

about her spiritual life and how she had never arrived at a destination. As soon as she'd gotten comfortable in some spot, the Lord had shaken her and moved her closer. That was no doubt in order to make her more like Jesus and conform her to His image. And the thing before her that was shaking her was the sale of her home.

"Leo, once I decided to move, I asked God to make the transition go smoothly. Now Elizabeth has been concerned and I've told her that God was going to work things out, but I'll admit to being a little discouraged. Even though I realize God brought Elizabeth into my life through this whole experience. I've thanked Him for that. But I don't understand why nobody seems to think our house is worth the investment. We've taken good care of the place. Elizabeth says it has curb appeal, whatever that is. I'm still flying Old Glory on the front porch—you would be proud of that flag.

"Here in the last few days I've kind of changed up my prayer, though. I was asking God to bring the right people along. But now I'm praying that God will bring someone to it so He can bless them.

"The other day I was reading the Eighty-seventh Psalm, looking at different translations of the same thing, and right at the end I read, 'My whole source of joy is in you.' I started meditating on that. Now the writer of that was talking about Zion, about the City of God. But I don't think it does too much damage to say that God Himself is our source of joy. You know how many times I've read the Bible cover to cover. And I believe there is no lasting joy outside of God's goodness. But when I read that verse, I saw something different. I was so focused on my house and getting it sold and helping out Elizabeth and her family with the commission she'd get that I forgot to pray for the *people* who would inhabit my new home.

"So right there I told God that He was my joy, He was my hope, He was my inheritance, and that I wanted to wait upon Him and His timing. And then I went to prayer for the family that would come along one day and see the house. I prayed, 'Lord, I want there to be a light in this neighborhood that comes in here and lives. I ask You to bring some believer to this home, Lord. I ask for someone on fire for You. Would You draw some Spirit-filled follower of Yours here so that You might bless them with this home?'

"I began to pray for that family like a father will pray for a godly man for his daughter. And I threw out some specifics to Him. You know I believe God loves to answer specific prayers, not the vague ones. So I prayed the people who came along would be godly and strong in the Lord. I prayed that there would be some kind of military connection, that somebody who had a love for the men and women who serve our country would take up residence. I asked that they have young children or grandchildren who could enjoy the big backyard that's been sitting there waiting for little children to come along. And I prayed that God would bring them this week, if it was His will, and that they would see it and fall in love with it just like I did.

"Leo, sometimes I get up from my prayer time and have this warm feeling like God is smiling, like He enjoys the time we spend together even more than I do. Other times I don't get a feeling and I just take it on faith that God heard every word I prayed and that He is guiding and leading me. But that day—it was yesterday—I had the sense that I'd broken through . . . or that He had broken through to me. And now it's up to Him to work, and me to wait on Him."

CHAPTER 20

✦ ✦ ✦

Elizabeth had never taken Danielle to a house showing and knew that it wasn't common practice or "professional." But since the client was a pastor, she felt like the man would understand. She gave her daughter instructions about what to do and what not to do while she walked through the home. "Just sit quietly in Miss Clara's living room while I give them the tour."

Monday morning Danielle was up early, ate her breakfast, showered, dressed, and had her hair ready by 8:00. Elizabeth stopped by the office before meeting her client, and Danielle spoke to Mandy and Lisa.

"How did the double Dutch competition go?" Mandy said.

"We got second place," Danielle said. "And you should have seen my dad. He did flips and twirled me behind his back."

Mandy applauded. "I wish I could have been there." She looked at Elizabeth. "Sounds like things with Tony are better?"

"Better than better," Elizabeth said with a smile.

Usually Elizabeth liked to drive a client in her own car and take them from one showing to another, but since the reverend only wanted to look at one house, they met at Clara's. He drove an older car that she guessed had a lot of miles on it, given the wear on the tires. He parked a little close to the fire hydrant, but she decided not to say anything.

She estimated Reverend Jones to be in his sixties and his wife to be about the same. She was pretty and greeted Elizabeth warmly. She made such a fuss over Danielle, and Reverend Jones got down on one knee and spoke to her, asking questions about school. He had to hear all about the double Dutch competition.

"I have a granddaughter about your age," he said. "We'll have to get her into that double Dutch thing of yours."

"Maybe she can be on my team!" Danielle said.

Reverend Jones walked down the sidewalk and peeked over the fence. "This backyard would be a great place for the grandkids. We could have picnics every Sunday afternoon."

They walked inside and Danielle skipped ahead,

running for the stairs. Elizabeth gave her a look and she obediently went to the living room and sat.

"How did you find out about the house?" Elizabeth said.

Mrs. Jones got a sly look her face and glanced at her husband. "He was doing one of his prayer drives."

"Prayer drives?"

"I talk to the Lord while we're driving around a neighborhood. Praying for the people we know, the needs that are all around. And since we were looking for a place to move, I thought we'd just drive through a few areas and see if anything stood out to us. The flag out front was the first thing I saw."

"Well, let me show you around. Would you like to start down here, go upstairs?"

"Lead the way," Reverend Jones said.

"This is such a unique property," Elizabeth said. "It was built in 1905 but updated several times. The widow that just moved out had been here fifty years. And let me tell you, she is an amazing lady."

"You don't see this kind of woodwork much anymore," Reverend Jones said, walking through the entry. He ran a hand along the wooden railing, admiring the craftsmanship, then glanced up. "Now right up there it looks like they had some work done. Some kind of patchwork to the ceiling."

Elizabeth smiled. "My client has a son who was rather rambunctious evidently. I never found out what happened, but Clyde was the one who made the hole and they had to repair it. That can be refinished, of course, if it's an issue."

"We have a son of our own who was like that," Mrs. Jones said, laughing. "He was built to tear things down, I think. Good thing he went into the military. Now it's a full-time job."

"Where's he stationed?"

"He's in Afghanistan," Reverend Jones said proudly. "We pray for him every day."

"The owner of the house—her husband was in the military as well."

"I wondered when I saw the flag out front," the man said. "My son's in the Army, so that definitely caught our attention."

"Well, let me take you upstairs," Elizabeth said. She and Mrs. Jones walked ahead as the reverend slowly took in everything. Elizabeth knew that one of the good signs of any home buyer was when they started picturing themselves in the house, where their belongings would go and who would sleep where. She wanted to give as much information as they needed without overloading them. Just let them breathe and feel the house.

"I love these old houses," Mrs. Jones said. "So much character."

"Oh, I agree. I'll show you the master bedroom."

They walked into the room and Reverend Jones kept to himself, thinking, looking around. Elizabeth wondered if he was that quiet in the pulpit.

She led Mrs. Jones toward the bathroom. "Well, the master bath was updated recently, but she kept the original tub. And all the tiles are brand-new. You know, I think this is best of all—the floor is original hardwood."

"I love hardwood floors," Mrs. Jones said.

"You know what's also great is that the neighborhood is mature, it's established, so it has that quiet feeling."

Elizabeth looked back to see Reverend Jones in Clara's closet. The papers had all been taken off the walls. The little window looked out on the backyard, but he didn't seem interested in the view. She found it so curious that the man was so taken with the closet. She'd shown a lot of houses, but this was a first.

"How long have you guys been in ministry?" Elizabeth said.

"Charles pastored the same church for thirty-five years," Mrs. Jones said. "We loved it, but we knew it was time for a change. And we wanted to be near our kids and grand-kids, to help mentor them."

Reverend Jones walked back into the closet. Mrs. Jones glanced at him. Finally she couldn't stand it any longer. "Charles, what are you doing?"

The man backed out of the closet like he'd been in a holy of holies, then turned to them and pointed behind him. "Someone's been praying in this closet."

Elizabeth hadn't told them anything about Clara's war room. She stared at the man. "That's right. That was her prayer closet. How did you know that?"

The man thought a moment. "It's almost like it's baked in."

Reverend Jones looked at his wife and something

passed between the two of them. Something that only years together and a strong marriage could create—this bond that helped them know each other's hearts. Mrs. Jones smiled at him and nodded. They didn't communicate words with those looks but sentences—paragraphs.

"Ma'am," Reverend Jones said, "we'll take the house."

Elizabeth looked at Mrs. Jones and they both smiled. She'd never had a situation like this. It was usually several days of showing home after home, then coming back and looking for the second or third time until one rose to the top. This was unprecedented. Within ten minutes of walking in the front door, they were ready to make an offer.

They stood in Clara's dining room, where Elizabeth had poured out her heart so often. This room had her tears baked in. Danielle walked in and Mrs. Jones hugged her.

"We're going to buy a house from your mom," the woman said.

Danielle's eyes grew wide. "But, Mom, you said people never buy houses on the first day they look."

Elizabeth looked sheepishly at her clients. "Well, I've never met a couple like this."

They drove to the realty office and the couple signed the contract. When they were finished, Elizabeth said she would present the offer in person and get back to them as soon as she had an answer.

Reverend Jones took Elizabeth's hand before they left. "I can tell this client of yours has made a big impression on your life."

"More than you'll ever know," Elizabeth said.

She hurried to Clara's son's house to tell the woman the good news. A man wearing glasses opened the door.

"Well, hello, come on in," he said with a slight drawl. "You must be Elizabeth."

"Yes, thank you," she said. There was something familiar about his face—and not just the pictures she had seen on Clara's mantel. She tried to connect the dots but had a hard time.

"Hey there, young lady," the man said to Danielle, smiling.

Then it clicked. His voice. She had heard that voice on a news report in the past few weeks. Something about the passing of an ordinance in town and the controversy it had raised. Opposing factions of the council had been brought together by the city manager . . .

"You're C. W. Williams," Elizabeth said. "You're the city manager."

He nodded. "I am."

The stories Clara had told her about her son, the trouble he'd been in, the ways he vexed her and sent her to her knees—they all came flooding back.

"You're Clyde?" she said incredulously.

He laughed. "I'm Clyde."

"You've got to be kidding me."

Behind her came a familiar voice. "Hey, Elizabeth!" Clara sauntered from the kitchen into the entry with the look of a queen. "Hey, Danielle!"

"Nice to meet you," Clyde said. "I'll let you all catch up."

Elizabeth shook Clyde's hand, then walked toward her friend. "You never told me that your son was the city manager."

"I didn't?"

Elizabeth shook her head.

"My son's the city manager," Clara said matter-of-factly.

Elizabeth couldn't stifle the laugh. Clara was full of surprises, and Elizabeth wondered when she'd get to the end of them.

"Okay, I've got some good news for you," she said.

Clara held up a hand to stop her. She closed her eyes in thought. "I bet you're going to tell me . . ." She opened her eyes and looked at the ceiling as if she were reading a script in heaven. ". . . that a retired pastor from Texas and his wife want to buy my house." She had a twinkle in her eyes when she looked at Elizabeth again.

"Now see," Elizabeth said, "that's the kind of relationship with God I want. I want Him speaking to me like that. What did He say?"

"Well, it was actually your daughter. She texted me on my new smartphone on the way over here."

Elizabeth gave Danielle a look.

"Don't be mad, Mom. I hardly get to text anybody."

"And this thing is so handy," Clara said, holding up her phone. "I've already downloaded a prayer app and a couple gospel tunes."

Elizabeth shook her head. She showed Clara the paperwork with the offer, but all she wanted to know was who the pastor was and why they liked her house. When she heard the man's son served in the military, Clara made a fist and shook it like she'd just heard the best news in the world.

"They talked about having picnics in the backyard and mentoring their grandkids in that house," Elizabeth said.

Clara closed her eyes. "God is just amazing. I had prayed for some specific things and He did even more than I could imagine."

Elizabeth went to the living room while Clara finished making coffee. She passed a plaque on the wall that read, *The Lord bless you and keep you. The Lord make His face shine upon you.*

He's surely done that, Elizabeth thought.

Clyde's daughter was a couple years older than Danielle. He opened the freezer and pulled out two Popsicles and unwrapped them. The girls headed for the back deck, giggling together.

Soon, Clara slowly walked toward Elizabeth, balancing the two steaming cups like they were an offering. "Here we go. Two *hot* cups of coffee."

"Well, if it's hot, then I'll drink it," Elizabeth said.

Clara set the mugs down on an end table and settled into her seat. There was something in her eyes, something in her heart that was ready to come out. Or maybe it was sadness at the close of a chapter of their relationship.

"Now we're still going to get together for our little chats, right?" Elizabeth said, reassuring the woman and herself.

"Oh yes. But it can't just be the both of us."

"What do you mean?"

"Oh, you need to find a young woman to invest in. And I'll do the same. We all need help every now and then."

Elizabeth pondered the change in dynamics. She didn't know if she could share Clara. She wanted her for herself. And just as quickly, she thought about Cynthia, her sister. She didn't live far and she needed a deeper relationship with God.

"Miss Clara, I really can't tell you how much your friendship means to me."

"That goes for the both of us."

"No, really. I wasn't willing to admit how much help I needed. And I needed somebody to wake me up from the insanity of doing the same thing over and over. You've been a gift from God to me."

Clara smiled warmly. "Don't you think that this is one-sided. You have meant more to me than you know."

"Well, good. I can't imagine how much your prayers and your passion for God must have meant to your husband. I wish I could have met him."

After a moment, Clara looked down. Her eyes began to fill with tears and Elizabeth realized she had touched some tender spot in Clara's heart. She wanted to apologize or take back the words, but before she could say anything, Clara spoke.

"No. No, you don't."

Clara was serious now, her lips pursed. Elizabeth thought this was a time for celebration, not tears. But she let Clara steer them toward memories tucked away and hidden in a secret room.

"See, I wasn't the same woman back then," Clara said with regret. "When Leo died, we were not on good terms. I always felt pushed to the back burner. And I was bitter, Elizabeth. I was so bitter." She clenched a fist and accentuated the feeling as if it were flooding her soul again.

"But even then God was showing me what to do. He was prompting me to fight for Leo, to pray for Leo, and I refused. And I kept pushing it back and pushing it back until it was too late."

The emotion came to her voice now and she choked out words that cut Elizabeth to the core. "There's no grief as great as denying the truth until it's too late."

Elizabeth felt herself on the edge of some emotional chasm. The clouds were parting between them, clouds of everything she hadn't known about her friend, about her motivation. The distance had closed so much in the past few months, but now they were even closer.

Clara paused, then continued with slow speech and punctuated words. "It was my pride, Elizabeth. It was my selfish pride! And I confessed it and I repented, and I begged God to forgive me. But I still have a scar. And then I started spending more time with the Lord and in His Word. And I learned how to fight in prayer first."

Every conversation Elizabeth could remember led back to this subject: prayer. Relying on God's power. Seeking Him above everything. This was the past Clara had come from, and she had let the pain and the regret do their perfect work to propel her forward.

"I'm an old woman now. And I realized that I have not passed on what I had learned. When I last visited Leo's grave, I asked God to send me someone that I could help. Someone that I could teach to fight the right way. And He sent me Elizabeth Jordan."

Elizabeth couldn't hold back the tears. Clara clasped her hands and leaned forward and kissed them. Then she sat back and tried to compose herself, reaching out a hand to tenderly touch Elizabeth's face.

"So you see, you were the answer to my prayer."

Elizabeth sat in stunned silence, tears running freely down her cheeks. Clara had seen her in the mirror of life, a reflection of herself. Elizabeth was not some project but someone to help guide along a different path than she had chosen. But Clara wasn't the only one looking in the mirror. Elizabeth was also looking at herself and where a few good choices in life could lead. And what a mirror it was. What a picture of the grace of God.

Clara wasn't finished. She seemed ready to charge another hill into battle. And with all the conviction she could muster, she reached out to Elizabeth once more with her words.

"Well now, you've got to teach other young wives how to fight."

Elizabeth nodded, her heart welling. "Yeah, I will," she said as if accepting a baton from a tired runner. And like a prayer she whispered it again. "I will."

CHAPTER 21

✦ ✦ ✦

After the double Dutch championship, Tony felt a letdown. He had been so involved with Danielle and the team that they practically lived at the community center. With no job and no prospects on the horizon—though he had sent résumés to six companies in response to online job openings he'd seen—he found himself growing closer to God and his family.

Michael met him for breakfast after he'd completed an overnight shift. "I've been keeping an eye out for a full-time jump rope position, but I haven't found anything for you yet."

Tony laughed. "You heard about that, huh?"

"Heard about it? It's all my daughter talked about. She was at the competition and said you were spinning all over that gymnasium. Flipping here and there and twirling Danielle like a baton. She said you rocked—that was the actual word she used, bro."

"There was some pretty stiff competition," Tony said.

"No, you're not getting it. Listen. My daughter is not into sports. She likes to read and draw pictures and stare out the window. But she came back that day and said, 'Dad, I want to jump rope like Danielle and her dad.'"

"What did you say?"

"I got her a rope and told her she could start practicing."

"What about you? You going to jump?"

"My point is, she saw what you were doing and it made her want to do the same thing. You motivated her—the whole team did. That's a gift, Tony."

"Well, if you find a double Dutch position—"

Michael interrupted him. "Take a look around this place. What is it all about? It's motivating people to get in the game. Exercise. Take care of your body. Build yourself up. This is like the sweet spot of your life, you know?"

"What are you saying?"

"My wife and I were praying for you last night. All of a sudden she says, 'Why doesn't Tony apply for the community center job?' Man, it never occurred to me, but you'd be a perfect fit."

Tony had thought about it, at least in passing, but he'd been so concerned about Ernie and his firing that he'd dismissed the idea. "I would think they're looking for somebody with a lot of experience running a place like this. I don't have any."

"You have experience bringing people together and working as a team. That's what they need. They don't need an egghead with ten degrees behind his name. They need somebody who can motivate others to take charge of their lives. What's the harm in applying?"

Tony didn't have a good answer for that one. There wasn't any harm at all.

"In fact," Michael said, "here comes Henry Peterson now. He goes to our church and he's the president of the board of directors of this place."

"Really? I've never seen him."

Michael cocked his head and gave him a goofy look. "There's a lot of people at church you've never seen."

"But that's changing," Tony said.

"Amen," Michael said. He stood and waved a hand at Peterson.

"Michael, stop it," Tony said, suddenly nervous. He wasn't dressed for an interview.

Peterson came to the table and shook Michael's hand. Tony stood as Michael introduced him.

"I want to nominate somebody to be director," Michael said. "A guy who would really be an asset to the community center and bring people together as a team. My friend Tony Jordan."

The man looked at Tony. "Weren't you in the double Dutch competition this past weekend?"

Tony smiled and nodded.

"That was an amazing performance."

"You were there?"

"My grandson jumped for the Speed Angels."

"They were really good," Tony said.

"Yes, they were. But I could see how you helped all the kids on your team work together. You did a great job with that."

Tony said Trish had been the real coach, and Michael shook his head.

"This is the problem with Tony. Used to be he wouldn't pass the ball at all. Now he throws it to everybody else on the court."

"Excuse me?" the man said.

Michael laughed. "Tony Jordan is the real deal, sir. He could get this place organized and running smoothly in about a week. And in a month he'd have a plan in place for growth in membership."

Tony couldn't believe what he was hearing from Michael, but the more they talked, the more vision he had for the center. It was close to home—he could ride his bike in the summer months. He wouldn't have to travel, so he could spend time with Elizabeth and Danielle like he wanted. Within a few minutes he'd gone from having no prospects to one big one that tugged on his heart.

"What about it, Tony?" the man said. "Would you be interested in the position?"

"Of course," Tony said. "I think I could help get the place in shape in a lot of ways."

The man thought a moment. "And are you currently employed?"

"He just left his position at Brightwell Pharmaceuticals," Michael said. "He was one of their top salesmen."

"Interesting."

Tony shook his head. "I didn't leave. I was asked to leave. You should know that going in."

"But you left on good terms?"

Tony nodded. "I think that's fair to say."

The man looked at his watch. "If you were a top salesman, you probably had a nice salary and benefits package. The salary here couldn't match that."

"How much are you talking?" Michael said.

Tony gave him a look as if he should stay out of it. Michael shrugged as if saying, *If you don't ask him, I will.*

The man gave the salary range and it was about half what Tony had made at Brightwell. He quickly computed what he might take home each month.

"I think I could make that work," Tony said.

Peterson took a card from his wallet and handed it to Tony. "There's an application online. Fill that out today and let's set up an appointment to talk at my office tomorrow. I want to get moving on this as soon as possible."

Tony took the card and shook the man's hand. When he

left, Michael grinned. "I knew I'd find you a full-time double Dutch position somehow. Congratulations, Director."

✦ ✦ ✦

Elizabeth arrived at the office early. With two closings scheduled that day at opposite ends of the city, she needed to budget her time and make sure all the contracts were signed and ready. Insurance was a common thing that held up a closing, so she made sure that both mortgage companies had what they needed. Melissa Tabor, her client with the two rambunctious boys and the software rep husband, had called her three times already. Hers was one of the homes closing later that morning.

She had driven all day yesterday, and in addition to the closings, she had showings of two different properties that afternoon. She was glad for the business and grateful that God was bringing clients her way. Clara had referred a couple people to her already. But she wondered if there would be time to breathe.

Her cell rang and she stared at the screen. Cynthia. She answered and asked how her sister was doing, how the job search was going for Darren.

"He actually has an interview today," Cynthia said. "No guarantees, but at least there's a little hope."

"I'm really glad. I'm going to be praying that this works out for him. For all of you."

There was silence on the line. Then Cynthia spoke. "Elizabeth, would you have time for lunch sometime?"

Elizabeth almost dismissed the request straightaway. She was so busy, so frazzled with her schedule, and Tony and Danielle were expecting her home that evening. But something about the pleading in her sister's voice moved her.

"I have two closings this morning—and I was going to skip lunch because of some showings this afternoon, but what about dinner? I'll need to let Tony know, but it shouldn't be a problem."

Cynthia let out a heavy sigh. "Oh, that would be great."

They agreed to meet at a restaurant at five thirty, and Tony was supportive of her meeting with Cynthia. By the time Elizabeth's last showing was completed, she was late. Cynthia was waiting at a table at the Italian restaurant chain, munching on breadsticks.

They ordered and Cynthia told Elizabeth about her family's financial struggles again, how hard it was for her and the kids, and what a heavy weight all of this was for her.

"I wish we could do more to help," Elizabeth said.

Cynthia shook her head. "I know you guys are struggling too, with Tony's job loss and all. That's really not why I asked to meet."

Elizabeth leaned forward. "Then why did you want to get together?"

"Something's different. Something's changed with you. I can see it in your face, what you say when you call. It's like something has come alive inside of you and is spilling out all over the place."

Elizabeth smiled. "Have you thought more about my offer?"

Cynthia nodded. "I wasn't sure at first, you know, about the God thing. I mean, I know this is important to you and is a big part of your turnaround . . ."

"It's not just a part of it," Elizabeth said. "It's everything. I can't explain the change in my life, my marriage, just the way I feel when I wake up in the morning—all of that is connected with the 'God thing,' as you put it."

The server brought their salad and Cynthia took the olives and hot peppers. Elizabeth smiled. They'd always fought over food as kids and here they were all these years later with some of the same issues. Cynthia ate hungrily until the salad was gone and they ordered another bowl. Elizabeth had known her sister would enjoy the endless salad.

"What scares you about my offer?"

Cynthia wiped her mouth with the thick green napkin. "I don't know. That you'll push me into something I don't want."

Elizabeth nodded. "That's a rational fear, especially with our history."

"Or that you'll hold this over me. You know, 'Read the Bible and we'll help you with your mortgage.'"

"I don't ever want you to feel that way. There are no strings attached to this. The goal is just to read the Bible, ask good questions about God and our lives, and draw closer to Him. That's my only agenda."

"The other thing that scares me is that it'll be like when we were kids. That you know everything and I'll feel like I don't know anything. I hated that."

"Cynthia, if you want to know the truth, I think I'm going to learn some hard things about myself through this. This is not me lecturing you and trying to get you to win Girl Scout badges, trying to get on the good side of God. This is about both of us moving toward God and toward each other, toward the truth. And the fact that you're being honest with me and saying some hard things right now tells me this is really going to be good. For both of us."

"You think so?"

"I know it. I've met this incredible older woman who has taught me so much about prayer and the Bible. And all through the process I thought I was the one growing—but she was growing too. God was stretching her in ways I couldn't know. So you'd be doing me a spiritual favor if you'd meet with me."

Cynthia's pasta came and Elizabeth ate her soup and salad. They talked and laughed like sisters who loved each other. They were different, they were miles apart in so many ways, but Elizabeth could feel them being drawn together.

✦ ✦ ✦

Tony had everything ready by seven. He ate his dinner and cleaned up the kitchen—he knew what it would feel like for Elizabeth to walk in and see dirty dishes in the sink. No way was he going to let that happen. When he saw her headlights on the living room wall, he ran some hot water into a metal bucket she used as a decoration.

Elizabeth walked in wearing the outfit she'd worn to work—a stunning dress. Her hair still looked great. He could tell by the way she walked that she was exhausted.

"Hey, what are you doing?" she said.

"Hey," Tony said softly.

"What's going on?"

"I'll tell you in a minute, okay? How was dinner?"

"It was good. Cynthia actually agreed to meet with me on a regular basis. We're going to try Tuesday afternoons to start."

"Did they forgive me for not helping them out?"

"Aww, yeah, I think so. You know they really appreciated the $500 we gave them, though. I told her we wanted to do more but we just couldn't right now with the way things are tight with money. She understood. But we did skip dessert."

Elizabeth's voice seemed softer to him somehow. Maybe it was how tired she was. Maybe it was the result of a little less pressure on their money problems. Or perhaps she was really warming to him. She was trusting again—especially the way she'd thanked him earlier when he said it would be great for her to meet with Cynthia for dinner. She really seemed to appreciate his understanding.

"Well, listen, I've got something I need to tell you,

okay?" Tony said. "Now I want you to think about it before you respond. All right?"

Elizabeth questioned with her eyes. "What is it?"

Tony smiled. "I had an interview today. And I got offered the job on the spot."

Her face brightened. "To do what?"

"To be the new director at the community center."

She glanced away and he could tell she was processing the news. It hit her out of the blue just like it had him the day before.

"Liz, we know this place so well. You know? I'm telling you, I can do this job."

She thought a moment more. "You would be closer to home."

"It's only half the pay, but if we're wise, I know we can make it."

She got a look on her face that was as determined as he was to pull through all the mess and struggle. She drew closer to him and lowered her voice. "Listen to me. I would rather have a man chasing Jesus than a house full of stuff."

It was exactly what Tony wanted to hear, what he needed to hear. He smiled and said, "Okay. All right then, I'll accept it." He squinted at her. "You know what? I'm kind of glad you didn't have that dessert tonight."

"Why?"

"You'll see. Why don't you just go to the couch."

"What?"

"Go ahead. Go to the couch. I'll be over there in a second. I'm right behind you."

Elizabeth obeyed, though it was clear she had no idea what Tony had in mind, which thrilled him. She sat on the couch and Tony quickly retrieved the metal bucket filled with hot water and brought it to the living room.

"Where's Danielle?" she said.

"She's over at Jennifer's house. They're having a sleepover."

He placed the bucket carefully at her feet.

"What is this?" she said.

Tony knelt and began to take off one of her sandals.

"No, no, no, Tony," she protested. "Don't touch my feet."

"Hey, just roll with it, okay? All right, come on now." He took off the sandal and put her foot in the water.

Elizabeth closed her eyes, enraptured. "Oh, my goodness, that feels so good."

Tony returned to the refrigerator and came back with a concoction he had made from ice cream in the freezer, some whipped cream he bought at the store, and some caramel and chocolate he had squirreled away without Elizabeth seeing. He held a spoon in one hand and a glass bowl with the sundae, complete with a cherry on top, in the other and stood before her.

"Now it's time you got what you deserve. This is for the woman . . . I don't deserve. You go ahead and work on that and I am going to get started on that foot massage you've been asking for."

Elizabeth took the bowl and spoon, in shock. She looked

at the sundae like the golden goose had laid a nest full of eggs. Then she dipped the spoon into the topping and took a small taste. "Really? Are you really doing this for me?"

Tony hit the Play button on the stereo remote and her favorite song played. When he scooted closer to her feet, she protested again. "Tony, I don't want you to smell my feet."

"Baby, look. I told you, I got this." He pulled out a white painter's mask and held it up so she could see. "You need to trust me, okay?"

Elizabeth laughed as he put the mask over his mouth and nose, then pulled the elastic straps and snapped them against the back of his head.

"I'm ready to go," he said, lifting his eyebrows.

He took the fragrant soap she loved and began to lather her feet, washing and massaging the stress and, he thought, all of the past away. Tony thought about the passage he had read at the men's study that week with Michael and the others. Jesus had washed the feet of His disciples, kneeling before each of them and doing what a servant would do. That was what Tony was called to do as a husband—serve his wife, give himself fully for her. And if he did that, how could she resist such love?

Elizabeth took a bite of ice cream and Tony looked up to see her laughing but also a tear running down her cheek.

"What's wrong?" he said, pulling the mask down.

"I'm eating my favorite dessert while my husband is rubbing my feet. There has got to be a God in heaven!"

He laughed with her and she sat back and relaxed, letting herself go. It was funny how he could feel her muscles loosening, like her spirit. And as he massaged, he spoke to her.

"Look, I know it's going to take some time. And I don't expect everything to be cleared up by one foot massage."

"You talking about my feet or about us?"

He smiled. "I'm talking about everything. For richer, for poorer, stinky feet and all the questions we have about the future. You know, I was thinking the other day how hard it would be to move from here, if we can't make it financially. And then I thought, if we have to sell, I know a pretty good Realtor."

Elizabeth chuckled and took another bite of ice cream.

"I love you, Elizabeth Jordan. And you're just going to have to spend the rest of your life letting me show you that."

She leaned forward and kissed him, and he could taste the chocolate and whipped cream and caramel on her lips.

"Think I could have some of that sundae?" he said.

She held out a spoonful and then quickly ate it when he leaned forward. "You get back to the feet." She took another bite. "That was pretty sneaky of you getting Danielle out of the house for the night. When did you come up with that idea?"

"I've been going through the Song of Solomon in my devotions," he said. Then he winked and Elizabeth howled, then kissed him again.

Miss Clara

✦ ✦ ✦

Clara held a pen in one hand as she picked up her Bible from the bed with the other. She let it fall open to a familiar passage in 2 Chronicles and read the words, knowing they were written in the Bible for the nation of Israel, but also knowing that God wanted to do the same for her and others today. She walked slowly into her darkened closet, praying the words she had memorized so long ago.

"'If . . . My people who are called by My name humble themselves, pray and seek My face, and turn from their evil ways, then I will hear from heaven, forgive their sin, and heal their land.'"

She switched on the little light in the room and knelt by

the wooden chair gingerly, her knees creaking and groaning from age. She had brought her pen to check off the last prayer request to be answered, the sale of her house. But she knew that God, who owned the cattle on a thousand hills, could do much more than that. Still, she thanked Him.

"You've done it again, Lord. You've done it again. You are good and You are mighty and You are merciful. And You keep taking care of me when I don't deserve it. Praise You, Jesus. You are Lord."

Like a prizefighter dancing around the ring, looking at some fierce enemy, she lifted her head, her eyes still tightly shut.

"Give me another one, Lord. Guide me to who You want me to help. Raise up more that will call on Your name. Raise up those that love You and seek You and trust You. Raise them up, Lord, raise them up!"

In her mind, she saw a family clasping hands at the dinner table to pray. A man on a tractor in the middle of his field. Two men with bowed heads praying in front of a world map.

"Lord, we need a generation of believers who are not ashamed of the gospel. We need an army of believers who hate to be lukewarm and will stand on Your Word above all else. Raise 'em up, Lord. Raise them up."

Clara saw streams of young people moving toward a flagpole, encircling the area with eyes closed. Others were heading for a church in the distance, carrying young children.

"I pray for unity among those that love You. I pray that You'd open their eyes so that they can see Your truth. I pray for Your hand of protection and guidance."

Clara thought of the police officers in her town and across the nation. Of the division between races and the struggles she had witnessed over the years.

"Raise up a generation, Lord, that will take light into this world. That will not compromise under pressure, that will not cower when others fall away. Raise them up, Lord, that they will proclaim that there is salvation in the name of Jesus Christ. Raise up warriors who will fight on their knees, who will worship You with their whole hearts. Lord, call us to battle, that we may proclaim You King of kings and Lord of lords!"

Clara pictured fathers praying over their newborn children. She pictured men and women in places of high power kneeling and praying for guidance. She thought of schoolteachers and business leaders and gas station attendants and mothers at PTA meetings. She thought of pastors and youth workers and missionaries and the faces all came together in her final words of petition.

"I pray these things with all my heart. . . . Raise them up, Lord, raise them up!"

ACKNOWLEDGMENTS

Chris Fabry

Thanks to Alex and Stephen for allowing me to be part of the process of bringing this book to life. What a privilege. And to those who prayed for this project and those who will be moved to prayer. With a grateful heart.

Alex and Stephen Kendrick

Thank you to Chris Fabry for a job well done. It was a pleasure working with you! To the Tyndale team, you guys are a blessing. Thanks for believing in these stories. To our wives and children, we love you dearly. It's time for a vacation! To our parents, Larry and Rhonwyn Kendrick, you've demonstrated over the years that daily prayer is an absolute priority. We can't imagine life without your love, support, and prayers. You taught us to stand firm and fight with the right weapons. We love you! To our ministry team, a thank-you would never be enough. You've worked with us, prayed with us, and stood by us. We are so grateful! May God get the glory, and may the name of Jesus be lifted high. He is Lord!

ABOUT THE AUTHORS

Chris Fabry is a 1982 graduate of the W. Page Pitt School of Journalism at Marshall University and a native of West Virginia. He is heard on Moody Radio's *Chris Fabry Live!*, *Love Worth Finding*, and *Building Relationships with Dr. Gary Chapman*. He and his wife, Andrea, are the parents of nine children. Chris has published more than seventy books for adults and children. His novels *Dogwood*, *Almost Heaven*, and *Not in the Heart* won Christy Awards, and *Almost Heaven* won the ECPA Christian Book Award for fiction.

You can visit his website at www.chrisfabry.com.

Alex Kendrick is an award-winning author gifted at telling stories of hope and redemption. He is best known as an actor, writer, and director of the hit films *Fireproof*, *Courageous*, and *Facing the Giants* and coauthor of the *New York Times* bestselling books *The Love Dare*, *The Resolution for Men*, *Fireproof* (the novel), and *Courageous* (the novel). Alex has received more than twenty awards for his work, including best screenplay, best production, and best feature film. In 2002, Alex helped found Sherwood Pictures and partnered with his brother Stephen to launch Kendrick Brothers Productions. He has been featured on FOX News, CNN, *ABC World News Tonight*, *CBS Evening News*, *Time* magazine, and the *New York Times*, among others. He is a graduate of Kennesaw State University and attended seminary before being ordained into ministry. Alex and his wife, Christina, live in Albany, Georgia, with their six children. They are active members of Sherwood Church.

Stephen Kendrick is a speaker, film producer, and author with a ministry passion for prayer and discipleship. He is a cowriter and producer of the hit movies *Courageous*, *Facing the Giants*, and *Fireproof* and cowriter of the *New York Times* bestsellers *The Resolution for Men* and *The Love Dare*. *The Love Dare* quickly became a number one *New York Times* bestseller and stayed on the list for more than two years. Stephen is an ordained minister and speaks at conferences and men's events. He attended seminary, received a communications degree from Kennesaw State University, and now serves on the board of the Fatherhood CoMission. He has been interviewed by *Fox & Friends*, CNN, the *Washington Post*, and *ABC World News Tonight*, among others. Stephen and his wife, Jill, live in Albany, Georgia, with their six children, where they are active members of Sherwood Church.

www.kendrickbrothers.com

DISCUSSION QUESTIONS

1. What factors contribute to the breakdown in Elizabeth and Tony's marriage? How does prayer turn it around? What applications could this have for your own relationships?

2. Early in the story, as she thinks about her relationship with Tony, Elizabeth concludes, "Maybe this was all she could hope for. Maybe this was as good as marriage got. Or life, for that matter." Have you ever been tempted to resign yourself to a situation or a relationship that seems stuck? What did you do? What encouragement would you give Elizabeth or someone you know facing similar circumstances?

3. Miss Clara thinks of prayer as "talking and listening and being excited to spend time with someone who loves you." How would you define prayer? In what ways does Clara's description match your view of it?

4. When Miss Clara brings Elizabeth a lukewarm cup of coffee, it serves as an effective illustration of Elizabeth's faith. Are you satisfied with how you would describe your own faith? (Hot, cold, or lukewarm?) What steps can you take to change things?

5. At the very moment Tony is about to make a decision that could destroy his marriage, he's stopped by a bout of illness that coincides with Elizabeth's prayers. Have you ever been surprised by an immediate answer to prayer? What happened?

6. After almost being robbed, Miss Clara tells the policeman taking her statement, "When you write that down, don't you leave out Jesus. People are always leaving Jesus out. That's one of the reasons we're in the mess we're in." What do you think she means? Describe a time in your life or the life of someone you know when Jesus was left out.

7. Once she sees her mother's prayer closet, Danielle decides she wants one of her own. What does that say about the effect of parents' actions on their children? What can you do to set an example of faith for the children in your life?

8. Miss Clara tells the friends in her Friday gathering, "The goal of prayer is not to change God's mind about

what you want. The goal of prayer is to change your own heart, to want what He wants, to the glory of God." Do you agree with her statement? Why or why not? How do you see the prayers of characters in *War Room* affecting their hearts? Can you think of a time when your own heart was changed in a similar way?

9. Tony is forced to make a tough decision: to tell his boss about the crime he committed or to keep it hidden. Does he make the right choice? Would it have been enough for Tony to simply pray for forgiveness and keep his secret?

10. When Coleman Young decides not to file charges against Tony, Tony is understandably relieved. Have you ever been given grace you didn't deserve? How did you respond?

11. *War Room* presents the idea that prayer is a powerful weapon in the battle against evil. Does this imagery change your perspective on prayer? How can it be used to strengthen your own prayer life?

12. Clara prays, "Raise up a generation, Lord, that will take light into this world. That will not compromise under pressure, that will not cower when others fall away. Raise them up, Lord, that they will proclaim that there is salvation in the name of Jesus Christ.

Raise up warriors who will fight on their knees, who
will worship You with their whole hearts." Does the
world need this kind of generation? How can you be
part of a generation of prayer warriors?